LAWRENCE C. CONNOLLY

VEINS

ILLUSTRATED BY STAR E. OLSON

Fantasist
Enterprises

WILMINGTON, DELAWARE

Text copyright © 2008 by Lawrence C. Connolly
Illustrations copyright © 2008 by Star E. Olson

Designed by
W. H. Horner Editorial & Design
www.whhorner.com

Published by
Fantasist Enterprises
PO Box 9381
Wilmington, DE 19809
www.FEBooks.net

VEINS

Trade Paperback:
ISBN 13: 978-1-934571-00-2
ISBN 10: 1-934571-00-8

ePub:
ISBN 13: 978-1-934571-06-4
ISBN 10: 1-934571-06-7

FIRST EDITION
August 2008

SECOND PRINTING
July 2014

10 9 8 7 6 5 4 3 2

PRAISE FOR

"For years I've been an admirer of Lawrence C. Connolly's exquisite and deeply affecting short fiction—he always writes with great skill, intelligence, compassion, and subtle lyricism; but with *Veins* he has done the impossible and surpassed his own high standards. This rich, mesmerizing, and darkly wondrous novel held me under its spell for days as I read it, and haunts me even now, weeks later. This is what grand story-telling is all about, regardless of genre. I began the novel as an admirer of Connolly; I finished it as one in awe—and so will you."
—**Gary A. Braunbeck,** Bram Stoker and International Horror Guild Award-winning author of *Destinations Unknown* and *Mr. Hands*

"One of the joys of my days at *Twilight Zone* was encountering the work of an extraordinarily subtle and imaginative writer, Lawrence C. Connolly, who brought enormous power to the shortest of stories. And now, in *Veins*, he's created something equally extraordinary—a supernatural novel that brings Native American magic to a crime thriller as intense and fast-moving as a Tarantino movie."
—**T.E.D. Klein,** World Fantasy and British Fantasy Society Award-winning author of *The Ceremonies* and *Dark Gods*

"*Veins* is haunting work, meticulously crafted by one of the genre's most masterful storytellers, writing at the top of his game. It is Connolly's crowning achievement: a multi-layered, intense exploration that scrapes away the surface of reality, excavating the wondrous and dreadful secrets that lurk in the twisting caverns beneath. In this harrowing, fast-paced novel, Connolly plumbs the depths of the dark side in a way that no one has done before. Some books are good, others are great, but a rare few are tremendous and beg to be read over and again. *Veins* is a tremendous and unforgettable read."
—**Michael Arnzen,** Bram Stoker Award-winning author of *100 Jolts*

MORE PRAISE FOR VEINS

"Lawrence C. Connolly writes with clear beauty and a purity of prose, his world not confined to the page, but breathing, soaring, sometimes kicking and cussing, but ever appealing to all the senses. *Veins* is both spiritual and physical, blending both this world and the world of that beyond with seamless grace. Connolly is a writer to follow, and his work a thing to savor."
　　—**Mary SanGiovanni**, author of *The Hollower*

"Much like the souped-up vintage Mustang that cuts through the heart of the story, *Veins* starts fast, accelerates quickly, and finishes with a flourish, fulfilling all the promise at novel length that Lawrence C. Connolly has been flashing for years in his outstanding short stories."
　　—**Robert Morrish**, fiction editor of *Cemetery Dance*, the World Fantasy Award-winning magazine of horror, dark mystery, and suspense

"Feels like some of the best magic realism that's been written lately . . . highly readable."
　　—*BookSpotCentral.com*

"With . . . expert imagery, Lawrence C. Connolly takes a reader on a different kind of magical mystery tour . . . about what drives people to extremes, and how destiny ultimately intervenes."
　　—**Sheila Merritt**, *HellNotes.com*

"[S]ubtly haunting, bringing together Native American myth with a crime thriller. The plot is fast and intense and the characters are wonderfully real."
　　—**Laura Lehman**, *BellaOnline.com*

AWARD NOMINATIONS FOR VEINS

Finalist for the 2009 Eric Hoffer Award.

Appeared on the Preliminary Ballot for the 2009 Bram Stoker Award for Superior Achievement in a First Novel.

Nominated for the 2nd Annual Black Quill Award for Best Small-Press Chill by the editors of *Dark Scribe Magazine*.

PRAISE FOR VIPERS

"[A] breakneck made-for-the-movies celebration of bloody carnage and black scheming . . . fans of summer blockbusters will be happy to crunch popcorn through the car chases, explosions, and brutality."
  —*Publishers Weekly*

"[J]aw-dropping, *Vipers* must be read by any serious follower of horror, crime, and dark fantasy."
  —**Gary A. Braunbeck,** author of *To Each Their Darkness*

"Connolly shows us once again just how imaginative, intelligent and skillful a writer he is."
  —**Simon Kurt Unsworth,** author of *Lost Places*

"[A] taut novel of horror and suspense that will have you reading chapter after chapter long after you meant to go to sleep."
  —**Alice Henderson,** author of *Voracious*

PRAISE FOR VORTEX

"Few writers understand their characters with the same depth, and empathy, that Connolly does. He leaves me in awe. Every time. I am a Connolly fan through and through."
  —**Joe McKinney,** Bram Stoker Award-winning author of *Dead City* and *Plague of the Undead*

"Writing with power and precision, Connolly evokes sights and sounds that haunt us. *Vortex* is a book you won't be able to put down."
  —**Jon Sprunk,** author of *Blood & Iron*

"Unbridled imagination meets impeccable storytelling. Connolly is amazing that way, like the bull and the matador rolled into one."
  —**John Dixon,** author of *Phoenix Island*

"[*Vortex*] will lose readers in a mystical and frightening world that they won't want to slither out of."
  —**Stephanie M. Wytovich,** author of *Hysteria*

"This is gleeful, intelligent stuff that deserves the widest audience possible. It's a hell of a ride, and I cannot wait to see where Connolly takes us next."
  —**Simon Kurt Unsworth,** World-Fantasy-Award-Nominated author of *The Devil's Detective*, forthcoming from Doubleday

ALSO BY LAWRENCE C. CONNOLLY

The Veins Cycle

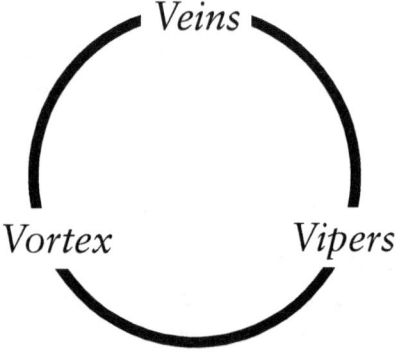

Short Story Collections
Visions: Short Fantasy & SF
Voices: Tales of Horror

From Ash-Tree Press
This Way to Egress

For V.

ACKNOWLEDGEMENTS:

I would like to thank Christopher Laughrey of the Pennsylvania Geologic Survey and Dawna Saunders of the Pennsylvania Department of Environmental Protection for their invaluable help in researching the geologic and industrial backgrounds for this novel. Equally helpful was Chris Stout, my weapons and pyrotechnics consultant, who made sure that the depictions of firearms and explosions were as accurate as possible. I also received terrific assistance from a number of auto experts and enthusiasts, among them James Wardrop, Bruce Houghtaling, Frank Brooks, Gwen Lewis, Scott Spehar and especially Dave Tournay, who kindly let me take his Dodge Viper out on the winding back roads of western Pennsylvania—all in the interest of research. Finally, I owe a generous and hearty thanks to my editor Will Horner, who provided both encouragement and insight through the manuscript's numerous revisions. If this novel works, it is because these knowledgeable individuals helped make it so.

AUTHOR'S NOTE:

Veins is a work of fiction, and as such it takes place in a parallel universe with its own unique topography and culture. Although many of the secondary locations mentioned in the narrative are real, the main locations (Windslow, Windslow Bottoms, and Windslow Mine) are not to be found on any real-world maps. Likewise, the Okwe, though elements of their speech have been derived from Mingo (an Iroquoian language once widespread throughout Pennsylvania, Ohio, and West Virginia), exist only in the fictional world of this book.

The land was ours before
we were the land's.

Robert Frost

PROLOGUE

The second time Kwetis visited her, she found him sitting outside the door of her trailer park home, wings folded against his back, clawed feet curled over the rim of a cliff. At first she wasn't sure which unnerved her more: seeing that Kwetis had returned to western Pennsylvania, or discovering that her front yard now ended at a sandstone precipice.

Kwetis looked back at her, head rotating to peer between his wings. "I've come to thank you," he said. "You did well, Yeyestani."

Yeyestani was an old word. It meant *teacher*. Kwetis was flattering her, which meant he had returned to ask another favor.

He stepped away from the ledge, walking on legs that bent backward at the knees, approaching until he stood just outside her door.

She didn't invite him in.

"Your friend performed well, Yeyestani."

"My friend?"

"Johnny Redwing."

"The Okwe boy?" She frowned. "He's no friend of mine."

"Still, he listened when you told him to take the job at the Frieburg estate. He did as you said. That was good."

"I heard he only lasted a week up there."

"Ten days."

"I heard they fired him."

"That's right. *Mr.* Frieburg fired him."

"So how's that good?"

Kwetis's eyes shimmered. An image rose within them, showing Johnny Redwing lying atop Mrs. Frieburg, riding her hard.

"So that's it? That's the reason you wanted him up there?"

"Not the whole reason."

"I don't understand."

"Yes, but that's because for you it's just beginning. Understanding comes later." He stepped closer. "You are helping our *oohaate*," he said.

"*Oohaate?*"

"Yes. Do you know that word?"

She had forgotten much of the old tongue, but a few words remained. *Oohaate.* She remembered her grandmother talking about that. *Oohaate.* The spirit path. The way that must be followed. It had no equivalent in English, though *fate* was an approximation.

"So I'm helping you cut a trail into the future?"

"Yes."

"And you've come back to thank me? That's all?"

Kwetis leaned closer. "No." His face crackled. "There's more." He touched her shoulder. His palm was hard, cold. His skin smoldered without heat. "I came to thank you . . . and warn you."

"About what?"

His eyes shimmered. "Your grandson Matthew is going to die."

Her heart skipped. Matthew was twenty-two, healthy, recently married. Kwetis rubbed her shoulder. "But through his death, you will gain a son."

"Me? A son?" She was seventy-four. "You're joking."

"I never joke. Jokes are for humans. I speak only what is, what will be. When Matthew dies, you will raise his son."

"But Matthew doesn't have a son."

"No. Not yet. But he will."

She felt disoriented. He was telling her too much too fast.

"Here," Kwetis said. "This will help." He took his hand from her shoulder and stepped aside.

In the distance, beyond the sandstone ledge, the landscape came alive with roaring machines: coal trucks, conveyors, dozers, draglines.

"Tell me what you see," Kwetis said. "Tell me if you recognize this place."

"I recognize it," she said.

It was the Windslow Surface Mine, a wounded valley that had once been pine-covered highlands. Machines had bulldozed the forest, diverted streams, and cut into the mountain until all that remained was a deep gash rimmed by a curved wall of sheared-off rock to the north and east, pine forest to the south and west. In between was a low wasteland of machine-gouged earth. The locals called it *the crater*.

But though it was familiar to her, it did not belong where she saw it now, a few dozen feet from her doorstep.

"I've moved it for you, Yeyestani."

"For me?"

"So I can show you another piece of the *oohaate*."

Her grandson Matthew worked at Windslow Mine, hauling coal along the ledge roads.

"I'll show you," Kwetis said. "I'll show you how he dies. But you mustn't try changing it. If you do, the *oohaate* will fail."

She watched a line of coal trucks ascending the face of the highwall, climbing a road that wound like a screw thread along the curve of vertical rock. Her grandson drove the lead vehicle, and even though she couldn't see him through the sun-glared windows, she nonetheless recognized his youthful vigor in the moving machine, as if his essence permeated the metal, radiating down into the steady motion of the massive wheels.

"Keep watching," Kwetis said. "This is how it happens."

Slowly, almost imperceptibly, the air quivered, trembling with a low-pitched sound, like the sustained ringing of a gong. Seconds passed. The ground stirred, vibrating beneath her. *The mine*, she thought, the realization coming the way insights sometimes do in dreams. *The sound is coming from the mine. The rocks are singing.*

To the east, the highwall trembled, its face shivering as the ringing welled into a jagged roar.

Then it happened.

The screw-thread road folded, crumbling beneath the trucks. Wheels lost traction as rock sheared away. And then, slowly at first, the convoy fell. . . .

By the time the full force of the thunder reached her, a quarter of the hillside had calved into the crater.

"Lose a grandson," Kwetis said. "Gain a son."

They were inside now, which meant that Kwetis could stay as long as he wanted. It was bad luck to ask a spirit to leave your home once you had invited him inside.

She realized now, studying him as he sat across from her, that he had changed since his first visit. The last time he had been more aloof, less personable. Perhaps this was a different Kwetis, a younger manifestation of the timeless spirit. According to the old stories, such things were possible.

The living room occupied the center of her trailer, positioned beyond a pressboard kitchen and ending at a darkened hallway. The hallway led to her bedroom, and from it came the sounds of her nightstand radio, the one she always played while she slept. She was sleeping now, but that didn't matter. Her awareness was here, in the living room, with Kwetis.

She looked into his eyes. "Tell me about him," she said. "Tell me about my great-grandson."

Kwetis had made himself at home. He sat across from her, wings draping the back of a chair, legs folded beneath him. She had offered him coffee, and he had accepted, the cup sitting beside him now, growing cold.

His gaze turned inward at her mention of the boy. When he spoke, he did so slowly, as if sharing information that was at once vast and personal. "Your grandson will name the boy Alex," Kwetis said. "But Alex will change the name. He will call himself *Axle.*"

"Axle? Like on a car?"

"Yes. That's the way he'll spell it."

She pictured the rearranged letters. "He will be a clever child?"

"No." Kwetis seemed to smile, though in truth his wolfish face lacked the subtleties of human expression. "Not particularly. Not at first. He will require considerable guidance, a lot of teaching."

"I take it he'll have an interest in cars."

"Yes. A big interest. It will be part of the *oohaate.* Very important."

"But why will I be the one to raise him? Surely his mother—"

"You will challenge the mother's right to custody," Kwetis said. "It will not be easy, but she drinks, and she will drink more after the accident. When you challenge her for the child, she will drink all the time."

"So maybe we should let her keep the child. Maybe it will help her, keep her from drinking."

"That doesn't concern us. The *oohaate* requires that you gain custody."

"And after custody. Then what?"

"Then you will teach him the old ways, the language and stories."

"I'm afraid I've forgotten those."

"You'll remember. They're in your blood. Trust your instincts. Old memories are like deep rock, there for the digging." He spoke with his hands, gentle gestures. "Raise the boy well. When he is nearly grown, I will visit you again. That will be our final meeting, Yeyestani."

She considered that. How old would she be when an as-yet-unborn child reached his teens?

Life is already too long, she thought, not sure she wanted to go another fifteen, twenty years. She was already weary, bone tired, worn to a nub.

Kwetis took her hand. "You look troubled."

Down the hall, something stirred: weight shifting against sagging springs. She felt the mattress beneath her shoulders, but tried ignoring it. She must not wake up now. It would be rude, possibly fatal.

"You have doubts," Kwetis said. "You're wondering if you will live long enough to raise the child."

"Will I?"

"Yes."

"Will I do a good job?"

He paused, his gaze softening. "Yes." Something moved across his face, a shifting shadow that conveyed a sense of respect and gratitude. He seemed poised to say more, but then he released her hand, unfolded his legs, and headed toward the door.

She followed him down a wooden step and onto a clay path that led past a small chain-link enclosure. The size and shape of a dog kennel, the enclosure held a generator and a large gasoline drum. A sign on the locked gate proclaimed that the contents were property of OSM, Federal Office of Surface Mining:

TRESPASSERS WILL BE PROSECUTED

A pole rose from the generator, supporting an overhead wire that ran toward a square shack with a boarded window. None of these things—fence, generator, wire, shack—were part of her real world. But she sensed they were important. Otherwise, Kwetis would not have put them in the dream.

He passed them without comment, advancing toward the brink of the now-silent surface mine. The machines were gone.

Windslow Mine, she thought. *As it will be in the future: quiet, overgrown, forgotten.*

Kwetis stepped toward the crater's edge, balancing precariously, pointing to the eastern slope where a carpet of trees and grass covered a wedge of collapsed wall: the killing ground as it would appear many years after her grandson's death.

"Other men will die in the slide," he said, speaking now with the shifting tension in his wings. He looked ready to fly. "There will be lawsuits, claims of negligence. The company will declare bankruptcy, leaving the workers with nothing while the owners walk away rich."

She stepped up beside him, letting him know that she wasn't afraid of the sudden fall. She felt safe in his presence, secure in the assurance that she would live long enough to raise a child who was yet to be born.

"This is the mine as it *will be*," Kwetis said. "One day, when your great-grandson is nearly grown, you will bring him here." He touched her hand, speaking with his grip. "You will raise him well."

She waited for him to say more, but instead he withdrew his hand.

"I'm wondering," she said. "You seem different from last time. Are you—"

He angled forward and leaped away. A concussive snap rose from his shoulders, the sound of wings catching the wind.

The blast hit her, pushing her back.

Dust rose.

She covered her face. Too late. Something had blown into her left eye, burning, becoming worse as she rubbed. She turned away from the ledge, still rubbing, the pain spreading through her, filling her head, traveling with her as she awoke in agony.

By mid-morning, the eye had hardened to a milky white.

Her view of the world had changed forever.

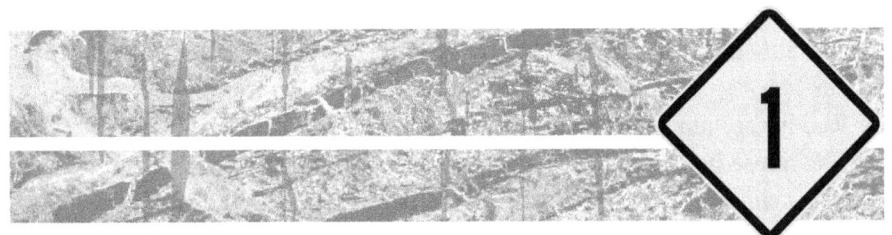

Moths hummed against the kitchen door, battering their wings as they struggled for the light. Inside, Reddy opened the refrigerator and frowned at the moldy food that his girlfriend Tejay had left behind when she'd stormed away two weeks before. Goddamn Tejay, aka Terry Jones, the girl who wanted to be something different. She had started with changing her name, but that was as far as it got. In the end she was still the same: cute and clueless, destined for doublewide adulthood in some nowhere trailer park.

Reddy frowned. He had to stop thinking about the past and focus on the future, or if not the future at least the promise at hand.

He pulled two Rolling Rocks from the bottom shelf and took a seat at a Formica-topped table. Spinelli was there, leaning back, looking at the checkbook and credit cards that Reddy had stolen from a car in Waynesburg.

"So?" Reddy removed the bottle caps and tossed them into an overflowing bin in the corner. One landed amid the bottles. The other ricocheted, skipping back to strike the breech of a 12-gauge pump-action Remington that leaned between refrigerator and wall. "You got a plan?" He thumped a bottle on the table in front of Spinelli. "I'm totally open to suggestions."

Spinelli flipped through the cards, looking them over front and back before setting them down. Then he opened the checkbook.

"Look at the balance," Reddy said. "It's almost a grand. But I'm thinking some of those checks haven't cleared. So it could be more. Know what I'm saying?"

Spinelli flipped through the register, studying it with eyes so intense that Reddy was sure the brain behind them was hatching something.

Reddy had met Spinelli ten days back at a Waynesburg bar, a smoky pub where Spinelli had shared stories of the profitable scams he had worked throughout four southern states. The two soon became fast if not close friends. Indeed, as near as Reddy could figure, close was a word that did not apply to

Spinelli. Friendly as he was, he seemed to keep a wall around himself, a permanent barrier like the long-sleeve jerseys he wore even on the hottest days.

"Listen, man." Reddy thumped his bottle on the kitchen table. "I've heard you can sell credit cards, the numbers, anyway. I've heard there are Internet sites for that."

Spinelli looked up from the checkbook. "You got a computer in this place?"

Reddy thought a moment.

The house belonged to his uncle, a semi-alcoholic mechanic who worked for a traveling carnival. When the man was on the road, Reddy got the house.

"Computer?" Reddy frowned. "No way. My uncle, he's totally old school . . . all switches and gears."

Spinelli put down the checkbook, took another drink. "You said there was money in the car, too?"

"Yeah. Thirty-seven bucks."

"That's the money you used to buy this beer?" Spinelli raised his bottle.

"Yeah," Reddy said. "I was going to use one of the cards, but I figured I'd better talk to you first. Like you said, if I ever need advice—"

"How much you got left?"

"Cash?" Reddy shrugged. "Couple bucks. Maybe five."

"And you want my advice? You want me to tell you what to do with this stuff?" He pushed the checks and cards toward Reddy.

"Yeah," Reddy said. "I figure you ought to know. I mean, you know about stuff like this, right?"

"I know a few things." Spinelli leaned forward. "And here's what I know about these." He pointed to the cards. "Each of these can get you ten grand."

"Cash?"

Spinelli nodded.

"Sombitch!" Reddy's pulse quickened. "Tell me how?"

"Just use them. Take them to Wal-Mart, Sears, the bank—doesn't matter where. If the cards have been reported stolen, and you can bet they have been, you'll be arrested on the spot."

Reddy sat back. "The hell you talking, Spinelli?"

"I'm talking fines of up to ten grand, ten years in prison, possibly both. And that's just for each card." He sat back. "What I'm saying is . . . dealing in stolen plastic isn't worth the risk. And checks are just as bad. They're like whores with AIDS. They look promising, but once you use them—"

"Shit, Spinelli. I just—"

"My advice?" Spinelli raised his Rolling Rock. "Pitch them and enjoy your beer."

Reddy didn't bother asking Spinelli to reconsider. The man in the long-sleeve jersey was an authority on just about everything. Reddy respected that, even if it did piss him off sometimes.

"You look angry," Spinelli said.

Reddy balled his fists, fighting the urge to fling the cards and checkbook at the kitchen wall. Doing that would solve nothing, and he didn't want Spinelli seeing that side of him. "Not angry," Reddy said. "It's just—" He slumped forward. "It's just . . . every sombitchin time I think I got something good—"

"Be patient, man. There'll be other things. Better things. That's the way life is. Just when you think things are going good, shit happens. But shit doesn't last. There's always a turnaround."

Reddy nodded, taking it in.

Spinelli had a way of talking that made his words sound like gospel truth, so Reddy was only mildly surprised when three or four beers later he heard a car crunching up his gravel drive.

"The hell?" Reddy cocked his head toward the screen door. "Sombitch!" He looked at Spinelli. "Sounds like Tejay's car." He cleared the cards and checks from the table, stuffing them into a pocket as he got up.

"What you ought to do is sit down," Spinelli said.

Reddy went to the door, put his face to the screen, and watched as headlights fanned the tailgate of his F-150.

"If she sees you standing there, she'll know you've been missing her."

Reddy pushed the door open, leaning out as Tejay's Escort crunched to a stop beyond the porch.

"Of course," Spinelli said, "there are advantages to letting her know you missed her. It's all in how you want to play it."

The Escort's door thumped open. Tejay stepped out, looking like she'd been poured into her tank top and cutoffs.

She closed the car door, pressing it with her hip when the gimpy latch didn't catch. That's when she noticed Spinelli's Yamaha Virago leaning on its kickstand beside the porch. "You buy a bike?" she asked.

"No."

"Got company?"

"Yeah."

"Is this a bad time?"

"No." He stepped onto the porch. "It's good as any." He paused as he reached the top of the short flight of sun-blistered steps. "Where the hell you been, Tejay?"

"Windslow."

"The whole two weeks?"

"Yeah."

"You know folks in Windslow?"

"No," she said. "I mean, I didn't. I do now. I found a temp job with a rich guy. That's why I'm back."

"You got steady work?"

"No. I quit." She climbed the steps.

"Damn, Tejay!" He hugged her. "I thought you were never coming back."

She pressed her lips to his ear. "We need to talk, Reddy. Private."

Reddy glanced back to find Spinelli watching them through the screen.

"Come here." She pulled his arm, leading him down the steps until they were out of sight of the kitchen door. Then, with her face in shadows, she whispered, "You need to help me do something, Reddy."

"A favor?" He wondered if that was why she'd returned, not to be *with* him, but to *use* him. "The hell you asking, girl?"

"Not a favor for me," she said. "It's for both of us. It's, like, a job. I need you to help me steal something."

This surprised him. Tejay had always been interested in bettering herself, in finding ways to move up in the world. Last year she had almost finished a semester at West Virginia Career Institute before dropping out to run through a series of temporary clerical jobs, most of which had ended in early termination. Reddy never understood why she didn't just go wait tables like everyone else. Now, here she was proposing they become partners in crime.

"It's a car," she said.

"What's a car?"

"The job. It's about a car."

"You want to steal a car?"

"Not steal it. Steal something from it. You've done stuff like that before."

"Not that you ever approved."

"That was before," she said. "And this job . . . it'll be worth it. But it's tricky. I can't do it alone."

"Where's the car?"

"Windslow."

"Where in Windslow?"

She hesitated. "That's the tricky part."

"Tricky how?"

"It's like—" She looked to the side, thinking. "It's not, like, a parked car."

"Not parked? Sombitch! You want to rob a car while it's moving?" He said it as a joke, certain that she must have meant something else.

But her expression remained serious. "We'll need to stop it first."

"Sombitch! Are you serious? We stop the car and rob it? With the driver inside?"

"We'll have to, like, tie him up, or something. The way I figure—"

"Wait a second. Hold on. The way *you* figure? Like you're some kind of authority?" He shook his head. "You've changed, girl."

Her features tensed, holding something back.

"What's wrong?" he asked.

"Nothing. You going to help me do this thing or not?"

"What thing? I need details, girl. When? Where? How much?"

So she told him, and when she finished, he was sure of two things.

First, the payoff justified the risk.

Second, he had no idea how to pull it off.

Reddy opened the screen door, led Tejay inside, and introduced her to Spinelli.

"Tell him," Reddy said, resuming his seat at the end of the table. "Tell him what you told me."

Tejay sat between them, looking uneasy.

"It's all right," Reddy said. "I trust him."

"You've known me less than two weeks," Spinelli said.

Tejay frowned.

"Sombitch, Spinelli! You're not helping."

"Just being up front," Spinelli said. He looked at Tejay. "I think it's best to be up front. Tell it like it is. It's my way."

Tejay looked skeptical.

Reddy picked up his nearly empty bottle. "She knows where we can get some serious cash."

"Is it legal?" Spinelli asked.

"No," Reddy said. "Definitely not." He looked at Tejay. "Tell him."

She gave an exasperated sigh, got up, walked to the fridge. Reddy watched her go, noting the way her butt cheeks peeked from the frayed bottoms of her cutoffs. It was good having her home. "Hey, Tejay!" He drained his bottle and tossed it toward the bin. "Get me one, too."

"I'm not getting beer."

A dry-erase board hung on the refrigerator. She took the pen from its magnetic holder, broke the string, and carried it to the table. "I'm drawing a map."

Spinelli nodded. "Good idea. I'm a visual thinker." He kept his voice calm, ignoring Tejay's attitude, sitting back as she pressed the pen to the top of the table.

"This is where the money starts." She drew a rectangle and labeled it: MAYNARD FRIEBURG.

Reddy looked at Spinelli. "Maynard Frieburg," he said. "That's the name of the guy . . . the guy with the cash."

Tejay kept writing, adding a second line beneath the rectangle: ESTATE.

"And that's where the sombitch lives." Reddy beat his hands against the table, drumming softly. "He's got a house in the hills outside Windslow."

"More than a house." Tejay drew a peaked roof above the rectangle. "More like a mansion. It was his dad's summer home. The family owns mines. They're, like, stinking rich."

"Frieburg?" Spinelli said. "As in Frieburg Coal Company?"

"Yeah," Tejay said.

"They've got mines down south—West Virginia, Kentucky, Tennessee—"

"That's the company." She still had an edge in her voice, but she sounded impressed, too. She glanced at Reddy. *All right*, her eyes seemed to say. *He's smart. That don't mean we need him.* Then she reached toward Reddy's side of the table—the side across from Spinelli. "Move your arms."

Reddy sat back while she drew and labeled another box: STRIP MINE.

"This is where Frieburg takes the cash," she said.

Spinelli looked intrigued. "He takes it to a strip mine?"

"No." Tejay kept writing, adding a second line: GENTLEMEN'S CLUB.

"Not a real strip mine," Reddy said. "It's a sex place."

"Like a Wal-Mart of porn." Tejay added an exclamation point after the word *mine*. "Get it? It's like some stripper saying, 'Get me naked!'"

"Yeah," Spinelli said. "I guess I've seen the billboards. It's in Windslow, too."

"That's right," Tejay said. "This map . . . everything I'm drawing . . . it's in and around Windslow." She pointed toward the Frieburg rectangle. "That's where the money starts. And this—" She touched the rectangle by Reddy's elbows. "This is where it goes."

"How's it get there?" Spinelli asked.

"I'll show you." She drew a line that curved away from the Frieburg estate. "This is Windslow Road." The line turned left, then right, then straightened as it crossed the expansion seam in the table's center. "I've been driving it, back and forth, making sure I know the turns." The line twisted a few more times, straightening out as it neared the sex club. "Six miles." She capped the pen. "Two lanes. Totally rural. You can drive it on Sunday nights and never pass another car."

"You've driven it on Sundays?"

"Yeah. Lots."

"You've watched Frieburg make this trip?"

"Yeah. He packs a briefcase, gets into his big-ass Escalade, and drives to the sex club."

"Packs a briefcase?"

"Yeah!" Reddy said. "Packs the sombitch with cash!"

Spinelli frowned. "He takes a briefcase of cash to a sex club?"

"Twenties," Tejay said. "All stacked and shrink-wrapped. It's like $100,000."

"Maybe more," Reddy said.

"Hold on." Spinelli looked at Tejay. "You're sure about this?"

Tejay nodded. "I've *seen* it."

"Seen the briefcase?"

"That's right. And the money."

"She worked at his estate," Reddy said. "She was a temp there."

Spinelli looked skeptical. "How long ago?"

"I quit, like, yesterday."

"*Like* yesterday?"

"I quit, all right?"

"How long were you with him?"

"What the hell?" She looked at Reddy. "Your friend's interrogating me." She folded her arms, glared at Spinelli. "Listen . . . you don't like my information, you can walk away. Reddy and me can do this ourselves."

"No." Spinelli held her gaze, his voice calm, matter of fact. "You've told me too much to let me go. If you get caught robbing this guy, I'll be an accessory."

"Heck with that," Tejay said. "We're not going to get caught."

"In which case you'll have to cut me in. Otherwise . . ." He shrugged. "I might sell what I know to Maynard Frieburg."

Tejay glared at Reddy. "Now he's blackmailing us."

"Chill!" Reddy looked at Spinelli. "Everybody just chill." But he was getting hot, too. "Sombitch!" He balled his fists, pressing them to the table. "I need a beer." He turned to Tejay. "Get Spinelli one, too."

"I'm not your slave!"

"It's my house."

"The hell it is. It's your goddamn uncle's. You can't even pay the utilities on time."

"Let's focus, OK?" Spinelli said, voice still calm, eyes still centered on Tejay. "I'll get the beer." He stood up and walked to the fridge. "I think we're all a little parched." He took out three bottles and returned to the table. "I have four questions. Nothing personal. It's all business, all right?" He opened the first bottle and passed it to Tejay. "First question is . . . why so much cash?"

Tejay took the bottle. "What do you mean?"

"What's Frieburg buying every week at the strip club for $100,000 in cash?"

Tejay took a drink, put her elbows on the map. "Nothing," she said. "The money's not for *buying*. It's for *gambling*."

"Gambling?" Spinelli opened the second bottle and passed it to Reddy. "Gambling at a strip club?"

"That's what he told me," Tejay said. "It's some kind of high-stakes thing. The club closes Sunday nights. The games are private. And all that money—" She waved her hand. "He's so rich, it's like chump change to him."

"But not to us," Reddy said. "Thirty-three grand a piece for one night."

Tejay frowned. "Split it two ways, it'd be *fifty* each."

"Right." Spinelli opened the third bottle and took a drink. "But it could never be two ways." He looked at the map. "This isn't a two-person job. Try it with two, it'll fail."

"You got a plan?"

"Getting one," Spinelli said. "But here's my second question." He tapped the table on either side of the straightaway section of road. "What's here?"

"Field," Tejay said. "Just a field. High grass."

"Any trees?"

"Not many. It's like mostly grass and weeds. And there's a creek. The water's not too deep. And there's a thicket."

"Growing along the creek?"

"Yeah. It's, like, all jaggers and sumac. At least, that's how it looks from the road."

"And what about here?" He tapped the twisting section between the straightaway and sex club. "All these curves must mean it's cutting through hills and forest?"

"That's right."

Spinelli nodded. "That's good." He stared at the map, thinking.

Tejay glanced at Reddy, then back at Spinelli. "What's the last question?"

"Right. One more." Spinelli got up, crossed to the screen door, and looked out to where Tejay's Escort sat between his Yamaha and Reddy's F-150. "I listened to your car as you pulled up. Your transmission slips. There's not much tread on your tires."

"So? Like, what's the question?"

He turned back to face the two of them. "Do either of you have access to a reliable car?"

"Reliable how?" Tejay asked.

"Fast . . . something that holds the road . . . doesn't stall."

"Sombitch! Could we steal one?"

"No," Spinelli said. "Doing a robbery to do a robbery is never a good idea. It compounds the risk." He sat down. "And cars are problematic. Stealing a car is as risky as stealing credit cards."

"What?" Tejay said. "Who's talking about credit cards?"

"No one," Spinelli said. "Not at the moment. And that's the beauty of this job. Cash is king. Easy to move, difficult to trace. But none of that matters if we're caught at the scene. This job is all about getting away fast."

"So you're, like, saying . . . what?"

"Sombitch! He already said it. We need a muscle car."

"Maybe not a muscle car, per se," Spinelli said. "Though it would be nice if we could find one. But it does need to be fast and reliable. And one more thing . . . and I'll just say it fast and get it over with. The car needs to come with a driver."

"Another person?" Tejay glared at Reddy. "We can't cut in another person. This is—"

"A sure thing," Spinelli said, calm and strong. "And the driver gets either a flat fee or a low percentage. That's the way these things work."

"You sound like you've done this before," Tejay said.

"I've done lots of things before."

"Do you have a driver in mind?"

"No. I'm not from around here. But I'll see what I can do. A driver isn't hard to find. It's all about knowing where to look." He studied the table. "Windslow is . . . what? Fifteen miles south?"

"More like twenty," Reddy said.

"All right, then. I'll take a ride down there in the morning, scope the location, make a preliminary plan, find a driver."

"So we're, like, on for this Sunday?"

"No," Spinelli said. "This Sunday's a stakeout. The three of us will watch the road, follow Frieburg, verify your story."

"My story's true," Tejay said.

"I'm not saying it isn't. The verification I'm proposing isn't about *proving*. It's all about *learning*, noticing details, making sure we can play the cards we're being dealt. If everything checks out, we'll tell our driver to have his car ready for the following week. It pays to be certain."

"Yeah!" Reddy said. "It pays! One hundred grand."

Tejay gave a cautious grin. At last, she seemed to be warming to the idea of working with Spinelli. "One hundred grand," she said. "Ours for the plucking."

They looked at her.

"Plucking," she said again, her grin widening. "Like plucking a bird. That's Frieburg's nickname."

"Sombitch calls himself *Plucking*?"

"No. He calls himself *Bird*. It's, like, an Indian name."

"The sombitch is an Indian?"

"No," Tejay said. "Not a real one, but that's something I learned about rich people. They can afford to be whatever they want. These days Maynard Frieburg wants to be an Indian, so he's, like, Maynard Bird."

"Bird!" Reddy knocked his bottle against the rectangle labeled STRIP MINE! "Gonna strip us a bird!"

The service bay brightened, filling with a glow of chrome and red enamel as Axle removed the flannel cover from his restored Mustang.

"My god!" Spinelli said.

Axle nodded, gratified by the reaction. "Five years," he said, stepping back from the unveiled Fastback. "She was nearly dead when I found her. Squirrels nesting in the engine. Floor rusted through. I brought her back."

Spinelli moved closer, looking but not touching. "The ad in the paper said it was fully restored." He shook his head. "But you've done more than that. You've perfected her. She's beautiful." He looked up. "Are you sure you want to sell her?"

Axle shrugged. "I'm desperate, man." He glanced around at his flood-damaged garage: water-logged files, mildewed walls, rusting equipment—all ruined earlier in the month when three days of pounding rain had forced Bottoms Creek over its banks. "It's like the ad says. *Must sell.* I got no choice." He dug out the keys. "What say we take her for a spin?" He swung the chain on his thumb, catching the keys in his palm. "I guarantee . . . if you drive her you'll buy her."

Spinelli frowned. "Got a better idea," he said. "You drive." He headed for the passenger side. "Show me what she can do."

They roared out of the garage, the chrome igniting as they steered into the glare of morning.

"We'll take her out on the highway," Axle said. "I'll show you—"

"No, not the highway. Turn here." Spinelli pointed toward the left branch of an oncoming intersection.

"Back roads?" Axle said. "You want to see how she handles dips and curves?"

"Yeah. For starters."

Axle cut the wheel, watching from the corner of his eye as Spinelli braced against the armrest. "You might want to buckle up."

"No. I'm fine." Spinelli grinned, listening as the wheels squealed beneath them. "Nice," he said. "She holds the road nice."

The bend continued, becoming tighter, setting the treads humming like bowstrings on an asphalt fiddle.

"It's the suspension," Axle said. "Weight distribution, engine—all custom." He steered through a series of tight curves, finally coming out on a long straightaway flanked by open fields. Not another car in sight. Only asphalt, high grass, and a lone tree standing way beyond the sloping shoulder.

"What's her top speed?" Spinelli asked. "How fast can she go?"

"Plenty fast." Axle shifted. "Hold on." He cut loose, throttling up until the roadside grass blurred and the speedometer shot toward the 3:00 position. For a moment they seemed to fly, the long hood cutting the wind, the engine roaring like a V8 hurricane.

"Oh, man!" Spinelli said. "Jesus!"

They shot between a pair of road-hazard signs, one for each lane, both fluttering like kites in the Fastback's wake. And then, just as rapidly as he'd accelerated, Axle geared back, revving down, braking hard before the straight road veered toward a succession of downhill bends.

"Oh man!" Spinelli's voice caught in his throat. "How fast?" He glanced toward the speedometer, doing a double take when he saw the numbers on the dial. "Wait a minute! That thing goes to 140?"

"Yeah. And there's no governor on the engine. Give her enough road, she'll get you there."

"So we were going . . . what? How fast?"

"Not sure. I was watching the road." He steered across the center line, bringing the nose around until it pointed back the way they had come. "But it was pretty darn fast." He shifted to neutral, revved the V8. "You want to try?"

Spinelli glanced out at the field, toward the lone tree growing beyond the thicket-lined creek.

"I'm telling you," Axle said. "You drive her, you'll want her. It's that simple."

Spinelli turned. "You *really* selling her?"

Axle shrugged. "It's like I said. I got no choice."

"There's always choices."

"Right, but in this case the choices are sell my car or lose my business. The landlord's giving me till the end of the month to clear the back rent. And then there's the cleanup from the flood. That's going to take money—more than I have."

"How much?"

Axle looked away. "Make me an offer."

"I mean how much do you *need*?"

"Need?"

"How much to keep the shop open?"

Axle swallowed. "Maybe—" He didn't want to give a lowball figure, but it was his nature. "I guess $2,000 would keep me open another month." He gripped the wheel, wishing he could hold on and never let go. "I mean, if I had $2,000 I could cover the back rent, stay in business through the summer, hope things turn around."

"But this car's worth a hell of a lot more than $2,000."

"Yeah, but you asked me what I *needed* . . . the minimum . . . and I'm not selling the car to cover my minimum. See . . . I'm thinking selling her would put me right. Maybe for the first time ever I could remodel, get some good equipment, hire a few people—"

"But you didn't bring this Mustang back to life just to sell her. Did you? I mean, she's yours, man. You have a right to keep both her *and* the shop."

"Tell that to my landlord."

"Maybe I don't need to." Spinelli spoke slowly, his tone full of possibilities. "Let me see if I've got the picture here. If you had $2,000, you wouldn't need to sell the car, not yet . . . maybe not ever."

"Yeah," Axle said. "But *if* is a big word." He looked into the distance. "*If* I had wings, I could fly. Know what I'm saying?"

"But if there were a way to get it . . . the money, I mean. If I knew how you and your car could earn a fast $2,000, you'd be interested. Am I right?"

Axle turned, looking at Spinelli, getting the impression that the man had never intended to make an offer on the car.

"Am I right?" Spinelli asked again, speaking softly, not pressuring so much as inquiring. *I understand*, the tone said. *I want to help*.

"What are we talking about here?" Axle asked.

"About getting you what you need."

"What I *need*?"

"I'm talking $2,000 for a few hour's work."

"Right," Axle said. "I heard that. But that tells me nothing." Deep down, he sensed it was time to end the conversation, drive Spinelli back to the shop, put him on his Yamaha and wait for a real buyer to call about the ad in the paper. That was the safe thing to do. But instead, Axle heard himself asking, "Two grand for doing what?"

Spinelli shrugged. *Nothing much*, the gesture said. *Hardly worth mentioning*.

Axle waited.

"Just driving," Spinelli said. "Driving me and a few friends."

"In this car?"

"Yeah."

"Where?"

"Here and there. I can spell it all out if you're interested."

"When?"

"Whenever you're ready to listen. Now's as good as—"

"I mean when's the job?"

"A week from Sunday."

Axle winced.

"Problem?"

"A week from Sunday? That's taking me right to the wire. If I pull this car off the market now—"

"Which is the idea, right? Think about it, Axle. Level with yourself. You need to be up front about these things. It's the best way." The words sounded rehearsed. "Listen, you do not want to sell this car. You brought her back to life. Giving her up now doesn't make sense."

"But if I take her off the market I'm risking—"

"It's all a risk, Axle. Anything worth wanting or fighting for is a risk. You know that, don't you?"

"Maybe . . . maybe I know that sometimes . . . other times I don't know what I'm thinking."

"Then don't," Spinelli said, his voice low and calm, the tone full of the confidence that Axle wished he had. "Don't think. Let me do that for you. And let me tell you how you can keep your car and your shop." He pointed south. "Take us back to those curves, the ones right before Windslow. I'll tell you how we can do this."

Again, Axle considered saying he wasn't interested. But there was something about Spinelli, something that made Axle want to trust him.

He put the car in gear.

"Just one thing."

Axle toed the brake.

"Remember what I said about taking risks."

Axle stared at the road, past the pair of diamond-shaped signs, one facing south, the other north: **CURVES AHEAD**.

"I need you to remember what I said. It's the truest thing there is, man. Some things are worth the risk . . . worth the gamble." Spinelli paused, then asked, "You with me?"

Axle took his foot from the brake.

"We cool?"

"Yeah," Axle said. He kept to the speed limit, steered by reflex, and listened to Spinelli.

Sitting in her parked Escort on the side of Windslow Road, Tejay watched as a black Cadillac Escalade roared around a tree-lined bend and onto the straightaway.

Reddy whistled. "Sombitch is moving!"

Tejay glanced in the rearview, making eye contact with Spinelli. "Should I follow him?"

"Not yet," Spinelli said.

"Sombitch, Spinelli! We'll lose him."

"Not likely." Spinelli raised a set of binoculars, watching the Escalade accelerate toward the end of the straightaway. "Just hold back, Tejay. Wait till he's out of sight."

"Sombitch must be doing eighty."

"It's an Escalade," Spinelli said. "Six-liter V8, 400-plus horsepower. But the bends will slow him down. That's where we'll stop him next week, when we do the job."

"So you've, like, got the plan worked out?" Tejay said.

"Almost."

The Escalade braked as it reached the end of the straightaway, climbed toward a bend in the road, and vanished around a fringe of roadside weeds.

Reddy slapped the dash. "Go!"

Tejay turned on the lights, gunned the engine, and stalled.

"Sombitch, girl!"

She put it in park and tried again. The engine sputtered, turned over, locked up.

"We're gonna lose him, Tejay!"

"It's OK," Spinelli said. "We know where he's going. Give it a second. Let the fuel settle. Then try."

Reddy shifted, getting antsy. "This is *exactly* why we need a car . . . a *real* car . . . sombitchin *muscle* car! Not some out-of-production piece of shit!" He looked back at Spinelli. "How come we're not doing this with the real driver?"

"Because the driver's only getting paid for one night. We agreed, remember?"

"How about now?" Tejay looked back at Spinelli. "Should I try it now?"

"Go for it."

She turned the key. The engine started.

"Accelerate slowly," Spinelli said. "The point isn't to catch him . . . not this time."

Tejay steered off the berm, gaining speed along the straightaway.

Minutes later, with the bends of Windslow Road behind them, they passed the entrance to the Strip Mine Gentlemen's Club and parked on an overpass that hummed with interstate traffic. From the shoulder they saw the sex-club parking lot, nearly empty except for Frieburg's Escalade and a small assortment of upscale cars. Frieburg, briefcase in hand, stood in the club's lighted doorway. He was a tall man, thin and muscular, dressed like a designer Indian.

Bastard. Tejay tightened her grip on the wheel, staring at Bird. *Going to get you, you rich-ass prick.*

She averted her gaze, afraid that her anger might give her away, clue Reddy and Spinelli to the fact that the heist was about more than the money in the briefcase.

"Who's the other guy?" Reddy asked.

Tejay focused on the second man in the doorway: fat face, tailored suit, gold watch that flashed as he slapped Frieburg's shoulder.

"The club owner," Tejay said. "His name's Kirill Vorarov."

"Hell of a name," Reddy said.

"It's Russian."

"Fat sombitch."

"And rich, too. Drives a silver Viper."

Vorarov opened the door, and the two men turned, vanishing into the club.

"Viper?" Reddy said. "That's a muscle car. Bet a Viper don't stall when you give it gas."

Tejay glared at him. "You mean like your truck stalls?"

"I mean like this sombitchin piece-of-shit Escort stalls."

"You two need to stop that." Spinelli put the binoculars away. "We can't do this job if you two are always at each other." He tapped Tejay's seat. "Let's go back to Windslow Road. To the lower bends."

Reddy looked at him. "You going to walk us through the plan?"

"Right. Provided you two are up for listening."

"Let's do it!" Reddy said.

Tejay started the car. "Works for me." She turned the wheel, swinging the Escort back the way they had come.

They parked beneath the cover of a leaning poplar, on a gravel shoulder that sloped into darkness. With the engine off, the air hung silent and still. No insect noises. No croaking toads. But the silence was temporary. August was coming. In a few more days the bends would hum with the songs of primeval courtship. Tejay had heard that some insects ate their mates. People did that, too . . . but in different ways.

"It's quiet," Reddy said. "And no traffic."

Tejay nodded. "Just like I told you."

"All right," Spinelli said. "Listen up. This is how we're going to do it."

Axle pulled to the shoulder and killed the lights. Darkness closed in, obliterating everything but the throb of the Mustang's V8, the whir of crickets, and the clatter of water flowing in a ditch beyond the road. Then, from the backseat: "Point that thing the other way, Reddy!"

"Chill! The safety's on."

"Don't care. Get it out of my face!"

Glancing at the rearview, Axle saw the barrel of a shotgun leaning between a couple of lowlifes who called themselves *Reddy* and *Tejay*. He didn't know their real names, and that was fine with him.

Reddy shifted, leaning forward. "The hell you looking at, Axle?"

It had been going like this ever since Spinelli got out of the car three miles back on Windslow Road. Reddy seemed to think that Spinelli's absence put him in charge.

"You got something to say to me, Axle?"

Axle tried thinking of a response, knowing that staying silent would give the impression that Reddy really was top dog.

"Talk to me, Axle, you sombitch!"

Sombitch was Reddy's all-purpose expletive, and like everything else about him, it was getting on Axle's nerves.

"Hey, Axle! I'm talking to you!"

Axle's cell phone flashed, defusing the moment with a country-western ringtone. He answered on the backbeat.

It was Spinelli: "Bird's on his way."

Axle closed the phone.

"Was that him?" Tejay said. "Was it Spinelli?"

"Yeah." Axle put the car in gear. "We're rolling!" He pulled onto the road, angling across the center line.

"Plucking time!" Reddy said. "Gonna pluck the *bird*!"

Axle set the brake while Tejay pushed the passenger seat forward and opened the door.

The dome light winked on, spilling over Reddy as he lowered his ski mask. "Like Spinelli told you, Axle." His pupils flashed through the eye-holes. "Don't screw up!" Then he followed Tejay out onto the shoulder, vanishing into the dark weeds at the side of the road.

The night shivered. Along the shoulder, leaves hissed with the sound of approaching rain. But there was no wind, at least not down here on the lower bends of Windslow Road.

Teyunies, Axle thought, recalling a word that his great-grandmother had used to name such sounds. *Teyunies*, the whisper of an earthborn guardian.

Axle wondered what Great-Grandmother would say if she could see him now. She had claimed he was destined for great things. He doubted armed robbery was one of them.

You will be a great leader. A caretaker of the land.

He resisted the memory. Such things were better forgotten, and this was no time for drifting, for losing focus.

But it was no use. The smell of the night, the sound of the trees, and the sense that he was caught in a process beyond his control—all conspired to take him back to the last time he had seen the old woman alive.

Great-Grandmother had arms like ropes: sinewy, long, tied off at the ends with weathered fists. She wore a sleeveless vest and denim jeans. Her hair was long, hanging in braids that she secured with clips of hand-tooled bone. The braids swung as she walked, slapping her back with soft rhythms.

"Come on!" She spoke without turning, trusting that he was behind her.

The long walk into the highlands was her idea. He had agreed to go along because she had bribed him, promising to give him the money he needed to rent a rundown garage in Windslow Bottoms, and because he had nothing better to do, having been suspended from school for stealing the glow plugs from his history teacher's Volvo. He was a troubled kid, eighteen and foundering in the deep end of adolescence. For some reason, Great-Grandmother thought that a walk into the highlands would straighten him out.

He turned as he followed her, looking back along the cracked pavement of Cliff Mine Run, the poorly maintained strip of asphalt that wound into the hills to the north of downtown Windslow. He could still see his neighborhood, a sprawl of corrugated steel and mossy fences, the hardscrabble trailer park that residents called *Coals Hollow*: a nowhere place on the edge of oblivion.

Past the park's entrance the asphalt eventually widened, becoming a proper street that extended toward a shopping district where plywood covered many of the storefronts and the clock above the municipal building remained forever stuck at half-past-four. Behind Coals Hollow, accessible by a dirt path, the bends of Windslow Road meandered toward the interstate. Both routes—south on Cliff Mine Run and north on Windslow Road—led toward freedom. If Great-Grandmother wouldn't give him the body shop money, Axle figured he'd soon take off along one of those roads, escape Coals Hollow, never return. . . .

"Akeo!" She called to him as the road steepened. "Hey, Akeo!"

He didn't answer. Didn't even bother looking at her. He hated when she called him that. *Akeo.* It wasn't even a proper name, just an Okwe word that meant *left behind.*

"Akeo!" Her voice turned jagged. "Stay close, Akeo. I have things to tell you." She turned toward him, walking backward, sneakers kicking dust as she veered onto the road's gravel berm. In a way he was glad to hear her sounding so strong. Her health had been failing for weeks, but now she was back to being her old self—ninety-four going on forty-nine. "Get up here, Akeo!"

He walked faster.

"Your father left you. Your mother left you. Don't think I won't do the same." She reached out, her long arm grabbing his shoulder, pulling him into a one-hand hug that smelled of earth and clay.

He didn't resist. Her warmth felt good, reassuring, and for a while they walked side-by-side, their shadows merging in the fading light.

"What's this about, Yeyestani?" he said, calling her by the old name, the one she preferred to *Great-Grandmother.* "Where are you taking me?"

"Windslow Mine."

"But this isn't the way." He had been to the mine before, always entering along a dirt trail that abutted a lower extension of Windslow Road. "The mine's in the other direction."

"The low part is." She took her arm from his shoulders. "But we're not going there. We're going to the highwall."

He pulled back, opening the distance between them.

"I need to show you something on the cliff."

"Show me what?"

"You'll see."

"What if I'm not interested?"

She slapped him hard across the back of the head, the sound resounding like a pistol shot. "Be respectful," she said.

He rubbed his scalp, falling back, moving out of range of her long arms.

"Someday you'll need the things I show you tonight."

He doubted that, but he held his tongue.

After a moment she looked back, studying him with the corner of her good eye. "A caretaker of the land needs to know the way to the Heart of the World."

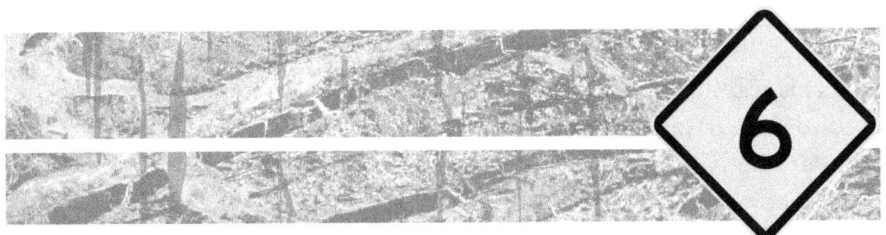

Axle hit the Mustang's flashers and opened the glove compartment. A plastic bag lay inside, stashed atop a roadmap of West Virginia. He retrieved it, opened the door, and stepped out into the soft clatter of the windless night.

Mist blanketed the wet asphalt, glowing in the dome light, breaking beneath his boots as he pivoted beside the car. It had been a strange summer, hot May followed by parched June. Early July had brought a three-day storm that caused more harm than good, but tonight the summer had delivered its first gentle downpour, the kind of shower that Great-Grandmother had called *female rain*: too brief to revive parched lawns and shriveled gardens, but enough to chill the air and coat the earth with low-lying fog.

Axle reached into the bag, pulled out a strontium flare, and struck it against the road. The top ignited. He tossed it. The flare traced an arc from his hand to a patch of asphalt beyond the Mustang's rear bumper. It landed with a spatter of sparks. Then it rolled, coming to rest in the downhill lane, staining the pavement with ruddy light. And all the while, Reddy and Tejay moved along the shoulder, getting into position.

Bird's SUV roared in the distance, still out of sight but coming on fast, high beams fanning a roadside fringe of laurel and sumac as it approached the downhill bend. Then its grill swung into view, swerving across the center line to avoid the flare.

Axle reached back into his bag, this time coming out with a high-powered flashlight. "Stop!" He clicked the switch, swung the beam, and raised his free hand to shield his eyes from the oncoming headlights.

The SUV roared closer.

He wanted to look, but he kept his face covered until the roar gave way to a locked-wheel shriek. The SUV skidded to a stop, heat from the grill wafting against Axle's raised hand. A power window whirred down. Music spilled out, American-Indian techno: cedar flutes, digital drums, chanting voices. "What the hell?" Bird yelled. "You trying to get yourself killed?"

Now, with the SUV stopped, Axle grabbed the hem of his ski mask and pulled it down across his face. The eye holes slid into position, and through them he saw Reddy racing out of the weeds to shove the shotgun through the SUV's open window.

"Hey!" Bird turned, head scraping the barrel.

"This way!" Axle yelled. "Look this way!"

Bird shifted, facing front.

"Put it in park!"

Bird complied.

Now Tejay approached, pulling herself up on the passenger-side door, banging on the glass.

Bird glanced at her masked face through the window.

"Open it!" Axle said. "Pop the lock!"

The automatic release clicked.

"That's good! Now put your hands on the wheel . . . up high . . . where we can see them."

Tejay opened the door. The interior lights came on, illuminating Bird. His hair was long, braided, clamped with clips of amber and bone. He wore a sleeveless vest, open in the front, fringed along the shoulders. Tattooed feathers covered his arms, becoming stylized flames as they reached his wrists. And his hands . . . there was something disconcerting about his hands. They should have been trembling with rage or fear, but instead they were as steady as his piercing eyes. Looking at them, Axle sensed Bird's power and privilege. Even now, with a loaded shotgun pressing his head, the man seemed poised to take control. "Listen," Bird said. "Do you *hatinyo* have any idea who you're messing with?"

Hatinyo was an Iroquois word. It meant *whitemen*, not that Bird had room to talk. Unless there were truth to the rumor that his mother had screwed an Okwe groundskeeper, his pedigree was about as indigenous as a jelly donut.

Tejay reached into the cab, grabbed something from the seat, and backed away.

"Hey!" Bird said. "What the hell are you doing?"

Reddy cocked the Remington: *Shk-SHK!*

Bird fell silent.

Tejay turned, raising her hands high to show Axle the briefcase: brown leather secured with combination latches. The brass accents flashed in the SUV's headlights as Tejay turned in place, doing a victory dance before tossing the prize to Axle.

Bird tried again: "Do you guys have *any* idea—"

Axle caught the briefcase. *Guys*, he thought. *Bird thinks we're all* guys.

The assumption was reasonable. In her mask and loose-fitting windbreaker, Tejay looked just like the rest of them.

"Do you guys have any clue who you're messing with?"

Tejay pulled a roll of duct tape from her pocket and returned to the cab. This time she hopped onto the front seat, right beside Bird.

"What the hell?" Bird said.

Tejay tugged the end of the tape—*Zzzck!*—ripped it with her teeth, slapped it down over Bird's mouth. Then she taped his wrists and eyes. *Zzzck! Zzzzzzzzck!*

Axle set the briefcase on the Mustang's backseat and climbed behind the wheel. *Clockwork!* He snapped off the flashlight, put it back in the bag, returned it to the glove compartment.

Everything as planned!

He slammed the door, shifted to reverse, and pulled alongside the SUV to find that Reddy and Tejay had moved Bird onto the floor behind the first row of seats, stretching him out in the aisle so that his legs extended into the rear cargo area.

Tejay worked quickly, binding Bird's ankles before scooting back toward the front of the vehicle. The plan was for her to return to the Mustang while Reddy released the break and sent Bird coasting over the sloping shoulder at the side of the road, but now Tejay was improvising, leaning back against the center island and kicking Bird with the heels of her western boots. She'd kill him if she kept it up, and Reddy didn't seem interested in stopping her. There was definitely something wrong with these two.

Spinelli had insisted that no one was to get hurt. Force was to be used only when absolutely necessary, and even then it was to be kept to a minimum. "If we do this right," Spinelli had said, "no one gets hurt. Not us. Not Bird."

Axle blew his horn.

Tejay turned, eyes flashing. Axle didn't need to see the face behind her mask. Her eyes said it all. The girl was out for blood.

After calling Axle to tell him that Maynard Frieburg's Escalade was on the way, Spinelli folded his phone and clipped it back onto his belt. By now the speeding SUV was out of sight beyond the bend in Windslow Road, heading toward the roadblock. If everyone stuck to the plan, the job would be over in a matter of minutes.

Spinelli stood up. He stretched cautiously, mindful that he was ten feet above the ground, perched on the branch of a dying oak. At his feet, a hooded windbreaker lay wedged against a juncture of trunk and limb. He had brought the jacket along in case the rain returned. But the sky was clearing now. Dry wind blew in from the west, pushing the clouds and stirring the thicket that grew along the banks of Saw Mill Creek.

Beyond the creek, standing atop the grassy berm of Windslow Road, a yellow hazard sign marked the spot where he would soon meet Axle's Mustang. In a way, that sign was the end point, the place where two weeks of planning would culminate in the perfect getaway. But it was also a starting point.

Combined with the cash he'd earned down south, tonight's heist would provide the extra cushion he needed to make a clean break. By tomorrow he planned to be a hundred miles east, starting fresh in Cumberland where a woman had agreed to put him up until he found a place of his own. Beyond that, he had no fixed plans. But he was good at putting things together. It would not take him long to think of something.

He knew he should get down from the tree and hurry toward the pickup point, but he felt momentarily lulled by the dark beauty of the land and sky.

Savor the moment.

He watched the drifting clouds. Wind stirred. Grass swayed.

Life is good.

He breathed deep, letting the night fill him with cool possibility. There was something invigorating about the prospect of starting over. He knew. He'd done it often enough. But this time felt different, better than the others, more certain and secure.

Time to make it happen. Get moving.

He scooped his windbreaker from the branch and tied it around his waist, letting it dangle like a backward apron as he swung down to land at the base of the tree. A flashlight dangled from his belt. He unhooked it, snapped it on, and froze as he heard something roar in the distance. He cocked his head, listening. The roar grew louder, changing pitch as a powerful glow rose beyond the thicket. It fanned out, swinging around to strike the road-hazard sign with a cold, blue-white glare.

Headlights!

He couldn't see the vehicle. The high thicket blocked it from view, forcing him to scramble back onto the overhanging branch where he raised his binoculars in time to see a sleek silhouette racing by, heading toward the lower bends.

"Shit!"

It was a Dodge Viper.

He dropped back to the ground, landing harder than before. The flashlight slipped from his hand.

Crack!

It fell hard, striking a piece of fieldstone, going out in a flash of arching filament.

"Christ!"

Darkness closed in, broken only by the ghostly flash of the arching bulb that repeated in his eyes each time he blinked. It followed him as he dropped to his knees, fading as he felt through the grass for the dropped flashlight. And all the while the Viper kept roaring along Windslow Road, changing pitch to a throaty snarl as it downshifted at the end of the straightaway.

Got to warn Axle . . . tell him to clear out now!

He gave up on the flashlight and grabbed his cell phone, flipping it open as he rose to his feet to find that he was now able to discern the gray trail of flattened grass that led back to the thicket. He hurried along it, hitting redial as he ran, stumbling when something grabbed him from behind.

"Goddamnit!"

A mass of low-lying thorns had snagged his hood.

"Shit!"

He tried tugging it free. No use. The beads on the drawstrings had swung like bolos, tangling in the branches. Only one thing to do. He untied the sleeves, abandoning the windbreaker.

By now, Axle's voice was buzzing in the earpiece, calling Spinelli's name, sounding confused. "That you, Spinelli?"

"Yeah. Listen up." He faced forward again, hurrying alongside the thicket. "There's another car."

Axle didn't respond.

"You hear me, Axle? It's a goddamn Viper. You've got to clear out now!" He gripped the phone, waiting for a reaction, getting only the sound of a loud thump.

The next instant, the earpiece went dead.

Bird lay motionless at Tejay's feet. Unconscious? Dead? Axle wasn't about to get out and check. He blew his horn again and gestured for Tejay to leave the cab. This time she moved, sliding across the seat, climbing down through the open door.

Axle didn't wait for her. It was enough to see that she was coming out. He shifted into reverse and smoked rubber through a U-turn that brought him around behind the SUV, facing uphill, ready to drive north over the six-mile stretch that led to the interstate's southbound ramp.

Almost there.

His phone chimed its country-western ringtone. He grabbed it, flipped it open. "Spinelli?"

The voice on the other end sounded distant, angry. "Shit!"

"Spinelli?"

The earpiece crackled: snapping branches, clattering leaves—sounds of a struggle.

"Spinelli?" Axle shifted the phone to his other ear. "That you, Spinelli?"

"Yeah. Listen up."

Axle listened, cupping the phone as he checked the rearview to see Tejay racing toward him. Reddy was nowhere in sight, but the SUV's brake lights were on, indicating that the red-haired bastard was behind the wheel. For now, at least, things seemed to be back on track.

"There's another car," Spinelli said.

The Mustang's passenger door flew open. Axle turned to find Tejay glaring at him, evidently still pissed at having been ordered out of the Escalade.

Spinelli's voice crackled in the earpiece. "You hear me, Axle?"

Axle gestured for Tejay to get in fast.

"It's a goddamn Viper. You've got to clear out now!"

Tejay shoved the front seat forward, banging it loudly as she climbed into the back.

Axle broke the connection. It was time to move.

"What is it?" Tejay asked, anger giving way to concern. "Was that Spinelli?"

"We have to clear out now."

"What's wrong?"

There wasn't time to explain. "Reddy needs to get in here!" Axle adjusted his rearview, looking back to see that Reddy now stood in the center of the road, raising his shotgun as the SUV coasted toward the shoulder.

Tejay turned in her seat. "What's he doing?"

Reddy fired, striking the SUV broadside as it plunged into a cover of trees.

"Hey!" Axle roared, calling out the side window. "*Get in the goddamn car!*"

Reddy turned, sprinted toward the Mustang, and climbed into the back next to Tejay. He closed the door. Then he grabbed the forward backrest, pulling it into place.

Axle met his rearview gaze. "Why'd you fire that gun?"

"Had to purge the chamber." The Remington thumped against the seat. "You got a problem with that?"

Axle just stared, wondering how such a pair of losers had ever gotten involved with a clever guy like Spinelli.

"We can't go riding around with a cocked 12-gauge," Reddy said. "I *had* to discharge it!" He pulled the ski mask from his head, red hair sparking in the darkness. "That all right with you, you freaking grease monkey?" He leaned forward.

"Sit back and buckle in," Axle said.

"Don't tell me what to do!"

"Have it your way." Axle kicked the gas and let out the clutch.

Reddy flew back, banging his head on the rear ledge. "Sombitch!"

Axle drove toward the flare that still burned in the downhill lane. He pulled alongside it, braking hard.

Reddy flew forward again, catching himself on the front passenger seat. "The hell you doing, Axle?"

Axle opened his door.

"You trying to piss me off, you sombitch?"

Axle grabbed the flare and tossed it into the runoff below the sloping shoulder. "I'm just sticking to the plan," Axle said.

The flare hissed as it struck the water.

"You know the drill, Reddy." Axle slammed the door. "Leave nothing in sight. Nothing to attract attention." He accelerated again, throwing Reddy back a second time.

"Sombitch!"

"I told you to buckle in."

"Hell with that! I don't buckle. Seatbelts are dangerous. I saw it on TV."

Tejay gripped Axle's backrest. "Something's wrong, isn't it?"

"Yeah," Axle said. "Big time."

"What?" Reddy kicked Axle's seat. "You're pissed because I fired my gun?"

"Not that," Tejay said. "Spinelli called back."

"And?"

Axle braced for the turn. "There's a Viper coming."

"A Viper? You telling me it's Kirill Vorarov's car?"

"I'm telling you Spinelli said it's a Viper."

"Don't make sense," Reddy said. "Vorarov's supposed to be back at his club."

The road brightened with approaching headlights, blue-white, full of xenon glare.

"Sombitch!" Reddy covered his eyes. "Ought to be a law against those things."

Axle glanced left as the Viper hissed by: top up, driver little more than a silhouette in the rushing night.

"Tejay," Axle said. "You get a look at that guy?"

"Yeah." She turned, glancing out the rear window as the taillights vanished around the bend. "Sort of."

"Was it Vorarov?"

"Yeah. I think so." She raised her ski mask, folding it over her forehead. "I mean, a car like that, who else it gonna be?"

"But that sombitch is supposed to be back at the club, right?"

"Yeah," Tejay said. "*Supposed* to be."

Axle sensed something in Tejay's voice, an odd tension as if she were holding things back . . . or possibly that she didn't really know as much as she claimed.

Bird regained his senses, rising from a well of pain to find himself lying on the floor of his SUV, on his side between the back seats, legs extending into the seatless rear. The people who had robbed him were gone. He could move without being kicked, but tape still bound his eyes, mouth, hands, and feet—and the SUV was moving, coasting from the cracked asphalt of Windslow Road, onto the gritty shoulder that sloped into the forest.

The cab tilted, moving faster.

He rose to his knees, flopping onto the seat beside him. He needed to get to the door, though he had no idea how to open it with hands lashed across his back and tape covering his eyes. And then—

BLAM!

Something hit the vehicle, blasting through the rear driver-side window. He ducked, clenching down as shattered glass peppered the interior. It sounded like high-velocity hail. The bastard with the gun had taken a shot at him!

A voice called from the road, audible through the shattered window. "Hey! *Get in the goddamn car!*"

It was the voice of the man with the flashlight, the only one of the three who had spoken during the robbery. *Face front!* the bastard had said. *Look at me!* But there had been nothing to see, only a man in a ski mask standing in front of a black car. *A Mustang?* He couldn't be sure. In his memory the thing was little more than a silhouette: no decals, racing stripes, or chrome. He wondered if the car's body had been coated with something, masked as thoroughly as the punks who had robbed him. And now the car was leaving. In a few seconds it would be gone, and Bird needed to know who was inside it, why they had messed with him, who they worked for.

He had no intention of letting this incident slide.

Bastards! Dead-meat bastards!

He knew he might actually have a chance of catching the pricks, but only if he made it back to the road in time to intercept the silver Viper.

He said he'd follow me. Got to be on his way by now . . . got to be!

Whatever that black car was—Mustang, Charger, GTO—the Viper could catch it.

But first I've got to get to the road!

Bird rose to his knees and threw his chin against the headrest. Cool air struck his face, blowing through the shattered window.

The SUV rolled faster.

Branches slapped the windshield, swinging back to scrape against the side panels. He wished he could still hear the voices from the road, maybe catch a spoken name as the crooks piled back into their car, but the only sounds now were the muted thumps and bangs of the SUV as it plummeted deeper into the forest.

Can't let those bastards get away.

He wiggled between the seats and into the wind from the shattered window.

Don't think about it. Just do it!

Shattered glass crunched beneath his moccasins as he pushed into the wind, through the jagged opening, and into a stretch of empty air.

WHUMP!

He landed hard. The slope was wet. He kept moving, sliding as the SUV coasted beside him, tires crunching close to his head. He kicked, dug his feet into the weeds, and rolled away. Then he crawled, working uphill as a crunching thud rose behind him. The SUV had struck something, stopping with the sound of an exploding headlight.

He crawled on, fighting toward the road.

Bastards!

He would get them. Whatever it took, he would find out who they were, who they worked for, why they had robbed him.

Prick bastards!

He'd catch them, make them pay. . . .

The car roared away, racing uphill as Bird crawled through a chill of shallow runoff. Then, inexplicably, the racing engine changed pitch, falling back into a well-tuned idle.

The car had stopped.

Bird rose to his knees, cocked his head, heard the click of an opening door. Had they seen him? He held his head high.

Come get me, you bastards! Don't leave yet! I'm expecting company!

He tried standing up, but his feet slipped on the wet ground. He fell, crashing sideways onto a grassy slope. The angle made it clear that he was still below street level. Whatever had stopped the punks in their tracks, it wasn't the sight of him. For all they knew, he was still in the Escalade.

He rested a moment, listening as the car's door banged closed again. The engine revved. Tires squealed, shrilling away.

His rage burned hotter.

Dead! You bastards are dead!

Had his lips been free, he would have screamed it.

You're all fucking dead!

He ascended the slope with a series of kicks, finally crunching down onto roadside gravel. He dropped to his knees, then onto his side. The surface beneath his face felt hard and smooth. *Asphalt!* He was in the downhill lane, gasping for breath, struggling to get up, dizzy from too much exertion, too little breath. And through the dizziness, he heard an engine roaring toward him.

Had the Mustang turned around?

He cocked his head, listening.

No. This engine was different, screaming like a jungle cat. He knew the sound. It was the Viper, racing full throttle, making up for lost time.

He'll run me over!

Bird wanted to scream.

Stop, Goddamnit!

But all he could manage was a duct-taped moan, a muffled cry lost beneath the V10's thundering roar.

Axle blinked, clearing the xenon glare from his eyes as he accelerated out of the turn. The Viper was gone now, racing toward the bend where Bird and his SUV lay hidden deep in roadside trees.

"Hell with it!" Reddy said. "So it was Vorarov! Like that even matters!" He lifted the briefcase from the seat, set it on his lap, and looked at Tejay. "Let's open this sombitch." He set his hands on the latches. "What's the combination?"

"Don't know," Tejay said.

"What the hell? You're supposed to know the combination!"

"It's probably zero-zero-zero," Axle said.

"Say what?"

"That's the factory default on those things. Most people don't bother resetting them. Try all zeroes."

"Yeah! Factory default! Hit the dome light. I can't work in the dark."

"Not now," Axle said. "Wait till we get Spinelli."

He downshifted through another bend, momentarily crossing the center line. He was tired of dealing with Reddy and Tejay on his own. Things would be easier once Spinelli was back in the car. After that, the four of them could cross the border into West Virginia where Spinelli had a friend living in a WVU frat house. The house had an attached garage: dark, windowless, reeking of beer. The space didn't get much use during the summer, but tonight Tejay's Escort and Spinelli's Virago were parked inside, awaiting their return.

The plan was to stop at the garage and divide the cash. After that, Axle would remain long enough to restore his Mustang's original color. Since Bird's memory of the night would center on the getaway car, Spinelli had insisted that Axle disguise it with a coat of body latex. The stuff sprayed on like paint. When it dried, it formed a black coat that completely masked the car's finish and accents. Removing the coat was easy.

It peeled away like skin from a sunburned back.

"Zeros!" Tejay reached for the briefcase. "Try zeros."

"Can't," Reddy said. "I can't see the numbers."

"Let me try."

"Hell with that! Hey, Axle. What about that flashlight? Where'd you put it?"

"Hold on!" Axle downshifted as he rounded the bend onto the straight-away. He studied the road. "Something's wrong." He hit the high beams as he neared the hazard sign.

Spinelli was not at the pick-up point.

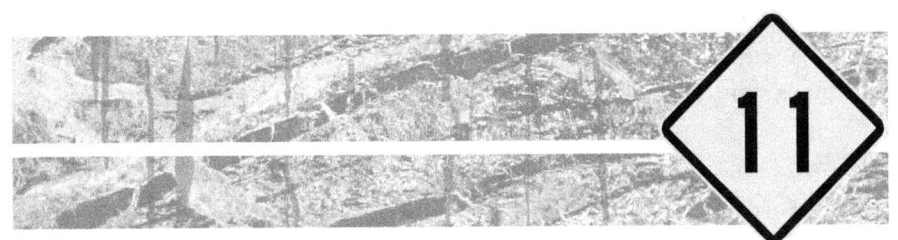

The Viper on Windslow Road notwithstanding, Kirill Vorarov was, in fact, right where he had always planned on being: five miles south of the hazard sign, sitting in his sex-club office, and contemplating one of his life's central ironies: sex. He was bored with it. It was all around him, but he couldn't be bothered.

People only want what they don't have, he thought, remembering a man who had once given him a lesson on wanting and having. He had last seen that man at a bar in New York City. It had been years ago, but the scene remained vividly clear in his mind.

"It's the truth," the man said. "A lot of people don't appreciate it, but it's the truest thing there is."

The man with the lesson was a chef at a three-star restaurant in Manhattan, but to look at him you'd never have suspected he had anything to do with food. He was nearly six foot, hundred-forty pounds, thin as a stick of vermicelli.

"The thing is, if you *got* it, why *want* it? See what I'm saying?"

Kirill shrugged. "I see it," he said. "I just don't get it."

Kirill did not know a lot about the chef's personal life, but he had tasted his *foie gras*: smooth as butter, laced with cognac, seasoned with cracked pepper and sea salt. It was perhaps the most exquisite thing Kirill had ever tasted, but the skinny chef claimed he never ate the stuff. Indeed, Kirill had never seen the chef eat anything.

"How can you not *want* to eat? Look at you. Like a splinter. You should eat something."

"And what about you, Kirill? You should go on a goddamn diet."

The chef wasn't being mean. He was just trying to sound like Kirill's good buddy, a dear friend from way back, the kind of person who could bust your balls and still be your brother. None of these things were true, of course. Kirill didn't even like the chef, but he let the comment slide. Business was business.

The bar where they were sitting was in an upscale bistro at 73rd and Lexington. The chef was off duty, but Kirill was working. Those were the days when Kirill ran collections for Uncle Ilya, and the chef, who hadn't picked a winner in weeks, was in deep.

"How can I diet?" Kirill said. "There's so much good food."

"For you, maybe. But that's because you aren't around it all the time. For me, it's nothing." The chef forced a smile, still trying to pretend that he and Kirill were friends, two chums having a couple of Upper-East-Side drinks, far from Shea Stadium where the Mets had lost again, far from Little Odessa where Uncle Ilya still ran the family business from a third-floor walk-up overlooking Brighton Beach.

"The thing you got to understand," the chef said, "the thing you got to realize . . . is the importance of anticipation. See, you only want what you don't have. That's the key. Me, I've got food. I'm surrounded by it, buried in it. White truffles, forest mushrooms, *perigord mousse*, *foie* fucking *gras*—what's to want when it's all right there?" He looked at Kirill, a cautious, sideways stare that was all about the things they were not talking about. "You know what I'm saying, Kirill?"

Kirill shrugged. The afternoon was winding down, and the chef was still delinquent. "You're saying food bores you?"

"Yeah." The chef sipped his drink. "You got it, my friend. My life's a fucking bore."

"So what are you telling me? You're ready to die now?"

The chef flinched.

Now, years later, sitting in his office on the ass-end of Pennsylvania, Kirill had to admit that the scrawny chef with the miserable betting record had known a thing or two about life.

Since opening the club in Windslow, Kirill had been surrounded by sex: by women who worked for him and danced on his stage and performed for the Internet porn sites that brought in more money than the club itself, by DVDs that filled his video racks, by magazines and toys that made up the bulk of his mail-order business—all of it was there for the taking. It was his. Anytime.

You gotta have what you don't have. That's the key.

And what were the things that the chef had wanted? Money? Time? If so, at least the skinny bastard had ended life with a hunger for something.

And what were the things Kirill wanted?

He sat back, looking across his paneled office toward a 1:240 scale model of a proposed resort called *Mountain Downs*: a sprawling mass of cantilevered architecture overlaying the former site of the Windslow Surface Mine.

Tonight he would be meeting with two people who were working to make that model a reality. One was an eccentric landowner who called himself *Bird*. The other was a Harrisburg attorney named Paul Peterson. They were an unlikely pair, but with any luck they would help Kirill realize a project that would at last put some distance between him and the babes and the DVDs and the toys. He would get what he didn't have. Then maybe he would actually want the things he had now.

Bird had called an hour ago to confirm the meeting. He and Peterson were supposed to be driving over from Bird's estate, and now the two of them were late.

Kirill checked his watch: ten minutes late.

His chest fluttered. Anticipation? "Screw it!" He pushed back from his desk. Perhaps he should go downstairs. It was quiet down there. He could drink a ginger ale while he waited, or maybe help himself to one of the bottles of Glenlivet or Ikon that he kept in a locked cabinet beneath the bar. He could—

His phone rang.

He checked the number. It was Paul Peterson. He took the call. "You're late, my frien—"

"Kirill!" Peterson sounded breathless, frightened. "Something's happened!"

A second voice shouted in the background, screaming as if in pain. And there were other sounds, screeching tires, howling wind.

"Something bad!" Peterson said, his voice falling away as if the phone had been yanked from his hand.

"Paul?"

No answer.

"Peterson?"

Screeching tires, howling wind, then nothing.

"*Peterson!*"

The connection failed.

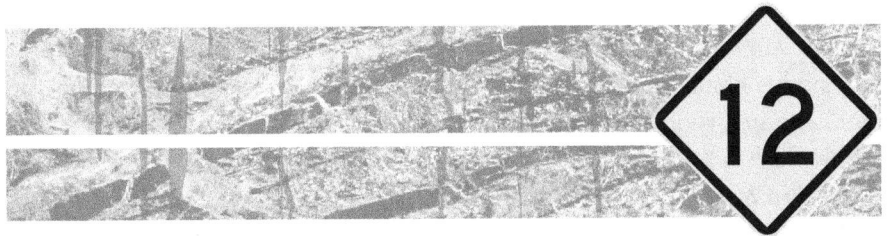

Spinelli's path stretched into the darkened thicket, past a choir of singing insects, toward the sound of flowing water and croaking frogs. He had crossed this same ground less than thirty minutes earlier, lighting his way with the flashlight that now lay broken in the field behind him. Could he find his way in the dark? Did he have a choice? He stepped forward, advancing toward the creek and the line of flat-backed stones that formed a dry path through the water. Beyond the stones, now cloaked in total darkness, a small clearing tapered toward a grassy slope and the hazard sign that marked the pickup point.

Almost there.

He pushed on until the creek appeared as a coal-black division between ebon banks. Overhead, branches hung low, weighed down by creepers and vines that formed a woven ceiling against the sky. And here he stopped.

How do I cross if I can't see the stones?

There had to be a way. Most problems had simple solutions. And he was a problem solver, an idea man.

So what's the solution?

He crouched by the water, taking stock of the things he carried: wallet, keys, pocket knife, binoculars, cell phone.

The phone.

He pulled the phone from his belt and flipped it open to check the brightness of the screen. No good. The pale glow barely extended beyond his hand. But the phone also had a camera . . . and the camera had a flash.

Worth a try.

He held the phone over the water and snapped a picture, squinting as the stones flashed into view. The first one waited just beyond the bank. Its likeness repeated when the flash winked out: a ghostly image floating in his vision, reappearing when he blinked, fading as he took his first step. Then, standing on the first stone, he raised the phone and hit the flash again, repeating the process, working his way across the creek until he saw something that made him stop. He glimpsed it as the flash ignited, a vague shape crouching on the edge of the bank. He blinked. The image repeated. What was it? A man? He blinked again, studying the details: tapered loin, crooked legs, clawed feet. . . .

Not a man.

Another blink. The image lost its definition. Maybe it was nothing: a gnarled trunk, twisted roots. He wanted to believe that. "Hello! Someone there?"

No answer.

Only a tree.

He looked at the phone, checking the captured image on the screen. Nothing unusual there. Only the shadows of trees. He punched up the contrast. One shadow stood out, different from the others. Tree-like, but different. He clicked to the previous shot. The shadow was there, too, but in a different position.

Christ!

He brought the phone closer, clicking through the photo record, checking all the shots. With each click, the shadow changed position, ambling backward until it slipped out of frame.

Not a tree.

He advanced the pictures again. The thing lumbered forward, toward the center of the screen.

It's right in front of me.

Yet it made no sound. Surely if there were something moving on the shore—something as big as the shadow on the screen—he would hear it. Wouldn't he?

Not if it's only a shadow . . . a trick of the light.

There was one way to be sure. He raised the phone, looked straight ahead, and hit the flash.

He saw it then, leering at him in the sudden blast of light, its face nearly touching his outstretched hand. There was no time to comprehend. It was suddenly there, then gone. And Spinelli, who prided himself on cool judgment, felt himself leaping away—jumping backward through darkness to land on the edge of a mossy stone. He lost his balance, fell, and plunged into the creek. A moment later he was sitting on his ass, wiping water from his eyes, and watching the image of the thing reappear behind his lids: wolfish face, human torso, hawk-like wings. . . .

The details made no sense, but there they were, pulsing behind his lids each time he rubbed his eyes. And now he heard the thing moving, stirring the air with giant wings. The sound rose. He looked up, glimpsing the creature's blurred shadow as it crashed through the canopy of leaves and vines.

Then it was gone.

There's an explanation.

He wanted to believe that.

A wild turkey . . . a trick of the light.

He stood up, shaking water from his hands, and realizing as he did that he now had something new to worry about. He'd lost his cell phone.

Goddamnit!

He crouched back down and felt along the mud and stones that lined the creek bed. The phone wasn't there, and he couldn't waste time looking for it. Axle's Mustang was already approaching, roaring in from the south bends of Windslow Road.

Screw it!

The phone was a prepaid disposable, purchased from a street dealer, cash transaction, no ID. Axle's number was in the memory, but so what? That was Axle's problem, not his.

Still shaking water from his hands, Spinelli slogged forward until he reached the bank. Then he climbed out, rose to his feet, and plunged head-long into a wall of jaggers and vines.

Where's the clearing?

He thrashed forward, fighting panic as something grabbed his neck. He turned, striking out against a mass of leaves, realizing that this time it was his binoculars that had become ensnared in the undergrowth. He jerked away, breaking the strap and pushing on as the Mustang approached the pick-up point.

I need to be there . . . need to be there now!

But he also needed to calm down. He could not appear frightened in front of the others. The four of them had miles to go before they divvied the cash and went their separate ways, and the rag-tag team needed a leader, a self-sure presence to hold them together a few more hours. They might have the briefcase, but plenty of things could still go wrong if the leader lost control.

Stay calm. They'll wait. They have to wait.

He kept moving, finally breaking through a wall of sumac and into the grassy field that led toward the steep shoulder of Windslow Road.

But it was too late.

Atop the slope, still hidden by high grass, the Mustang was rumbling away.

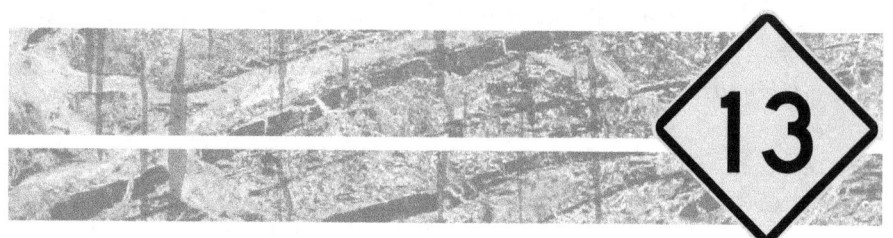

A xle continued a few hundred feet beyond the sign, looking to see if Spinelli was farther up the road.

"The sign," Reddy said, looking through the rear window. "Sombitch was supposed to be at the sign!"

Tejay knelt on the seat, peering back beside Reddy, the briefcase momentarily forgotten. "What now? Do we leave without him?"

"Damn straight!" Reddy said. "That's what he told us. We wait for no one, including him. We follow the plan, right?"

"We can't leave him," Axle said.

"Why not?"

Axle glanced at the rearview, meeting Reddy's challenge eye-to-eye. "Because it's wrong."

"Screw that!"

"We waited for you, didn't we?"

"When?"

"When you were taking your pot shot at Bird's SUV."

"That was different. You knew where I was."

Axle stopped, put the Mustang in reverse, and roared back to the hazard sign.

"So what the hell?" Reddy asked. "What now?"

Axle swerved into the southbound lane and stopped beside the sign. "I guess we wait." He rolled down the side window, looking out, studying the landscape: tall grass, weedy thicket, weathered oak.

"This is where we left him, right?" Axle opened his phone and hit callback. The earpiece hummed, ringing four times before switching to voicemail.

Axle closed the phone and opened the door. The dome light came on, spilling onto roadside gravel.

"Light!" Reddy said. "Now we can see." He grabbed the briefcase. "Leave the door open, man!"

Axle's shadow stretched before him as he stepped from the car and scanned the high grass below the slope. He heard something moving. "Hey!" He peered down the steep decline. "Hey, Spinelli! That you?"

Behind him, Tejay and Reddy argued in the backseat, their voices venting through the open door as they struggled with the briefcase:

"Sombitch!"

"I almost had it, Reddy!"

"Sombitch! Move your fingers!"

Axle took another step, away from the voices, toward a lumbering shape that materialized out of the high grass. And then: "It's me!" The shape stumbled forward. "Give me a hand, Axle."

Axle descended the slope, reaching out to grab a soggy sleeve. "What happened?"

Spinelli's shoes made farting sounds as Axle pulled him onto the berm. "Fell in the creek!"

"Hurt?"

"No. Drenched is all."

"Didn't you have a windbreaker?"

"Yeah," Spinelli said. "And a flashlight and binoculars. *And* a cell phone." He shook his head. "I lost my goddamn phone."

"What happened?"

He turned away. It was clear he didn't want to talk about it. "Doesn't matter." His voice trembled.

"You all right?"

"Yeah, just cold is all. That water was cold." He looked toward the thicket, then up at the sky. For a moment he just stood that way, as if searching for something in the air.

"Sky's clearing," Axle said. "I think it's done raining."

"Yeah." Spinelli turned toward the car. "Let's get out of here." He sounded stronger, his voice no longer shaking, back to business. "Did you see that Viper? The one I called you about?" He rounded the front of the car, heading for the passenger door.

"Yeah," Axle said. "We passed it. Tejay thinks it was Vorarov."

"Probably was. Who else would it be?" Spinelli paused, looking south. "Did you get Bird's SUV off the road?"

"Yeah. Reddy did that. Over the shoulder, completely hidden."

"The flare?"

"Gone. I tossed it in the runoff. Like you said."

"The briefcase?"

"Reddy and Tejay got it."

Spinelli looked through the side window, frowned a moment at what he saw, then looked back at Axle. "I appreciate you stopping for me. I won't forget that."

"No way I'd leave a man in the middle of nowhere."

Spinelli nodded, then opened the door and climbed in, shoes flinging mud across the floor mat, pant legs making soggy skids as he settled into the seat.

Axle climbed behind the wheel.

"Sorry about this mess, Axle."

"Nothing soap and water won't fix." He slammed the door.

"*Sombitch!*" Reddy said. "Put the light back on. We're working here!"

Axle gunned the engine and steered into the northbound lane. His mind raced ahead, contemplating the ground they had to cover once they left the straightaway: one bend curving away from the Frieburg Estate, a second veering past the rear entrance to the Coals Hollow Trailer Park. The next turnoff after that was the interstate, barely two miles away. They were almost home free.

Spinelli looked back at the briefcase. "You open that yet?"

"Sombitch is locked. And it ain't *zeros*!"

"Zeros?"

"That's what Axle said. Factory default. Fucking zeros!"

Axle said nothing.

Spinelli reached into a back pocket. "Try this." He pulled out his pocket knife. "Use the screwdriver. Pop the latches." He passed the knife over the seat, hesitating as the blue-white glow of xenon headlights dawned beyond the rear window.

It was the Viper, top down, high beams blazing.

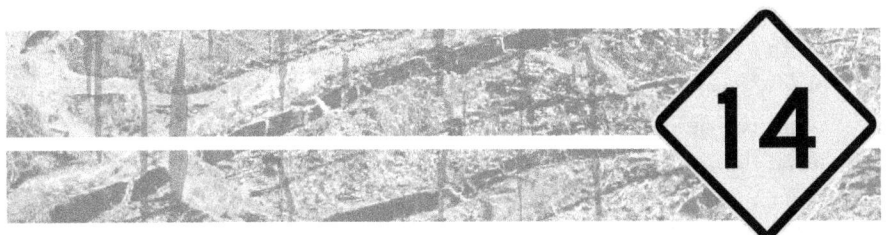

Paul Peterson could not believe how fast the night had raced out of control. Twenty minutes earlier he had been standing in the gun room of a highland estate, admiring a collection of artisan-made pistols and accepting yet another not-entirely-legal gift from the client who called himself *Bird*. Previous gifts had included imported vodka, Cuban cigars, and a custom Dodge Viper. Peterson always made a point of driving the latter when he came west to consult with Bird on the Mountain Down's project. But even that extraordinary gift had not thrilled Paul the way tonight's present did. More than any of the others, tonight's gift, an artisan's copy of a Soviet-era handgun, was a clear sign that Bird and his partner Kirill Vorarov regarded Paul as their equal. He wasn't only their attorney. He was one of them.

From the beginning, Paul had been intrigued by his eccentric clients, and although he'd been hired to do the grunt work required to secure their casino license, he had often found himself wanting to become a bigger part of the fast-lane world in which they lived.

And now, racing north on Windslow Road with his Viper's top down and Bird in the passenger seat, he was getting his wish.

"Floor it!" Bird screamed, ripping duct tape from his wrists and tossing it into the wind. "Drop that fucking phone and drive!"

But Paul couldn't drop the phone. It was too late for that. He had called Vorarov, and now Vorarov was talking, chiding him for being late.

"Kirill," Paul said, gripping the phone as he steered one-handed through a turn. "Something's happened!"

Bird screamed again. No words this time. Just a pained shriek as he yanked duct tape from his hair.

Paul tried focusing, concentrating on breaking the news to Kirill. "Something bad—"

Bird lunged, grabbed the phone, snapped its lid, and banged it down into the cup holder in the center console. "Just drive!" he said. "Kirill can wait until—" He straightened up, peering through the windshield as the bend brought them onto a hill above a straightaway. "That's them!" Bird pointed to a car idling beside a hazard sign. "Faster, man! Catch them."

"And then what?" Paul asked, maintaining speed.

"We get my fucking briefcase."

"Get it? Just like that?"

"No. We use persuasion." He grabbed a brush-metal case from the floor.

"What're you doing?" Peterson asked.

"What do you think?" Bird lifted the case onto his lap.

"You can't be serious."

Bird opened the case. The artisan-made gun lay inside, resting in a sponge bed beside a full magazine.

"No." Paul took his foot from the gas.

"I told you to drive, goddamnit!" Bird picked up the gun. "Those bastards stole my briefcase, and I don't intend to negotiate." He slapped the magazine into the grip and turned the gun on Paul. "Drive!"

Paul hesitated.

"I am *so* not kidding!" Bird racked the slide, chambering the first round. "Drive!"

Paul hit the gas. The V10 roared.

"That's all you've got to do, Peterson. Drive. Just drive, fast as you can."

"And you? What are you going to do?"

"Me?" Bird gripped the top of the windshield. "I'm going to show you why I made you drop the top on this fucking car." He pulled himself up onto the seat, braids whipping in the wind as he rested the gun atop the convertible's windshield.

Up ahead, the Mustang accelerated off of the straightaway and toward the hairpin bend that wound past the entrance to Bird's estate.

"Flash your beams," Bird said. "Get them to stop." He steadied his aim.

Paul flashed the beams.

In the cup holder on the center console, the cell phone started ringing.

15

A xle checked the mirror. The Viper was coming on fast, top down, beams flashing.

"Sombitch!" Reddy knelt backward on the seat, squinting into the glare. "Sombitch is signaling us!" He shielded his eyes, trying to get a good look. "This is fucked!"

Axle hit the gas, hurtling full throttle toward the first downhill turn.

"It's the same one," Reddy said. "It's the one that passed us before. Vorarov's car."

Axle downshifted as he hit the bend, burning rubber through a sideways skid, putting the bend between them and the Viper.

Spinelli looked back as the road went dark. "It might not be him," he said. "Might not be the same car."

"Screw that," Reddy said. "You saw his lights. Sombitch was flashing us!"

"Maybe he wanted to pass."

"No! No way! Sombitch wanted us to *stop*. It's the same car. I know. I got a good look."

"But its top is down," Spinelli said. "The top was up on the other one, the one I called you about, the top was—"

"Right! *Was* up. Now it's down. It's down because the sombitch put it down!" Reddy grabbed the headrest, pulling himself forward.

Spinelli turned away, facing front. "Sit back, Reddy."

"No, man. Listen to me!" Reddy's shotgun slid from his grip, landing in the gap between the seats. "You got to listen. I saw—"

The Mustang hit a dip. Reddy's chin struck the backrest, but he kept talking, spit misting in the dashboard's glow. "I saw him. I looked back and I saw him leaning forward. That's why the Viper's top is down now, so he can lean forward and aim across the windshield."

"So *who* can aim?" Spinelli asked. "Aim *what*? Who're you talking about?"

"Who the hell do you think? Maynard *fucking* Bird!"

"You saw Maynard Bird in the Viper?"

"Damn straight. In the passenger seat."

"You looked into those xenon high beams and saw Maynard Bird?"

"I saw *someone*. Who else would it be?"

Spinelli looked at Tejay. "Did you see any of this?"

"Shit. I ain't seen nothing." Tejay rode scrunched against the seat, head below the window, arms wrapped around Bird's briefcase. "And I ain't looking."

"It was him," Reddy said. "I bet you anything it was Maynard Bird aiming at us across the windshield."

"Aiming what?"

"What do you think? A gun, you sombitch!"

"How'd Bird get a gun?"

"Like that even matters. The point is he got it. I know what I saw!"

Axle reached for the stick shift. The 12-gauge was still there, resting between the seats, getting in the way. "Damnit, Reddy! Move this piece of shit!"

"Who the fuck you talking to?"

Spinelli grabbed the shotgun, pushing it back. "Damnit, Reddy. The man's got to drive!" He shoved the barrel toward Reddy as Axle shifted onto a straightaway.

Reddy grabbed the barrel and sat back. "Find a turnoff, Axle! Get us off this road."

Up ahead the pavement veered again, curving past a break in the trees. Beyond the break, a dirt path. Beyond the path, a grid of gravel roads and incandescent lights. It was the turnoff leading down to Coals Hollow.

"Do something, man!" Reddy kicked the seat. "That's what we hired you for! You know these roads. Get us out of here!"

The asphalt turned. Axle continued straight, crashing down the unpaved trail and onto a gravel street lined with rusted mailboxes and mossy fences. He swerved, losing control. *WHAM!* He clipped a post, sending an oblong shadow arcing past the side windows. It was a mailbox: flag up, door open, tumbling like a low-orbit satellite.

"Sombitch, Axle! You're in someone's yard!"

Axle steered into the skid, regained control, roared back onto the gravel lane. The end of the park lay straight ahead, gravel intersecting with the lower bends of Cliff Mine Run.

He couldn't turn left. That way led into town and a half-dozen out-of-synch traffic lights. He'd never lose the Viper that way. The only chance lay to the right, into the highlands, toward the place that Yeyestani had called *the Heart of the World.*

16

"Why are you calling it that?" he asked.

She kept walking, away from the trailer park and into the highlands until she came to a point where Cliff Mine Run veered sharply to the right. He expected her to follow the asphalt, but instead she stepped onto the shoulder and toward a weedy slope that descended into a wall of trees. "Why am I calling it what?"

"The Heart of the World," he said, still standing on the edge of Cliff Mine Run, not sure he wanted to follow. "Why are you calling it *the Heart of the World?*"

The sun had set, filling the forest with premature night, blotting out Yeyestani as she entered the trees. "I'm calling it that because that's what it is."

"*Was,*" he said. "But not anymore. The mountain's *gone.*" She had made that point often enough, reiterating it in the stories she had told him since he was old enough to listen. Why was she changing things now?

"*Was,*" she said. "*Was* gone."

"What's that supposed to mean?"

She kept walking, invisible now, a voice in the shadows.

He stepped forward. "Am I supposed to follow you?"

No answer.

He kept moving, crossing the shoulder until he stood before a path that had not been visible from the road. Gouged by truck wheels, the path rose in the middle, rutted on the sides, covered with a blanket of knotted weeds. It was an old coal-hauling road, cut before he was born, probably abandoned since the death of his father.

The ruts extended through an arch of trees that thinned on one side after a few dozen feet. He saw a stand of low weeds where the trees fell away. Beyond the weeds, a steep slope descended toward the sound of running water. *A creek,* he thought. The countryside was riddled with them:

shallow rills meandering through the highlands, gradually wending their way toward Windslow Bottoms and out to the Monongahela River. Some of the creeks had names: Saw Mill Creek, Bottoms Creek, Cliff Mine Creek. But most were nameless ruts. There was no way to keep track of them all.

The trail continued past the slope, running parallel to it for a short distance before curving into a wide, level clearing.

He moved forward, down the trail, past the sound of running water, and onto the oval patch of cleared ground. The rutted trail extended beyond the curve, bisecting the clearing and passing beneath a chain that hung suspended between concrete posts. Riveted to a center link, a rusted sign claimed the site as property of OSM. The name meant nothing to him.

Beyond the chain, the wheel ruts continued straight for another hundred feet before curving again, this time into total darkness.

"Hey!"

No answer.

"This is stupid, Yeyestani! I'm going home!"

Silence.

Of course she didn't need to answer. They both knew what was at stake. If he turned back, she'd keep her money and he'd never get his body shop. It wouldn't matter to her that his life held no other prospects and that not getting the body shop would keep him on the fast track to nowhere. She was belligerent that way.

He stepped over the chain, followed the trail, and soon came to a place where the forest thickened to his left, becoming a woven fortress of creepers and brambles. To his right, a rocky wall curved inward, forming a shale alcove. Looking up, he saw that the alcove's wall rose thirty feet or so, ending at an overhanging ledge and a giant tree that tilted beyond the brink. A gibbous moon lay in the tree's branches, glowing through brittle leaves, mottling the forest floor with silver light.

The old woman couldn't have scaled the cliff any more than she could have pushed her way into the bramble forest. She had to be somewhere on the level path. But where?

"Yeyestani!"

The rock wall amplified his voice, and this time, when the reverberations died, something stirred: the windless hiss of branches and leaves—spirit sounds.

Whispers of an earthborn guardian.

He shivered and cupped his hands to his mouth, pushing his voice as loud as it would go. "Yeyestani! Where are you?"

The hissing stopped.

Silence returned.

And then, within the silence, a voice from beyond the bend: "This way!" It was Yeyestani. "Come on!"

He did as she said, hurrying forward until the path straightened and the forest opened before the edge of a deep abyss. She was there, waiting for him, standing at the mouth of a ledge road that led down along a face of sheared-off rock. He knew where he was now. Although he had never seen it from this angle, he recognized the terrain. Looking beyond Yeyestani's silhouette, he saw trails running like screw threads toward the floor of a man-made valley and, way down on the valley floor, an unpaved road stretching south toward Windslow.

He walked toward her.

"Careful," she said, keeping her back to him, her face toward the wide hollow of the abandoned Windslow Surface Mine. "This is the ground that swallowed your father."

17

Kirill Vorarov hit the callback button on his desk phone.

The earpiece hummed. Once. Twice. "Pick up, Paul!"

A third ring, and then: "*Kirill!*"

Kirill pressed the phone hard against his ear, trying to distinguish Paul's voice from the other sounds coming through the earpiece: howling wind, racing pistons, and a ranting voice that sounded like Maynard Frieburg.

"Bastards!" Maynard roared. "Bastards robbed me. Kicked me in the head. Took my briefcase. You tell him that. Tell him they're going to pay!"

"Paul." Kirill tried sounding calm. "Is that Maynard? Are you with Bird?"

"Yes. I found him lying on Windslow Road, bound and gagged."

"Tied up?"

"*Taped* up. They used silver-backed tape. That's how I saw him. The backing reflected my headlights. If not for that, I would have–"

"They shot my Escalade!" Bird shouted louder. "Tell him! Tell Kirill what they did, goddamnit!"

"They shot out one of his windows," Paul said. "He had to crawl through broken glass. Now he's all cut up . . . and he's pissed."

Tires squealed.

"Paul." Kirill was pacing now. "Are you driving?"

Tires squealed again. "Yes." The squeal seemed to go on forever. "We're driving . . . going after them."

"After who?"

"The men who robbed Bird—"

"My briefcase!" Bird screamed. "Bastards took my briefcase. Tell him!"

Kirill returned to his desk, leaned against it. "Who?" he asked. "Who did this thing?"

"Don't know. Three men in a black Mustang. Bird says—"

"Let me talk to Bird."

There was the muffled sound of the phone changing hands, and then: "Three guys with masks!" Bird said. "They stopped me on Windslow Road."

"You have any idea who—"

"None. But they were punks. Little guys."

"Where are you now?"

"North bends of Windslow. We just passed my estate. The Mustang— *holy shit*!"

"Hold on!" Paul shouted.

Something thumped, a deep jolt that Kirill felt right through the phone, the sound of Paul's Viper bottoming out on unpaved ground.

Kirill gripped his desk, holding on as the thumping gave way to the roar of tires on gravel.

"Coals Hollow!" Bird said. "They've taken a back entrance into the trailer park. Christ! I didn't know that ramp was there. The bastards must be local. They know their way—"

"Bird, listen to me."

"They're cutting through to Cliff Mine Run."

"Can you stop them?"

"I intend to do more than stop them."

"No. Stop them. That's all. Stop them. We need to find out who they're working for. We need to know—"

"I know enough," Bird said. "I know they fucked me over. I know they shot a hole in my Escalade. I know they took my fucking briefcase!"

"Listen to me." Kirill was pacing again. This conversation was going on too long. The line wasn't secure. "Just stop them, Maynard. And if you can't stop them, stay with them. Find out where they're going. That shouldn't be hard to do. A Viper against a Mustang. No contest. Just stay with them."

"I'll do more than—"

"Just stay with them. Help is on the way." He broke the connection.

The problem in doing business with a man like Bird was that he lacked a clear sense of identity. He wanted to be a businessman, but he dressed like an Indian. And he didn't understand that men like him, men with money and power, were supposed to keep their hands clean. Dirt and blood were for soldiers, not generals.

Kirill had plenty of soldiers, but something like this required special skills.

He cleared the line, opened his directory, scrolled down until he found the name he needed: Calder, Sam.

Then he punched in the number and awaited the automated prompt that screened the soldier's calls.

She believed in the virtues of a simple life, a cabin built from trees that she had felled with the help of a man and two boys who no longer shared her world, a stream for washing, a well for drinking, and a patch of cleared forest on which to grow enough vegetables to get her through the year. When necessary, she purchased additional supplies in Huntersburg. And of course there was a forest full of rabbit, turkey, pheasant, and deer— all of which she hunted and trapped in season. It was important to obey such laws. She did not like being hassled.

The cabin had power, supplied by a waterwheel built by an Austrian company specializing in off-grid hardware. The wheel produced enough juice to run a pair of LED lamps, a laptop computer, and a few low-energy appliances. In winter, a wood stove provided heat.

A bank of batteries ensured a reliable power reserve, and, when the stream froze over, she had a gasoline generator in a shed abutting her cabin. It was all top-of-the-line. She liked the simple life, but keeping it simple required a degree of reliable technology. The hardware was expensive. But she had money. She didn't work often. When she did, the pay was good.

Her office took up most of the cabin's main floor. Here she stayed in contact with the world via a high-speed satellite connection, monitoring national and international news and maintaining a blog that she called *The Self-Reliant Woman*.

A rack behind her workstation held a trio of guns: a Remington 700, a Benelli 12-gauge, and a high-powered M40A1. The first two were for hunting. The latter, hand-built by Marines at Quantico, Virginia, was for work.

Above the guns and workstation, a sleeping loft stretched beneath the cabin's peaked roof. A pair of windows opened out of the front and back gables. On all but the coldest nights, she slept with the windows open. She liked the feel of open air. But tonight, something felt wrong.

She noticed it while still asleep, a sudden updraft accompanied by a whistling in the trees. Leaves turned belly up, rising skyward, intimating a return of the passing rains that had swept through the region a few hours earlier. But the air smelled wrong: too dry for rain. The strangeness of it roused her, pulling her awake as the hissing grew louder.

Rolling onto her side, she opened her eyes and peered through the screen. A shadow skirted the ground, cutting the moonlight, too fast and close to be a passing cloud.

The cabin shivered, walls creaking, lilting westward. She was sure of it now. The wind felt wrong. She knew the forest. This was not its normal voice. . . .

She rolled away from the window and onto the ladder that led to the lower level. Moon shadows danced along the floor, spilling onto her face as she crossed to her workstation window. The wind came from behind the trees, from beyond the storage shed. Nothing else moved, only those trees. The rest of the forest, as much as she could see of it, appeared rigid and still.

She turned, grabbed the Benelli, and headed to the door.

A porch extended from the front of the cabin. She crossed it and hurried down the stairs, running now, pivoting on bare feet as she reached the ground. And then, with a sound like the snap of an unfurling sail, a shadow rose from behind the cabin. It blurred skyward, straight up, a cruciform silhouette backlit by the moon.

Her nightshirt billowed in the updraft. And then everything went back to normal. The forest sighed. Branches relaxed. Leaves drooped, hiding their bellies.

What was that?

She stepped forward, out of the gable's shadow and into the light of the cloud-streaked moon. And then, from the empty cabin, a voice: "It's Kirill!"

She turned, listening.

The voice came again.

"It's Kirill!"

Her phone seldom rang. Unless she were in the field with the ringer set to vibrate, its software prompted each caller to record an announcement that played until she answered, or until the phone disconnected.

"It's Kirill!"

She cradled the shotgun. "What does he want?"

She returned to the cabin, climbed the narrow stairs, and pushed through into the first floor. The phone sat on her workstation, flashing in its charger. She grabbed it, flicked it open, pressed it to her ear. "Damnit, Kirill. It's late."

"There's trouble," he said, sounding shaken. "I need you out here."

"Your office?"

"Yes."

"Tonight?"

"Now."

She crossed to the back of the cabin, returning to the workstation window. Everything looked as it should, the view forcing her to rethink what she had seen. The thing had to have been a bird, a turkey perhaps—its size exaggerated by darkness. She wanted to believe that. But there was one problem. Her militia training had given her calibrated eyes: 20/20 vision, acute night perception, and a reflexive ability to size up points of reference. She wasn't given to visual error.

So what did I see?

"Sam?" Kirill said. "You there, Sam?"

She turned away from the window. "I'm here." She closed her eyes, letting her internal senses give her the time before checking it on her workstation clock. *10:13 PM.* She opened her eyes, checking the dial, seeing that she'd been correct. Her inner clock rarely let her down. Again, she said, "It's late, Kirill."

"I understand."

"If I come out now, it's going to cost you extra."

Kirill already had her on retainer.

"We'll discuss that later," Kirill said.

"Should I pack for business?"

"Yes."

"Urban or field?"

"Field."

"Night?"

"Yes. Tonight. Right now."

"Targets?"

"Three."

"Category?"

"I'll tell you," he said. "I'll tell you what I know when you get here." He sounded tense. "Damnit, Sam. We're wasting time."

She returned the shotgun to its rack. "Half an hour," she said. "I'll be there in half an hour."

"Make it sooner." He broke the connection.

She dressed quickly, putting on a set of woodland BDUs: jacket, pants, and hat—all with camouflage patterns of forest green. Then she pulled on her boots, grabbed the M40A1, and headed back outside. The rifle wasn't loaded. Keeping such a precision weapon in a constant state of readiness would wear down the mag spring, and she never used the gun around the property anyway. There was ammo in the Jeep. She would load in the field.

Rounding the cabin, she paused to take another look at the clearing behind the shed. She had seen giant birds out west when she had bivouacked with a survivalist named Incendiary Ray. But the largest bird in these parts was an occasional golden eagle. Their wingspans were impressive, sometimes approaching eight feet. That was big, but this thing tonight had been condor size, and it had flown like no bird she had ever seen. Straight up! But what was that to her? The thing was gone, and she had work to do.

She shouldered her rifle and turned toward the car.

A person who lived in the wild had to accept the odd encounter. Whatever the winged creature had been, it had posed no threat. One look at her, and it had leaped to the sky. Odds were she'd never see it again.

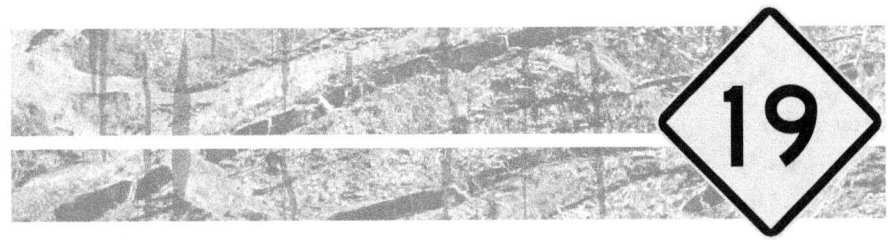

19

Axle accelerated around an uphill bend and onto a short, level stretch. Straight ahead, Cliff Mine Run crossed a patch of subsided ground, the pavement disappearing momentarily beneath a sheet of runoff that pooled from a roadside ditch. He gripped the wheel and splashed through. Waves rose beyond the side windows, fanning out like gigantic wings. The front wheels lost traction.

Hydroplaning.

That was all he needed, to spinout with the Viper hot on his tail. He took his foot from the gas, cutting his speed. And then he was through, back on dry asphalt, accelerating toward another uphill bend as the Viper's lights flared again in the rearview.

"We got to blast the sombitch!" Reddy thumped his shotgun. "Blast him good!"

The Viper hit the flooded pavement, slicing through like a powerboat. The driver didn't cut his speed. He just kept coming, closing the gap between himself and the Mustang.

"I have to blast him," Reddy said. "You hear me, Spinelli? Blast him good!"

"Blast him how?" Tejay asked. "You gonna hang out the window?"

Reddy braced the Remington's stock against the floor. "Whatever it takes." He raised the barrel, gripping the breech with one hand, reaching for the slide with the other.

"Don't!" Spinelli said. "Don't cock that thing in here."

Shk-SHK!

"Goddamnit, Reddy!"

"Chill! Safety's on . . . for now."

Spinelli turned to Axle. "You'd better get us off this road."

"I'm working on it."

"Work faster!"

Axle watched the asphalt unfurl in his headlights. He was looking for the sloping shoulder, the point where roadside gravel angled toward a wheel-rutted trail. He had not revisited this spot in years, not since the weeks following his highland journey with Yeyestani, when his young psyche had struggled to make peace with the events of that long-ago spring night. Most of what he knew about the terrain came from those subsequent visits, all of which had been during the day. Not once had he dared return to the place after dark.

The cab brightened as the Viper drew closer, the scream of the racing V10 drowning out the Mustang's roar, and it was then that Axle saw the turnoff, the break in the trees, the rutted trail leading into darkness. He downshifted and jerked the wheel, flew from the pavement, hit gravel, and hurtled forward.

Sparks flashed above the Viper's windshield.

Pop-pop-pop!

The man in the passenger seat opened fire, spraying the Mustang with bullets that pinged against the trunk and shattered the rear window. Reddy and Tejay dove for the floor, slamming into each other as the Mustang bounded toward the trees. Axle tensed, back and shoulders clenching as the pistol rang with semiautomatic fire: *pop-pop-pop!*

One of the shots whizzed through the cab, hitting the dashboard, sinking deep into the padding. And then the Viper was gone, racing away on Cliff Mine Run, taillights blazing like demonic eyes.

"*Told* you!" Reddy leaped up, raising his Remington, pointing it at the ceiling. "I *told* you he had a gun!"

The Mustang bounded forward, momentarily bottoming out as it hit the hump of the rutted trail—

BLAM!

The night vanished with a blinding light. Something slammed Axle's ears: a terrible sound, a noise like fists against his skull. For a moment he was transported, out of the car, out of himself, into a weightless place where he drifted through glaring deafness.

And then. . . .

WHAM!

The front end bottomed out again.

Suddenly he was back in the moment, surrounded by ringing chaos: people bouncing and shouting with muffled voices.

Spinelli turned, mud flying from his pants and shoes as he reached into the backseat to grab Reddy's Remington. "Damn you, Reddy!" His voice sounded flat, nearly inaudible beneath the ringing in Axle's ears. "Put the fucking shotgun away!"

"Away?" Reddy's hair blew in the sudden breeze from the Mustang's ceiling. "Away where?"

Axle glanced toward the source of the wind, a jagged hole that opened into darkness. *The shotgun.* He put it together, coming to grips with what had just happened. *The shotgun discharged, blew the dome light right through the ceiling.*

The Mustang continued moving, barreling between the trees.

Axle blinked, trying to clear the barrel flash from his vision as the front end bottomed out a third time.

WHAM!

And all the while, Reddy and Spinelli went right on arguing:

"Put it away? What do you mean, you sombitch? Away where?"

"Don't care where!" Spinelli tried pulling the gun from Reddy's hands. "Just get rid of it!"

"Screw that!" Reddy twisted the barrel, bending it back until Spinelli let go. "My gun's not the problem!" He pulled the weapon toward him, cradling the stock. "And I was right about Bird. It was him, like I said. And he had a gun, just like I *told* you."

"Yeah? And you told me your safety was on. What about that?"

"Fuck it!" Reddy said. "So I made one mistake. That don't mean I'm wrong about Bird." And then, as if it settled everything, he added: "Kiss my ass!"

Axle kept blinking, watching the trail until a clearing emerged beyond his bouncing headlights. He took a hard right, continued a short distance, and hit the brakes. Straight ahead, a rusted chain and a pair of concrete posts blazed in the high beams.

Spinelli looked at Axle. "What's this?"

Axle killed the lights and engine.

"This is it?" Spinelli said. "This is your plan? Park here, turn out the lights, hope they don't come after us?"

Axle wiped his forehead, trying to get it together. He felt sick, light-headed, disconnected.

"Damnit it, Axle, I'm talking to you!"

Then, beyond the ringing in his ears, Axle heard another sound: the roar of the Viper approaching the forest trail.

"Sombitch!" Reddy kicked Spinelli's seat. "Let me out!"

"What?"

"Damnit man, let me out!"

Beyond the shattered rear window, darkness gave way to a refracted blue-white glow.

"Goddamnit!" Reddy said. "I'm gonna blast that sombitch. If you want to keep your eardrums, you'll let me do my shooting outside!" He kicked the seat again. "Let me the fuck out of this car!"

"Shit!" Tejay said, looking back across the trunk. "Here they come."

Spinelli opened the door, making room as Reddy climbed out, crouched, and took aim at the approaching glow.

"Come to Reddy, you sombitches."

20

Standing on the ledge of Windslow Mine, Yeyestani pointed toward a portion of the collapsed highwall. "Your father is still under there," she said. "They tried digging him out, but the rocks kept shifting. In the end, they decided to leave him."

Axle tried imagining his father beneath all that fallen dirt and rock. "Doesn't seem right," he said.

"But it's the way it is, Akeo. Sometimes it's easier to forget about a little man."

"Is that why we're here?" Axle asked. "To talk about him?"

"Yes," she said. "And other things." She lifted her gaze away from the collapsed wall and out to where the land rose before descending again toward the interstate. Axle knew what she was looking at, and *knowing* made him uneasy.

"Those spotlights," she said, indicating twin beams that blazed behind a pine-capped rise. "You know about them?"

"Yeah." He shifted. "So?"

The source of those lights was legend among the boys of Windslow, all of whom had seen the windowless building on the hill beside the highway. And they had seen the billboards too, signs displaying hot babes beneath electric-pink banners reading: STRIP MINE!

The signs only showed the women from the shoulders up, but their expressions made it clear that they were totally naked. Axle did not want to discuss such things with Yeyestani.

She seemed to understand. "I'm not talking about *tekhakahat*." She always used the old words when broaching matters of sex. It was her way of moving the subject out of the present, giving it a context beyond transitory urges. "I have other things in mind." She lowered herself, sitting on the ledge, legs dangling into the void. "I need to tell you about the man who owns those lights." She touched the ground beside her, motioning for Axle to join her on the brink.

He hunkered down, easing forward until his legs dangled with hers.

"His name is Kirill Vorarov," she said.

Axle frowned at the strange sounding name. "Say what?"

"It's Russian," she said.

"He's from Russia?"

"Yes, by way of New York."

Axle shrugged. "So what's he doing here?"

"He wants to develop this land . . . this mine . . . the surrounding hills."
She kept her eyes on the distant lights. "You need to know his name, Akeo."
An edge entered her voice as she turned to study him with her dead eye.
"Someday you'll cross him."

"I don't know what you mean."

"You will." She turned a little more, both eyes looking at him now. She
had told him about her dead eye, the one that bulged from its socket like a
polished stone. She claimed that it saw the future. If that were the case, she
was seeing him twice: as he was, and as he would be.

"You'll understand," she said. "Maybe not tonight, but in time. Big
changes usually take time." She turned away, looking again at the wedge of
fallen rock. Parts of the slope were overgrown with trees, fast-growing sumac and poplar whose roots had found purchase amid the jagged scree. In
places, the intertwined branches formed forest islands, the largest of which,
a quarter acre patch of dense canopy near the top of the slide, resembled
the shoulder of a glacial hill—more like a portion of ancient hillside than
an eighteen-year-old fall of rock. "But other times," she continued, "big
changes can occur in an instant."

He knew she was thinking about his father.

"He was driving," she said. "Hauling 50 tons of dirty coal, leading a
four-truck convoy. When the haul road gave way, the thunder of it carried
clear to Mt. Morris."

Axle studied the slope, looking for his father's face among the leaves.

"It was company greed that killed him. The wall was unstable. Engineers
had recommended cutting a new ramp along the northern end, but man-
agement didn't want that, not with the easy coal nearly gone and the mine
ready to close within a year."

"So they killed him."

"That's what I say, but I'm no lawyer, and the lawyers said there wasn't
enough proof." She sighed. "It was dirty business, Akeo. When it ended,
the mine closed and the owners walked away. They kept their money, too.
Nothing for the workers' families, nothing for the land . . . and soon the son
of one of those owners will return to his father's highland home and join
forces with Kirill Vorarov. Once that son returns, things will happen fast."

"What son?"

"Maynard Frieburg. His father built a summer mansion on a rise off Windslow Road. The place is closed now, but the son will return. He'll move in, renovate the place, begin a partnership with Vorarov." She coughed, deep and throaty, a sound of disgust. "It's only a matter of time before they get together." There was no speculation in her voice. She spoke as if stating fact.

"Why are you telling me these things?"

"Because they're important."

"To me?"

"To everything." She stared at him, her face bent into a pensive frown that seemed almost as weathered and scarred as the surrounding landscape.

"What?" he said. "What are you looking at?"

She leaned sideways, tilting until she seemed on the verge of losing her balance. The moon hung behind her now, her face in shadow, her voice a whisper between backlit braids. "Remember," she said. "Dream and remember."

"What?"

She touched him gently, though for a moment he feared she might grab him and lose her balance, hauling them both down into the mine. "You'll understand." She withdrew her hand. "Someday. Trust me. You'll dream the memory of now, and you'll understand."

She turned away, pulling herself back from the abyss and springing to her feet with an agility that belied her age.

"Come on," she said. "I need to get back."

"Back home?"

"Yes, back home." She turned, but instead of retracing her steps toward Cliff Mine Run, she moved along the brink until she came to a steep decline, a ledge road that angled down along a portion of sheared-off highwall.

He called after her. "I thought you said we were going home."

She kept walking.

"Yeyestani!"

She answered with her back, giving him no choice but to follow her down into the hollow that had once been a great mountain at the Heart of the World.

hk-SHK!

Spinelli flinched at the sound of Reddy's 12-gauge cocking beyond the Mustang's open door. But he said nothing. It was time to let the red-headed punk have his way.

To Reddy's left, the Viper moved along the forest trail, advancing toward the clearing, rumbling like a jungle cat.

"This isn't worth it," Tejay said. She pulled the briefcase from the glass-strewn seat, lifting it onto her lap. "I say we give it back. He wants it so bad, he can have it."

"Shut up," Reddy said.

The blue-white glow grew brighter, coming nearer. But the Mustang remained hidden, in shadows to the right of the approaching beams.

Reddy steadied his aim.

Spinelli covered his ears.

BLAM!

A xenon headlight exploded, spewing shards and sparks as the Viper lurched to a stop.

Reddy held his aim as he worked the pump.

Shk-SHK!

Bird didn't duck for cover. He stood on the passenger seat, pivoting toward the shotgun's ratcheting click as Reddy fired again.

BLAM!

The blast hit Bird in the chest. He went down, falling from the car, vanishing into a tangle of ferns and sumac.

"One sombitch down!"

Shk-SHK!

Screams rose from the Viper. It was the driver, shouting into a cell phone, shrilling: "They shot him! They shot Bird!" The voice couldn't be Kirill Vorarov's. It was too young, too frightened.

"They shot Bird! We're off Cliff Mine . . . above the site . . . and *they fucking shot him!*"

The V10 roared back to life.

Reddy waited a moment, picking his shot as the driver tried steering out of the line of fire.

BLAM!

The Viper's windshield shattered.

Shk-SHK!

Reddy shifted his weight to his other knee, keeping the Viper in sight as the driver lost control. "C'mon, you sombitch. Give me a shot!"

The engine revved. Tires spun, lifting the front end free of the rutted trail and into the side of a tree. The second headlight shattered, misting into darkness.

Reddy aimed at the side of the car.

BLAM!

The air rang with the thump of imploding fiberglass, clearly audible beneath the gun's roar, and then, just as suddenly, silence.

Reddy gripped the pump, about to reload.

"Enough!" Spinelli said. "You got him."

"Don't hurt to make sure."

Spinelli took his hands from his ears. "No!" He leaned through the Mustang's open door, grabbing Reddy's neck. "Wait!"

Reddy pulled away. "Hands off, man."

"All right," Spinelli said. "Just no more shooting." He sniffed the air. "Christ, can't you smell that?" He got out of the car, standing between Reddy and the open door.

"What?" Reddy said. "You mean gun smoke?"

"No." Spinelli sniffed again. "I hope to hell that isn't what I think it is."

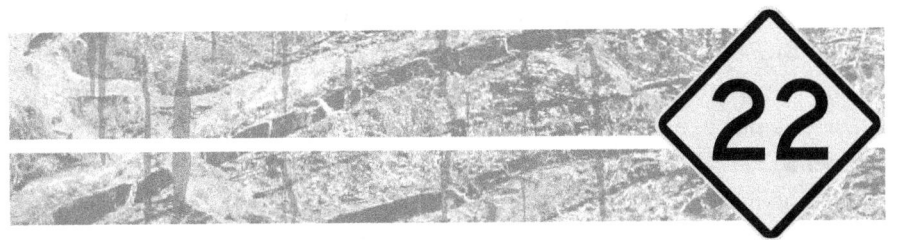

22

Axle's ears ached from the shotgun's roar. His eyes burned, throbbing with the adrenaline-charged panic that still lingered after the chase. Now, in the sudden calm, he felt sick: pulse racing, throat dry and thick with fear. He forced a swallow. His spit tasted bitter, like the stink from Reddy's gun. He hadn't counted on anything like this when agreeing to be Spinelli's driver. This was supposed to have been a night of easy cash. He had not bargained on a high-speed chase in the forest highlands. And he certainly had not anticipated winding up here.

But here he was: drained, frightened, and parked on the edge of the chained path that Great-Grandmother had led him to nine years earlier.

He considered telling Spinelli how shitty he felt, but at the moment Spinelli's attention focused on something else.

"I smell it, too," Tejay said, sniffing as a slow breeze drifted through the car. "Smells like gas."

Spinelli stepped away from the open door.

"Phew!" Reddy rubbed his nose. "It's gas, all right." He lowered his gun. "Is it the Viper? Did I shoot its tank?"

"No." Spinelli walked toward the back of the Mustang. "Not the Viper. It's us!" His voice caught in his throat. "Don't anybody light anything."

"The hell?" Reddy shouldered his gun. "We're leaking gas?" He hurried after Spinelli, slipped on the wet ground, landed with a smack. "Ow!" The car reverberated with the thump of his head striking the rear fender. "*Sombitch!*"

"Careful!" Spinelli said. "Ground's wet."

"Christ!" Reddy pulled himself up, leaning against the car. "Fucking gas!" He shook his arms, spattering the fender. "I'm covered!"

Spinelli shouted into the car. "Tejay! Get back here. We need your tape!"

"What tape?"

"The stuff you used on Bird. The stuff you taped him with."

"The hell?" Reddy said. "Duct tape? You can't duct tape a gas tank"

"Who says?"

Tejay knelt on the seat, looking back through the shattered window. Everyone was focused on the leaking tank. Everyone but Axle. He couldn't move. It was as if the stink of the air and the throbbing in his ears had glued him to the seat: one hand on the wheel, the other on the stick, eyes staring straight ahead toward a trail that he had once walked with Yeyestani. He knew this place. But he did not like thinking about it. Troubling things had happened here. Things better forgotten. Things that had nothing to do with the life he had made for himself after Yeyestani's death.

Got to get us out of here . . . off of this trail . . . back on the road . . . out of Pennsylvania.

But he stayed right where he was, paralyzed, staring past the chain that blocked his way. Beyond the OSM sign, a wave of dust moved along the trail, cresting and spreading out as it reached the Mustang. But nothing else stirred. It was as if a single burst of wind had blown down among the trees, spread out, dissipated.

He blinked, trying to focus.

The dust settled.

Something's out there. Something more than wind.

The air turned still, and in that moment he sensed something rising along the side of the car, a steady, soundless movement that he felt without hearing. He didn't turn to look at it. Too frightened to move, he remained as before, facing front, neck hairs bristling, swallowing a scream as a dark hand curled through the forward corner of his rolled-down window. Something was standing right beside him, leaning on the door, peering in. He felt the weight of its stare, the chill of its breath, the earthy smell of its skin.

"It's all right," the thing muttered. It had a voice like breaking shale: dry and brittle. "It's all right to remember." It reached in, touching Axle's shoulder with a hand that was at once hard and gentle. "It's all right." It leaned forward. "You need to keep going. You can't stay here. More people are coming . . . people who want you dead. You need to get away while you can, before your gas tank runs dry, before swelling sets in."

"Swelling?" He had missed something. "How can the tank swell if it's leaking?"

"Answers come later," the thing said. "Just drive."

"Where?"

"You know." The thing took its hand from Axle's shoulder. "The seeds were planted long ago. You know the place. Go there while you still can."

Axle shivered.

You know the place.

Axle remembered it now: straight ahead, beyond the forest, out where the ground gaped like a jagged wound.

He shifted in his seat, preparing to drive.

"Hey!" Spinelli called from behind the car. "Hey, Axle!"

Axle sat forward, looking at the rearview to see a red glow rising beyond the shattered window. He had moved his foot onto the brake, preparing to put the car into gear.

"Hey, Axle! Foot off the brake. We don't want any current in the system. Axle! You hear me?"

Axle took his foot off the brake. It was easier than arguing. Then he glanced back at the side window, but there was nothing there now. The shadowy figure was gone.

I imagined it.

The explanation didn't feel right, but it was the only one he had . . . the only one that made sense.

"Tejay!" Spinelli said. "Bring us the tape!"

"Won't work," Tejay said, still kneeling on the backseat, looking out through the shattered window. "What good's a patched tank if it's empty?"

"It's not empty yet."

"Will be! By the time you patch it!"

"We'll siphon what we need from the Viper."

"No," Axle said, speaking up at last. "No one goes near the Viper." The shadowy figure might have been a dream, a hallucination, but its warning rang true. "We can't stay here." He put his foot back on the brake and started the engine.

"Hey!" Spinelli slapped the fender. "Shut her down, Axle!"

Axle flipped on the lights, illuminating the dash. The fuel needle showed he still had a quarter tank. "Get in!" Axle shouted. "We're leaving!" He shifted into reverse, forcing Spinelli and Reddy to leap aside as he backed over the muddy ground.

"Axle!" Spinelli ran to the open passenger-side door, grabbing it as Axle hit the brakes. "I said *shut her down*!"

"No, man! Get in." Axle tried sounding as if he knew what he was doing, thankful that it was too dark inside the cab for Spinelli to see the fear in his face. "I know a place that might have gas."

"Where?"

Axle remembered: chain-link fence, gas generator, fifty-gallon drum. But there was no time to explain it to Spinelli. The needle on the fuel gauge kept falling, creeping toward E. "Trust me!" Axle said. "Get in!"

Reddy moved first, slogging into the backseat, bringing with him the stink of his gas-soaked clothes.

"Christ!" Tejay moved away. "Gas me out!"

"Shut up!"

Spinelli hesitated before climbing in and slamming the door. "This better be good, Axle!"

Axle reversed again until his wheels cleared the spill, then he shifted to low and floored it, driving the Mustang into the chain that spanned the rutted path. The links broke, whipping away beyond the side windows. . . .

Then he drove, straight ahead, down the dark trail that led back to the place where he had last seen his great-grandmother alive.

23

Yeyestani led him down the road that ran along the face of the mine's highwall. No berm. No posts. No guardrails. Nothing to prevent either him or Yeyestani from falling to their deaths if they stumbled or veered off course in the dark. Just thinking of the drop made him queasy. *It could happen*, the feeling said. *A few steps to the right, and you'll join your father.*

"Don't think about it," Yeyestani said, as if reading his thoughts. "Keep walking. We're almost there."

"Almost where?"

She didn't answer.

"You said we were going home." If her plan was to follow the screw-thread path into the crater and return to Coals Hollow by way of Windslow Road Extension, they would surely be walking for another hour, maybe longer.

"You need to trust me," she said. "You'll see the place soon enough."

"What place?"

She walked on, her gait making it clear she had finished talking for now.

They came to a protruding vein of rock that ran down along the face of the wall. The path curved around it, narrowing as it reached the outer edge, widening again as something new came into view: a wide shelf of machined sandstone and weedy clay that lay at the end of a long, steep stretch of road. And in the middle of the shelf, equidistant from the wall and the lip of the abyss, stood a boxy building with fresh patches on its roof and a bright padlock on its door. In front of it and off to one side, a chain-link fence enclosed a gas-powered generator. This, too, was padlocked. Above the lock, a sheet-metal sign displayed an OSM logo and a warning that trespassers would be prosecuted.

The place was clearly not anyone's home, but once Yeyestani started talking in riddles there was no getting her to give up a straight answer.

He resigned himself to playing along. It wasn't as if the night would go on forever. Sooner or later they'd be back in Coals Hollow, and he'd have his body-shop money. It would all be worth it then. He could afford to humor the old woman a little longer. Nevertheless, he held back as she reached the end of the narrow road and started across the wide shelf of level rock. He wanted to see if she would keep walking, past the building and onto a continuation of the ledge road that led into the lowlands. If she did that, there was a good chance they were heading home.

She didn't look back as she passed the fenced-in generator. A moment later, she mounted the shack's single wooden step and paused before the padlocked door.

"What're you doing?" he asked.

She touched the padlock. "What's it look like?"

"It looks like you want to open that door."

Now, at last, she turned to face him. "What're you doing back there?"

"Waiting to see what you're doing."

"I told you what we're doing."

"You said we were going home."

"And so we are."

"So why stop here?" he asked. "What is this place?"

"This shack?"

"Yeah. What is it?"

To his surprise, she answered directly, no riddles. "Field office." She tightened her grip on the lock. "It used to belong to Windslow Coal. Now it's property of OSM."

"What's OSM?"

"Office of Surface Mining. They reclaim old mines, ones that closed before the laws changed, before mining companies were held responsible for cleaning up their messes. The owners of Windslow Coal abandoned this site just in time."

Axle gazed out at the chasm beyond the cliff. Things looked different here than they had from the ledge above. The crater appeared larger, rougher, more threatening. The moonlit rock glowed with rippled scars, marks left by earth-shearing machines. To the northwest, just visible behind a sandstone outcrop, a broken trestle stood rusting in the shadows. He had seen this place many times while growing up, but always from below, always from a distance. Now, for the first time, he sensed its pain.

"So how come OSM hasn't reclaimed this place?" he asked.

"No need," she said. "The wall appears to be stable. There's no problem with runoff. Vegetation keeps erosion in check. The site isn't causing any trouble, and OSM has plenty of nuisance mines to contend with before they can worry about the ones that mind their business." She turned again to face the padlocked door. "Surveyors come here now and then, look around, move on. It's for the best. This is one site that can fend for itself." She shifted, holding the lock in both hands now.

"You have keys to this place?" he asked.

"No." The lock clicked, falling open. "Something better."

Although she had learned her trade in the jagged crags of Colorado, Sam had deep Appalachian roots. Born in a Blue Ridge holler, raised in the Allegheny foothills, she considered the region an extension of her soul, more intimately tied to her than any person had ever been.

Weeds grew thick along the unpaved trail that led from her cabin to the nearest road. She liked it that way. People tended to ignore no-trespassing signs. The best way to keep a road private was to make people think it wasn't a road at all.

She drove with only her parking lights on, feeling the way as much as seeing it, getting her bearings from the dips and curves of the living earth.

A mile from her cabin, the ground declined sharply, angling along a tree-lined scarp to intersect with a mountain road that the locals still called *Indian Kill Trail*. It had been paved once, but the blacktop had long ago crumbled to gravel.

Farther on, Indian Kill brought her onto an old coal company road that cut through the lower regions of a reclaimed surface mine. Here she skirted the base of a slope that had been machined into an unnatural succession of bench cuts, right-angled steps and risers that gave the terrain a serrated edge. Beyond the slope's highest tier, highway lights played through a fringe of hardy lespedeza grass and freshly planted pines. Stunted trees grew here, trunks encased in protective tubes, branches brittle and thin. The result was neither natural nor pleasing, but that had not prevented the mining company from fashioning a scenic overlook along the interstate's northbound lanes. Complete with paved lot, coin-operated binoculars, and little else, the facility existed solely to support the coal company's assertion that the land had been reclaimed for public use.

The overlook was one of the reasons Sam drove without headlights. She liked keeping her comings and goings private, and although it was unlikely that anyone was watching, she chose to err on the side of caution.

From the southern edge of the reclaimed mine, another old coal road ran a quarter mile to a wooden bridge that connected with a dark section of Route 19. That's where she hit the lights, snapping the high beams and accelerating into the northbound lane. The way was clear. No traffic. No cops. She had the road to herself until she reached the interstate, and from there it was open highway to the Mason-Dixon Line and the clapboard monstrosity that Kirill Vorarov had erected alongside the interstate's southbound lanes.

The pavement deteriorated markedly as she crossed the border into Pennsylvania. The speed limit changed, too, dropping from seventy to sixty-five. No matter, her laser and radar detectors showed the route was clear, and if anyone was going to get stopped it was the highballing truck in front of her. She kept the needle on eighty until she neared Windslow.

She passed Kirill's billboard shortly before the exit. It had changed over the years, becoming bolder: a naked woman lying on her side, covered only by a raised knee and descending arm. Along the upper edge of her body, following the glacial curves of her shoulders, waist, and hips, pink letters rose and fell like a parodied Hollywood sign, spelling out the club's name: STRIP MINE!

The woman's face did not show in the picture.

In many ways, the image represented everything Sam despised about Kirill Vorarov. But without him, life as she knew it would have been impossible. She needed his money. He needed her services. Out of necessity, she chose to be at his beck and call.

She approached the exit, a highway off-ramp illuminated by service station signs. And beyond the signs, sitting in a cleft cut back into a rounded hill, stood a low-slung building with stark white walls. The sex club had no windows. The parking lot was large, plenty of room for tractor trailers. Usually, when the place was open, Kirill kept two searchlights blazing on a truck bed in the front lot. But tonight was Sunday. The place was dark, with only a yellow bug light glowing over the windowless door.

She studied the place as she took the exit and passed beneath the overpass, detecting the shadow of a man standing in the club's doorway. It was Kirill. Her sniper eyes glimpsed him for a moment: head bowed, arm raised, apparently talking on a cell phone. Then he vanished, eclipsed as she raced past the plate-glass front of a mini-mart service station.

The station's owner had modified the message on his readerboard since Sam's last visit to Windslow. She glanced at it as she hurried by, noting how he had replaced some of the letters with dollar signs to drive home his point:

$AVE WIND$LOW
$UPPORT
MOUNTAIN DOWN$

Like most area business owners, the station manager believed that Kirill's proposed casino complex on the former site of the old Windslow Mine would bring economic revitalization to the region. But there were plenty of locals who felt otherwise, and their readerboards (primarily outside churches and private homes) urged people to fight the plan. Sam doubted the dissenters would succeed any better than they had a few years earlier when they had tried to prevent the opening of Kirill's sex club. What the well-intentioned opposition failed to realize was that morality and logic seldom informed such decisions. It was money that made things happen, upfront money in the form of bribes, deferred money in the form of promises to local businesses. And if there was one thing that Kirill had in spades, it was money.

Sam continued straight after the service station, racing past a dark stretch of undeveloped land that had already been purchased for virtually nothing by Kirill's associates at Mountain Investment Enterprises, Inc. The land as it was had little value: too narrow for farming, too close to the interstate for housing, too much in the shadow of Kirill's sex-superstore to attract the kinds of businesses that often sprang up around highways. But for a proposed four-lane access road, one leading from the interstate to the casino resort at Mountain Downs, it was ideal.

The purchase of the site was one more way in which Kirill's people had been quietly moving ahead on the project in advance of approval from the Gambling Commission. Indeed, they had been moving so quietly that few people outside Windslow paid much attention to the Mountain Downs project.

So what was going on tonight? Was someone trying to muscle in on Kirill's action? Had a new competitor surfaced, one who could not be wheedled or bribed into concession? Perhaps that was what tonight's summons was about. Sam had already helped Kirill through two such impasses. Each had been easy work, requiring her to do little more than place a high-powered round through the window of an unoccupied room. Each time, the warning had been heeded and the competitors pulled out, no doubt encouraged by some carefully applied grease and a not-too-subtle assurance that a second shot, should it be necessary, would end up in someone's head.

But why the urgency tonight? Kirill had sounded strange on the phone. He had seemed distracted, agitated, almost frightened.

She wondered about these things as she took the left onto the two-lane drive that rose toward the empty parking lot of the club.

Kirill folded his phone as she pulled alongside the door below the bug light. He was a heavy-set man, his girth muted by the folds of a well-tailored suit. Armani had a way of making dumpy men look stylish.

She opened the Jeep's door and started to get out.

"No." He raised a hand. "Stay there." He walked to the passenger side and climbed in.

"What's going on, Kirill?"

He pointed, out of the lot, toward Windslow Road. "Go!" He held the phone, clutching it like the end of a lifeline. "North. Toward the site."

She put the Jeep back into gear. "The Mountain Downs site? Windslow Mine?"

"Yeah." He pressed his hands together, cradling the phone. "Hurry. I'll explain."

She preferred working alone, but he was footing the bill. Ultimately, he could have it any way he wanted.

She toed the gas, cleared the speed bump at the end of the lot, and accelerated toward the winding bends of Windslow Road.

25

Bird lay bleeding beside the ruined Viper, spread eagle amid tangled weeds. Somewhere, people were talking.

"Ow! Sombitch!"

"Careful. Ground's wet."

Bird tried looking toward the voices. No good. His muscles didn't respond. His body seemed locked in the throes of a lucid dream.

. . . but I'm not dreaming . . .

His chest burned.

. . . dying . . . not dreaming . . . dying . . .

Time passed. The voices grew louder, then faded beneath a thundering engine. Was it the Viper?

No. The Viper's dead.

The thunder came from the other car, the stealth-black Mustang that he and Peterson had followed into the clearing.

It's leaving . . . leaving me for dead.

The engine roared away, fading in the distance. Silence descended, lingered a moment, then gave way to a rhythmic, twittering ring.

Peterson's cell phone.

It pulsed four times before falling silent. Another sound followed, closer.

My phone.

It was probably Kirill calling back.

Bird pictured the big man in his office, pacing, growing agitated as he waited for someone to answer. The image lingered as Bird lost consciousness. Soon he was dreaming. Kirill became a lumbering beast advancing through tangled undergrowth. Bird heard the sounds: snapping branches, thudding feet. They seemed too real to be part of a dream. . . .

He opened his eyes.

The rustling continued, emanating from the edge of the clearing, coming closer. He squinted, watching as a dark shape lumbered into the moonlight.

Animal? Human?

It stared at Bird, then hunkered back and leaped forward, soaring through the glade to land beside the Viper. Bird saw it more clearly now, but seeing didn't help. Even as it crept nearer, coming close enough to touch, Bird still had no idea what it was.

"This isn't your time to die," it said, touching Bird with a hand that smelled of moss and stone. "You need to follow the people in the car."

Bird coughed. A moment ago he had wanted nothing more than to follow the Mustang, but now, although he remembered being angry enough to kill the people who had robbed him, he could not remember what that anger felt like or why such a thing would be worth the effort. He wanted to say these things to the creature, but blood filled his throat, gagging him as he opened his mouth. He could not speak without choking.

"Don't struggle," the creature said. "I can't have you choking to death." It turned Bird's head, letting the blood in his throat drain out onto the ground. "Kwetis did not arrange your birth just to have you die here."

Blood bubbled from Bird's lips. "Kwetis?" He had studied enough of the old stories to know that name. But what did it mean? How could a legend arrange someone's birth? "How—"

"Don't talk. Listen." It leaned closer, speaking softly. "I am the earthborn guardian of *Awenyahsa*. Do you understand? Do you know what that means?"

A student of all things Okwe, Bird had acquired a scattershot knowledge of the tribe's language and legends. He knew the term *earthborn*. It identified a class of resurrected servants, people brought back from the grave, remade to serve as caretakers of the land. During their existence, the earthborn served another class of guardians called *the skyborn*—powerful spirits who could infiltrate and alter human dreams. That much Bird knew. The rest was strange, confusing. "I don't understand," he said.

"You will."

"When?"

"Soon." The guardian ran its hand over Bird's chest, letting it linger on the place where leaking breath bubbled from a ruptured lung. "I need you to get up, follow the Mustang. Keep walking until you find a ledge overlooking the mine. The people who shot you will be there. One of them is your future master. Find him. You need to be with him when it comes down."

"What?" Bird coughed. "When *what* comes down?"

"The wall."

"What wall?"

"Just find him."

"I don't understand."

"You don't need to. Just walk. You'll get there. Your future master will wait until you come."

"Then what?"

"Just get to him. Stay with him until I come for you both. After that, everything will be clear."

Bird felt his strength returning.

The guardian backed away, standing up until its head seemed to rest against the moon. It flexed its shoulders, throwing them back. A pair of gigantic shadows unfurled behind them. *Wings*, Bird thought. *The guardian has wings*. He recalled another piece of folklore. An earthborn guardian was flesh and bone, but its wings rode on spirit wind.

"Are you leaving me?" Bird asked.

It crouched, looked at him, and then leaped upward, shaking the trees as it ascended into darkness.

26

Spinelli and Tejay lowered their windows, venting the fumes from Reddy's gas-soaked clothes.

"Where are you taking us, Axle?" Spinelli said.

Axle didn't answer. He felt sick, disoriented.

We screwed up. There's no going back.

The trail veered into a shale alcove. He knew this place, but it had changed since the night Yeyestani had brought him here. The once-unobstructed path was now partially blocked by a fallen tree, a monster oak that lay with its branches imbedded in the ground and its roots smashed against the wall of stone. No doubt it was the same tree that had once clung to the ledge above. Now it formed a diagonal slash across the trail, just high enough to grant clearance to the speeding Mustang.

The aerial *twanged* on a branch as Axle sped beneath the trunk. The sound reverberated through the hole in the roof, buzzing like a giant moth.

Again, Spinelli asked, "Where are we going, Axle?" He sounded impatient, pissed that Axle wasn't answering. "Damnit, Axle! This car's full of fumes. I do not want to stay in it any longer than we have to. Where are you taking us?"

But still Axle said nothing.

A moment later, when the forest opened, the land answered for him.

"What the hell is this?" Spinelli sat forward, peering through the windshield as the Mustang rumbled toward the brink of Windslow Mine. "Christ, Axle! Where are we?"

Axle kept driving, right to the edge where the ground fell away and the mine's dark expanse opened like the mouth of hell.

"Axle," Tejay said. "This is a cliff!"

Axle steered right, driving along the precipice, heading toward the trail that angled down along the wall.

"Sombitch!" Reddy pushed his head over Spinelli's seat. "Tell me we aren't going down there." His voice shrilled. "Tell me we are fucking *not* going down that ledge."

"It's a road," Axle said, toeing the brake, checking his speed. "A haul road. Trucks used to drive it." He downshifted. The engine revved, fighting gravity as he started down.

"Trucks drove this narrow sombitch?"

"It used to be wider."

"Screw what *used* to be," Spinelli said. "Where the hell are you taking us?"

Axle downshifted again, grinding into first as the road steepened into a seventeen percent grade.

"There's a shelf beyond that vein of rock." He didn't bother pointing. The column that bisected the trail already towered before them, backlit by the moon, coming on fast. "You need to trust me," he said. "You'll see it in a minute."

"Why not give us a preview, you sombitch. Tell us. Let us decide if we even want to go there."

Axle swallowed, clearing his throat. "It's a shelf . . . level ground over-hanging the mine. There's a place there . . . a shack. It's—"

"A shack?" Spinelli said. "I thought we were going to a place with gas."

"The shack's got a generator. The generator's got fuel. We can—"

The engine sputtered.

Spinelli flinched, bracing. "Axle!" The engine pinged but kept running. "Does this car have power steering?"

"Yeah."

"Brakes?"

"Yeah. Power steering. Brakes. It's loaded."

"And if you lose power? What then?"

"What then?"

"What happens if all that power shit loses power?"

"Happens?" Axle didn't need this conversation. He needed to concentrate.

"I'm asking if you can control the car if you lose power."

"Yeah." Axle hugged the wheel. "But it's a bastard. If it—" The engine pinged again . . . backfired . . . stalled. "Shit!" The wheel tightened.

"I don't believe this." Tejay's voice came from low in the backseat. She had gone back to scrunching down, sparing herself the sight of the drop beyond the side windows. "This is *so* not happening!"

The Mustang picked up speed, drifting toward the outer edge of the road.

"Cut it, Axle!" Spinelli slapped the dash. "Cut left! We're going over!"

Stones popped beneath the wheels, tumbling into the void as Axle steered closer to the wall.

Spinelli looked out his open window. "There's nothing there." His voice caught in his throat. "I can't see the road beneath the car. We're like right on the *edge*. The fucking *edge*!"

They reached the vein of rock, the haul road curving around its base like a hat brim.

"Sombitch! No way!"

The road narrowed, diminished by years of erosion, forcing Axle to steer closer to the wall . . . closer . . . closer. . . .

kkkkkkkssssssssttttttttTTTZZZCH!

The side mirror struck rock, spewing sparks.

"Sombitch!"

PING-clunk!

The mirror broke, bouncing away, thumping between car and wall.

Axle ignored it and watched the curving road.

"Too fast!" Reddy said. "You got to slow this sombitch down. Slow it *down*!"

Axle worked the parking brake: holding the release, depressed the pedal, checking his speed as he entered the turn.

"Awfully tight," Spinelli said, pressing a hand against the dash. "Ledge doesn't look wide enough, Axle."

But Axle was already angling the Mustang's fender and door against the wall of rock, making the side panels ring with the screech of metal on stone, igniting a new shower of sparks that spilled through the open window.

"*Fire!*" Tejay said, recoiling from the sparks. "We're on *fire!*"

Spinelli balled his hand against the dash. "Shut up, Tejay!"

"We're on *fire!*"

The car jerked to the right, easing away from the wall.

The door stopped sparking.

"It's out!" Tejay said. "Fire's out. Not that you bastards give a rat's ass." She rose in the seat to have a look, but slumped down again when she saw the crater still looming beyond her side window. "I swear to shit . . . if I get out of here . . . I'm going to do something. No more hanging out with assholes. You know what I'm saying?"

They ignored her: Axle working the wheel and brake, Spinelli gripping the dash, Reddy hugging his Remington.

They were nearly halfway through the turn, still alive, still descending.

"Jesus!" Spinelli arched his back, bending it away from the door, as if the extra distance would matter should the car plunge over the edge. "Jesus, Axle." His hair blew in the wind from the crater. "Jesus." Some of the tension had left his voice. "The road . . . it's getting wider." He looked down along the fender. "I can see it. There's like a six-inch margin . . . wider . . . maybe a foot . . . maybe more."

Axle released the brake, letting the car pick up speed as he steered onto a descending straightaway.

"You did it," Spinelli said, a little too loud, trying to sound like the man in charge. "Listen, just do me a favor, Axle. If you need to start riding the wall again . . . put up your window first. All right? We do not want sparks in this car. Do you hear me?"

Axle didn't answer.

"Sombitch, Spinelli. That's fucked up. He needs both hands to drive."

Spinelli looked back at Reddy. "You've evidently never been burned."

"Don't go preaching to me, you sombitch. We wouldn't even be here if you'd been at the pickup point. If you'd been where you were supposed to be—" He leaned forward, his attention snagged by something that lay beyond the protruding vein of rock. "Is that it?" He pointed. "That the shack?"

The structure was much as Axle remembered, a gabled box with a fenced-in generator. It sat on a table of rock that had been cut back into the highwall. But the shelf had changed. It looked smaller. The shack stood right on the brink, nothing behind it but empty air. Were his memories wrong, or had the landscape changed?

"Don't look like much," Reddy said.

"Don't have to." Spinelli kept his hands on the dash, holding on as the road leveled out. "We're here to get gas, not move in."

Axle worked the brake again, slowing their descent, easing past the generator and into the moon-tossed shadow of the weather-beaten shack.

27

The interior of Sam's Jeep smelled of wilderness, dark and feral. It wasn't a bad smell. Under better circumstances, Kirill might have found it pleasant.

He had always sensed something alluring in Sam's earthiness, her self-sufficiency. Perhaps, as the scrawny New York chef might have explained it, Kirill desired her because he knew he couldn't have her.

People only want what they don't have.

"Turn here," Kirill said.

Sam braked, taking a hard right onto Old Coal Creek Trail, a meandering strip of asphalt that connected Windslow Road with Cliff Mine Run. "I thought you said we were going to the mine, Kirill."

"We are. But not the lower part. We're going to the forest above the wall."

"What's there?"

"A lawyer." Kirill realized he was still holding the phone, gripping it tightly in his fist. "My lawyer and my business partner, they're both up there." Kirill clipped the phone to his belt and sat back. "They're in trouble."

"Define trouble."

Kirill reached for the seat's shoulder harness, pulling it around him as he tried putting his fears into words. "I think they're dead." The seatbelt clicked. "Shot."

"By whom?"

"Three guys in a Mustang."

The Jeep hit a pothole. The thud resounded through the cab. Sam maintained speed, racing toward an intersection.

"Turn right," Kirill said.

Sam took the turn, and for a while they drove in silence, Kirill trying to collect his thoughts. He looked out the side window, watching his reflection race over a backdrop of trees. A minute past. The forest opened. A raggedy trailer park appeared, the gravel of its center road still bearing the tracks of a high-speed chase.

"You know who they are, Kirill?" Sam asked, breaking the silence. "The three guys in the Mustang? Any idea?"

"No."

The trailer park vanished as Sam continued into the highlands.

"Any idea what they're packing?"

"A shotgun. My partner said they had a shotgun."

"That all? One shotgun?"

"He didn't say that was all. He just said they had a shotgun."

"What were your lawyer and business partner doing in the forest above the highwall?"

"Chasing the Mustang."

"Why?" She cut her speed as they reached a stretch of flooded pavement. Water drummed against the floor. "Goddamnit, Kirill. Talk to me. Start from the beginning."

He did, starting with what he knew about the robbery, letting the pieces fall together as he spoke. The more he talked, the clearer it all became, but he didn't have time to finish. He stopped the story abruptly before getting to the shootout. "We're almost there." He studied the road. "Slow down."

Sam toed the brake, cutting her speed.

Kirill studied the forest beyond the side window. "There's a turnoff."

She downshifted.

"I told Bird to follow the bastards, not confront them."

"But he confronted them anyway?"

"Right. Opened fire on them. Then chased them into the woods."

Up ahead, fresh skids appeared on the asphalt. She stopped, lowered her window, and snapped on a spotlight above the side mirror.

"There's an old coal-hauling road cutting through those trees." Kirill looked beyond the sloping berm. "I've been down it with the surveyors. It's right around here."

She swung the beam, angling it onto a break in the forest wall.

"That's it," Kirill said.

"Not much of a road." She kept her hand on the spotlight, pivoting its beam as she steered the Jeep over the shoulder.

Chrome flashed in the distance.

"See that?" Kirill said. "There's something back there."

"Right. I see it. Let's have a better look." She snapped on a row of roof-mounted safari lights, illuminating the Viper.

"Christ!" Kirill's voice came from deep in his throat, an animal growl. "They're going to pay."

The trail ran a hundred feet toward the battered car. Someone was still sitting behind the wheel. But he wasn't all there. Most of his head was gone.

"They're going to pay for this, Sam. Understand? Whoever did this, you're going to make them pay."

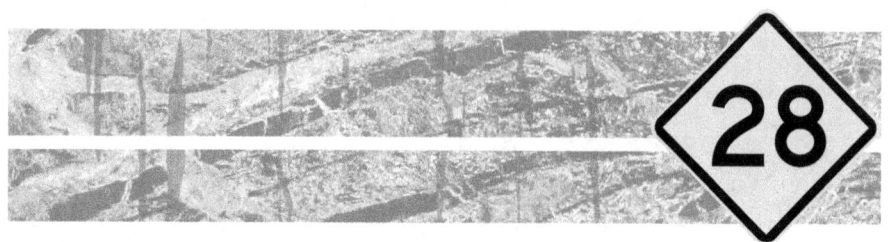

pinelli opened his door. "Everybody out!"

"Don't have to tell me twice!" Reddy grabbed the gun and briefcase.

Axle set the brake and killed the lights.

Spinelli climbed out, stepping aside for Reddy and Tejay. "Hey!" He grabbed Reddy's arm. "Briefcase stays in the car."

"Screw that!" Reddy pulled away. "This shack is as good as a frat-house garage for counting money." He kept moving, pausing when he reached the chain-link enclosure that held the generator. "This baby's padlocked." He dropped the briefcase, stepped back, and cocked the Remington. "Good thing I brought a 12-gauge key." He aimed at the lock. The barrel flashed, releasing a roar that echoed through the abandoned mine. "It's open now!" Reddy kicked the gate. It swung inward, flying back to clatter against the fence. "Go on, Tejay. Start the generator." He picked up the briefcase. "Meet me in the shack."

"No!" Spinelli said. "We're not going inside."

Reddy kept walking.

Spinelli called after him. "We're here to get gas and patch the tank. That's it. I need you to stay outside. Air out those gas-soaked clothes!"

"Already did that!" Reddy paused beside the shack's padlocked door, dropped the briefcase between his ankles, and raised the shotgun. *Shk-SHK!*

"Reddy!" Spinelli's voice went ragged. "Goddamnit, Reddy!"

BLAM!

The report echoed through the mine.

"Damnit, Reddy! Why don't you just send up a goddamn flare?"

"Flare?" Reddy snorted. "I ain't got no flare. The hell you talking?"

"You can hear those gunshots all the way to Waynesburg."

"Yeah!" Reddy slapped the breech. "12-gauge!" He turned and kicked the door, forcing it inward.

Axle watched it all from behind the wheel, feeling a strange sense of detached foreboding. This was the place Yeyestani had brought him on the night she died. Strange things had happened here, things he could not account for, things that were better forgotten.

"Hey, Axle!" Spinelli peered into the darkened car. "Where's your flashlight?"

"In the glove box."

Spinelli pushed the button and reached inside.

"It's in a bag," Axle said. "Big plastic bag."

Spinelli pulled it out and removed the flashlight. Then he turned to find Tejay standing beside him.

"You want this, right?" She handed him the roll of duct tape.

"Thanks. Check the generator. See if there's gas."

She turned and walked away.

Spinelli shoved the spool of tape over his wrist and snapped on the light. "C'mon, Axle." He swung the beam toward the back of the car. "Give me a hand." His shoes, still wet with creek mud, gurgled as he walked.

Axle swallowed. His spit tasted worse than ever, like high-test and gunpowder. Perhaps if he got out of the car he would feel better. Like Reddy, he needed to air out.

Spinelli called from the bumper. "Hey, Axle! You coming?"

Axle opened the door and stood up, realizing at once that he should have remained sitting. The world spun. He lost balance, catching himself by grabbing the roof. His arm gave a hollow thump.

"Hey?" Spinelli said. "You all right?" His voice came from beneath the car. He was on his back, checking the damage to the tank.

"Yeah. Just . . . dizzy." His outstretched hand lay inches from the hole that Reddy's shotgun had blasted in the metal. The hole's sides curled up and back like the petals on a flower, with patches of bright red where the black latex had peeled away. It looked oddly delicate, more like a work of art than a shotgun blast. And beyond it, the larger wound of Windslow Mine stretched wide and far away.

"Hey, Axle!" Spinelli slid out from beneath the car. "I could really use some help back here."

But Axle kept staring, across the mine and into the deep southern sky. No double searchlights tonight. Sunday night at the sex club was a time for maintenance: restocking shelves, disinfecting stalls, skimming cash, cooking books, and (according to Tejay) doing something that required large amounts of cash from Maynard Frieburg. . . .

"Axle! C'mon, man. What are you doing?"

Axle pushed away from the car, trying to stand. "I was just . . . just thinking."

"I'm thinking, too. I'm thinking it's a good thing we didn't catch fire. Scraping the wall . . . all those sparks . . . the car full of fumes—" His voice trailed off. He seemed to be remembering something . . . something painful and long ago. "Damn!" His voice tightened, suddenly afraid. "Come here and take a look at this."

Axle tried walking, but once again he lost his balance, falling against the car.

Spinelli looked up. "Axle?" He stood. "You sure you're all right?"

Axle shivered, feeling cold. "Spinelli, there's something—" He swallowed. The fresh air had done nothing to improve the burning in his mouth and throat. His spit tasted worse than ever. "I'm done in." He coughed. "I need to sit down." He kept his grip on the roof as he turned back toward the driver's seat. "I . . . I need to rest." His sleeve squeaked against the roof's latex skin. "Just . . . for a minute."

"No way!" Spinelli moved toward him. "We've got to patch—"

The generator thundered to life.

"Got it!" Tejay said from inside the fence. "Started right up!"

Lights winked on within the shack, spilling out through the open door, throwing an incandescent wedge across the weedy ground.

"Tejay!" Spinelli turned toward the generator. "I didn't want you to start it. I told you to see if it had gas."

"Yeah, well, I did. It does." She looked toward the shack, pivoting to get a look at what Reddy was doing inside. A moment later, she was heading toward the lighted door.

Axle couldn't watch her. The light seemed strangely bright, blinding him. "Christ!" He covered his eyes and turned toward the back of the car, toward Spinelli.

"Axle?" Spinelli said, voice catching in his throat. "Damn, man!" He moved along the side of the car, coming closer. "What hap—"

"It's my eyes," Axle said. "The light. It burns." Even now, having turned from the glare, he had to squint through splayed fingers. "Burns like a bastard." He closed his eyes and rubbed them, pushing against the pain.

Spinelli reached for him. "What the hell, man?" He touched Axle's face. "What happened to you?"

"My eyes."

"No, man—it's more than your eyes." Spinelli took hold of Axle's hands. "Axle . . . Christ, Axle! Let me see."

Axle resisted. "Nothing to see." He kept his hands pressed to his face. "It's just the light. It burns."

Spinelli raised the flashlight.

"Stop it, Spinelli. That hurts."

Spinelli lowered the beam and turned Axle toward the glow from the shack's open door. "Jesus, Axle!" He tugged Axle's hands. "You're all—"

Axle jerked away, steadying himself against the car, throwing his arm across the wet roof.

Wet?

Axle squinted at the latex coating beneath his arm. It was slimy, streaked with. . . .

"It's your arm," Spinelli said. "Jesus, man! It's your whole right side! You're soaked!"

Axle squinted, looking at his sleeve, his hand, the roof of the car. He bent his arm, drawing it toward him, noticing how it smeared a trail across the latex-covered metal.

"That bastard shot more than your car, Axle." His voice tightened. "Jesus, man! You're covered with blood."

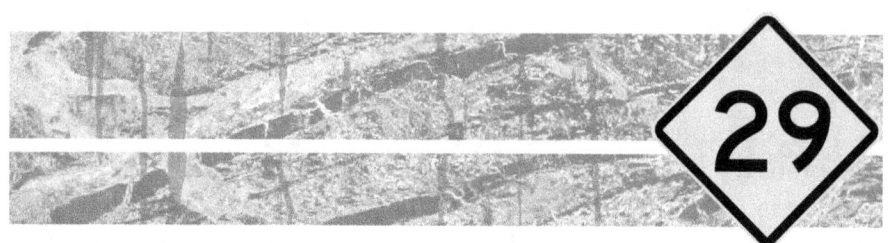

Sam kept the safari lights on as she pulled into the clearing. She set the brake, kept the engine running.

Paul Peterson's nearly headless body sat in the Viper, leaning back, one hand on the wheel.

"Bastards," Kirill said. "I want you to get the bastards that did this."

Peterson's head lay strewn across the Viper's trunk, streaking like a rusty skid over the platinum paint.

"You hear me, Sam. I want you to get these bastards. Get them good."

The windshield was shattered, tires flattened, airbag deployed and hanging like an apron over Peterson's lap. Enraged, Kirill looked into the clearing, noting how the rutted trail curved toward a pair of concrete posts and a wide spill of gasoline. He smelled the stink of it, heavy in the windless night. "Bird must have shot their tank," Kirill said. "They can't be far." He turned to find Sam looking the other way, hand out the window, panning the spotlight over the weeds on the edge of the clearing.

"We've got a new problem," she said, steadying the light.

"What kind of problem? What do you see?"

Sam took her rifle from the rack behind the seat. Then she opened her door and stepped down from the cab.

"What is it, Sam?"

She left the door open.

Kirill couldn't see anything out there, just ferns and sumac glowing on the edge of the spotlight's beam. But Sam had evidently found something. She quickened her pace, moving out of sight as she rounded the door.

Kirill got out and crossed behind the Jeep to meet her on the edge of the clearing. "What the hell are you looking at, Sam?"

She stepped aside, revealing a patch of blood-stained ground. "Your partner," she said. "He must have fallen here." She crouched, getting a closer look. "You said he had a gun, right?"

"That's right. Looks like he used it, too." He gestured across the clearing. "You see that gas spill?"

"I'm more interested in what I don't see, Kirill." She sat back, resting on her heels. "Where's your partner?"

"Must have gotten up."

She studied the ground. "Someone else was here with him." She ran a hand across a patch of flattened grass. "Someone knelt beside him. Then they both got up. One of them went that way." She pointed at a line of footprints, dark and shiny in the Jeep's lights. Someone had stepped in the blood before walking away, leaving a trail of diminishing smears.

"Was it Bird?" Kirill asked.

Sam stood and walked a few paces to kneel beside one of the prints. "No heel," she said, inspecting the impression. "Flat sole."

"Bird wears moccasins."

She set a hand beside the print. "Size twelve."

"That's about Bird's size. Big feet."

"So these could be his." She returned to the patch of flattened grass. "But what about the other guy? He was kneeling here, beside your partner. Then he got up." She stepped away, following a trail of flattened ferns that ran perpendicular to the tracked blood. "He walked over here. Then—" She looked around. "His trail ends."

"What? He flew away?"

"Hell if I know. But he was big. I can tell you that. He was big, and I have no idea where he went." She looked up at the trees.

"But we know about the Mustang," Kirill said. "We know Bird shot its tank."

"Do we *know* that?"

"We know it's leaking gas."

"It appears that way."

"And if it's leaking, you can track it."

"Right. And so can your partner." She paused. "That's a problem."

"A problem how? What're you saying?"

"Your partner." She looked toward the rutted trail that ran toward Windslow Mine. "Three people on the run with a shotgun is one thing. A wounded man out for blood with a semiautomatic, that's another." She frowned. "Things just got a lot more complicated."

30

Tejay entered the shack to find Reddy throwing the locked briefcase onto a makeshift table, two sawbucks supporting a sheet of half-inch plywood. Behind the table, a rear door stood closed beneath a pair of two-by-fours and a hand-lettered sign that read:

DANGER
NO EXIT

Bare bulbs dangled from the ceiling, each suspended by a chord that ran along an overhead beam and down a pressboard wall to connect with an outlet box. Beside the box sat two wooden chairs, one stacked atop the other. Across from them, a hatchet hung in the shadow of a cast-iron stove.

"Give me that sombitch." Reddy pointed to the hatchet.

Tejay got it for him.

He set one hand on the briefcase, held it steady, and brought the hatchet down hard beside one of the latches. Leather snapped. Wood splintered. "Zeros my ass!" He pulled the hatchet free and swung again.

At this rate, it wouldn't take long.

She stepped away from the table, glancing outside to see if Spinelli and Axle had started patching the tank. They stood together beside the car. Axle gripped the shotgunned roof. Spinelli held Axle's arm. The pose looked intimate. What were they doing?

Reddy kept swinging, faster and harder, making headway. "Almost!" He swung again—*WHAM!* "Almost got you—" *WHAM!* "—you sombitch!" He threw the hatchet on the table and tried lifting the lid. It shifted, rising enough for him to curl his fingers inside. He pulled harder. Wood splintered. The lid swung upward, toward Tejay, blocking her view as Reddy stared inside.

She tried reading his expression. "Reddy?"

He just stared.

"Reddy?" She had a bad feeling about the look in his eyes. "It's all there, right? Just like I told you."

"Like you told me?" He turned the briefcase toward her, letting her see for herself how thoroughly the night had gone wrong.

31

Blood," Spinelli said. "You're covered with blood."

"No!" Axle braced against the car. "No way, Spinelli! That's crazy, man. The bullet hit the gas tank."

"Bird fired more than one bullet, Axle."

"But he hit the tank."

"He also took out the rear window. That bullet kept moving, man. It could have—"

"No! It hit the dash. I saw—"

"And how many times did Bird shoot? Six times? Ten?"

"I don't know. But what you're saying is screwed up. How could I—"

Spinelli leaned closer, inspecting the wound.

Axle flinched.

"Looks like it hit you above the ear." He pushed Axle's hair, bending it back in a stiff clump. "That's where the blood's coming from." He ran a hand along Axle's forehead. "There's no exit wound." He looked at Axle's eyes, studying them, avoiding their gaze. "Your eyes are black. Fully dilated." He turned Axle's face into the light, making him squint. "The bullet's still in there."

"In my head?"

"It looks that way."

"Is that good?"

"I don't know."

"Am I going to be all right?"

"I'm no doctor, Axle."

"But I kept driving!" Axle looked inside the car, seeing the interior in the harsh light from the shack's glowing door: the cushions, gearshift, steering wheel—all covered with the same smears that stained his arm, the same glossy darkness that his sleeve had left on the Mustang's roof. Just like the gas tank, his head had leaked all the way from Cliff Mine Run.

He shivered again, more violently, almost convulsing. "But how could I drive if I got shot? That's crazy, right? I mean, *I kept driving*!"

"You were terrified. Fear kept you going."

"But in the *head*? How could I—"

"Listen, Axle." Spinelli's voice faltered. "The important thing . . . the thing that matters—" He tightened his grip on Axle's arm. "We need to get you inside. We'll stop the bleeding. Then we'll patch the Mustang and get you to a hospital." He tossed the flashlight onto the passenger seat. "C'mon." He gripped Axle with both hands. "Walk with me."

Axle slumped forward, falling against Spinelli's shoulder.

"Stay with me, Axle."

Axle could no longer feel his legs. "Something's happening. My head . . . there's—" He was slurring now. "Pressure . . . getting worse . . . it's like—"

"Trauma," Spinelli said. "You're bleeding inside, swelling . . ."

Swelling.

The creature in the clearing had warned about that.

You need to get away . . . before swelling sets in.

"Keep walking," Spinelli said. "We're going inside."

"Can't feel my feet."

"You're doing fine. Stay with me. Stay awake."

But he couldn't. The world went dark. He felt himself falling, and then. . . .

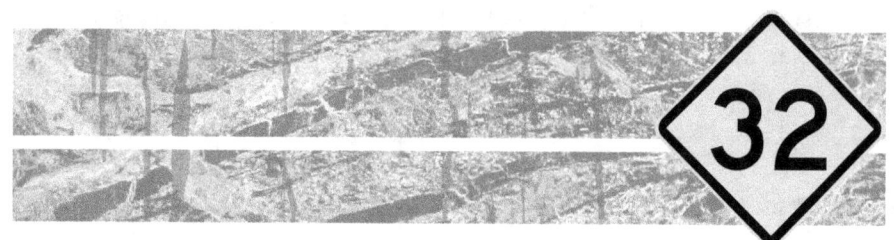

Yeyestani paused before a padlocked door.

"You have keys to this place?" he asked.

"No." She spoke without turning. "Something better." *Shk-SHK!* The lock fell open in her hands. The sound reminded him of something. Not something he had heard before, but something that he would hear in the future. The impression was undeniable, oscillating like the memory of a dream.

She glanced back across her shoulder, staring with her normal eye, the one that saw things as they were. "What's wrong, Akeo?"

He felt confused, disoriented. "I want to go home."

"You are home."

"What's that supposed to mean?"

"What do you *think* it means?"

"I think . . . it means you're messing with me. You're messing with me and I'm tired of it. If you want to tell me something, why don't you just—"

Her shoulders shifted as she pushed against the door, easing it inward. Light spilled out, fanning in a wedge across her shoulders.

There was nothing unusual about the glow itself. Nothing strange or magical. It was simply the pale yellow of incandescent light, but who had turned it on?

"Does someone live here?" he asked.

"Yes. Lives. And dies." She gestured for him to follow. "C'mon. Things will be clearer when you come inside."

And yet. . . .

He already *was* inside.

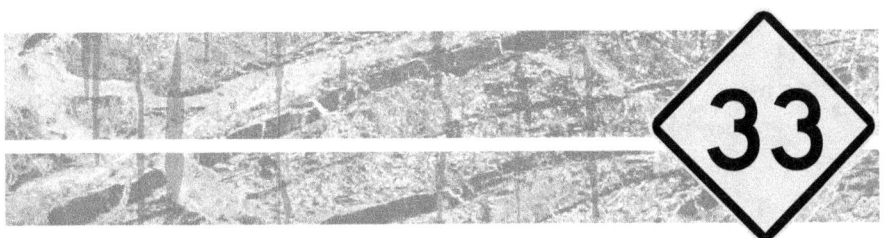

Tejay turned from the table to see Axle coming through the door, leaning against Spinelli, covered with blood. He looked unconscious, possibly dead.

Reddy saw it too. "Sombitch!" He backed away from the table. "The hell happened to him?"

"Shot."

"Shot?" Reddy grabbed his Remington and headed for the door, moving as if he expected to find the shooter outside.

"Take it easy, Reddy. It didn't *just* happen." Spinelli grabbed a chair from against the wall and threw it down in the center of the room. "It happened when we left the road." Axle's head flopped to the side as Spinelli eased him into the chair.

"Sombitch got shot and kept driving?"

"That's what I'm telling you."

"How?"

"I don't know." Spinelli slipped the spool of duct tape from his wrist, set it and the flashlight on the floor beside the chair, and began studying Axle's wound. The temple was swollen, the cheek beneath it black with blood. "All I know is that he's getting worse. He'll die if we don't get him help."

"Sombitch! Looks like he's dead already."

Spinelli knelt beside the chair. "Bandages," he said. "We need bandages."

"Bandages?" Reddy snorted. "The hell we gonna find bandages?"

"You wearing a T-shirt?"

"What the hell, Spinelli?"

"We need to do something."

"Yeah? You want something? Use your own goddamn shirt!"

Spinelli started to respond, reconsidered, then turned and grabbed the hem of his own jersey, pulling it up and over his head in one quick motion. His undershirt came off, too, and in that instant Tejay saw the reason why

Spinelli always wore long sleeves.

He turned away, giving Tejay a clear view of the mottled flesh that covered his back, shoulders, and arms. It looked like hardened wax—rippled, discolored, nothing like skin.

She winced but said nothing.

Reddy was not so tactful. "Sombitch, Spinelli! What happened to you?"

"Nothing."

"Don't look like nothing."

"Was a long time ago. It's nothing now." Spinelli wrapped the undershirt around his hand. "Axle's the one hurt here, not me." He brushed the shirt over Axle's face, wiping the blood.

"Burn scars!" Reddy said.

Spinelli kept his attention on Axle.

"Sombitchin *third-degree* burn scars, that's what those are. Must've been real bad, too. What was it? Grease fire?"

Spinelli held Axle's head steady as he applied pressure to the wound.

"The hell you doing now, Spinelli?"

"Stopping the bleeding." He still wouldn't look at Reddy.

"Won't it stop on its own?"

"Damnit, Reddy. I'm trying to keep him alive."

"Yeah, right."

"And you're not helping."

"Yeah? Screw that." Reddy returned to the table.

Tejay stepped aside, letting him pass.

"Listen, Spinelli. I hate to tell you, but Axle's not the problem here . . . not the *big* problem."

"He's dying, Reddy."

"Yeah, but he's not the reason we're out tonight, is he?"

"Damnit, Reddy. You got something important to say, say it. Otherwise—"

"I'm saying Axle's not the problem we need to worry about!" He rapped his knuckles on the plywood table. "Come here. I'll show you." He set his hand on the open briefcase. "You really need to take a look at this."

Spinelli turned. "You got the briefcase open?"

"Yeah." Reddy reached down. "It's open." He grabbed a piece of what lay inside. "But it ain't what you think." He raised his hand, holding up a manila folder, legal sized, fastened at the top with a bulldog clip. "It's papers." He reached down again, this time picking up a blue-backed envelope embossed with an official-looking seal. "Sombitchin papers."

"Papers?"

"Yeah. Just papers." Reddy dropped the envelope. "No cash."

Spinelli let go of Axle's head, put the bloody undershirt on the floor, and stood up. "How?" He glanced at Tejay. "You said—"

"I thought—"

"You said you *knew*!"

"I did!"

"She set us up, Spinelli."

"No," Tejay said. "It's not my fault. It was supposed to be cash. It's always—"

"Not *always*!" Reddy shouted. "Not *tonight*!"

Spinelli stepped to the table.

Reddy pushed the briefcase toward him. "Go through it, man. It's papers. Papers all the way down."

Spinelli looked at the contents, documents clipped and banded into neat bundles.

Tejay looked at the floor. "It was *supposed* to be money."

"That gives us nothing," Reddy said. "If it was *supposed* to be, where is it?"

"I don't know."

"How can you not know? You worked for him."

"I did!" she said. That much was true. "I worked for Bird. I *saw* the money."

"But not tonight."

"No. Not tonight. I didn't see it tonight. But before . . ." She steadied herself. She didn't dare cry. Crying would show weakness. Weakness would make things worse. Reddy was like one of those wild dogs she had seen once on the Discovery Channel, dogs that skirted the edges of direct confrontation, running in circles, making noise until they detected weakness. When that happened, it was all over. Let them sense fear, and they went nuts. "Listen, Reddy." She looked at him now. "I'm telling you, it *should* have been there."

Reddy stared back at her, eyes wild and glazed. It was the same look he had fixed her with in the moment before Spinelli had brought Axle into the room. Their little dance had gone full circle. They were right back where they had been when Reddy got his first look inside the briefcase.

She tried another approach. "Listen, Reddy. It's not like—"

He leaned toward her.

"It's not like I set you up."

He was close now, close enough to strike her. It was a dangerous place for her to be, but she dared not back away. "We're all in this together, Reddy." She glanced at Spinelli, but he was too focused on the briefcase to realize what was happening.

"Listen, Reddy. Maybe—" Her voice cracked. It was all Reddy needed to hear. The next thing she knew his hand was on her face, striking her hard, sending her spinning. She tried catching herself on the table, reached for it, missed, and went down hard, banging her head on the stove.

Reddy rounded the table, coming toward her. She heard the squeak of his gasoline-soaked shoes, and then Spinelli was on him, pushing him back. "Jesus, Reddy! Cool it, man."

She tried getting up, her senses still reeling. And it was at that moment, as she gripped the base of the iron stove, that she got the overwhelming impression that there was someone else in the room. It was not a presence she could see or hear, but it was nonetheless real: approaching from behind Spinelli and Reddy, moving past her. . . .

She turned.

The presence continued through the room, paused in front of Axle, then drifted out through the open door. . . .

She blinked, recovering her senses, the impression fading. But still she stared, across the room, into the night.

"The hell is it now?" Reddy said.

She looked around to see him and Spinelli staring at her.

"You see something outside?" Spinelli asked.

Reddy grabbed his Remington and hurried back to the door.

Spinelli bent down, giving her a hand.

"I'm all right," she said, recoiling from the scars on his arms. "I'm fine." She pushed him away. "He slapped me, is all. Just a dope slap. I'm OK." She didn't want Spinelli touching her. She wished he would put his shirt back on. "Really, Spinelli. I'm fine." She stepped away, turning to see Reddy looking out at the ledge, his shoulders blocking her view.

"Spinelli!" he said, leaning forward, gripping his gun. "Christ, Spinelli! There's someone coming down the wall!"

Yeyestani's shadow crossed Axle's face as he stood outside the shack. "What's wrong, Akeo?"

"I want to go home," he said.

Yeyestani backed away. "You are home."

"You keep saying that."

"Because it's true."

Axle frowned. He had never been to this part of the mine before, had never stood on this ledge or seen the one-room shack with its padlocked door and fenced-in generator. Moreover, until tonight, until following Yeyestani into the highlands, he had not even known the shack existed.

"True?" he asked. "How is it true?"

She stood with her back to the light, her face in shadow. And yet he knew she was smiling. He heard the grin in her voice as she said, "Why don't you see for yourself." And with that she took one step back and another to the side, vanishing behind the doorframe, giving him his first unobstructed look of what lay within.

His breath hitched.

"Akeo!" She spoke from around the corner. "Come inside, Akeo. Come *home.*"

Nothing could have prepared him for what lay within the box-shaped shack. He remained on the ledge, unable to move. Before him, beyond the lighted threshold, stood a cupboard, stove, and sink. Two stools faced each other across a narrow counter. A refrigerator lay almost hidden beneath magnets, memos, and old photos. He knew this room. It was the kitchen of Yeyestani's singlewide trailer.

The shack's exterior remained as before: a wooden box lit by the moon, a concrete foundation planted on weedy clay. The trailer's interior had no business being inside the pressboard shack. And yet here it was, framed within the splintered door, luring him with the soft light of home. He considered fleeing back along the ledge and toward the road that led to Coals Hollow. But why? Why go to all that trouble when home lay three feet in front of him?

He stepped toward the front door, wondering if the place held only the kitchen. The exterior was too small to contain the full length of a singlewide trailer. And yet, as he crossed the threshold, he saw the interior stretching away to his left—a long, narrow space that started with the living room and ended with a closed bedroom door at the end of a darkened hall.

He looked for Yeyestani, expecting to see her settled into her favorite chair or standing near the bedroom. But she was gone.

He turned, looking back the way he had come. If this were really Yeyestani's home, he would see a wooden gate outside the door, and beyond the gate a gravel lane leading toward Cliff Mine Run. But instead he saw the rocky shelf ending abruptly at a jagged abyss.

Outside: Windslow Mine.

Inside: home.

Only the door seemed to be part of both worlds: one side aluminum, the other roughhewn wood. What would happen if he closed it? Would the mine remain? He shivered. The question made him feel sick, strangely dizzy. But the answer didn't matter. What he cared about was being home. And if he couldn't be there, at least he could *seem* to be.

He eased the door back into its frame, then turned and entered the living room.

Everything was as he had left it before following Yeyestani into the highlands. A pillow lay on one end of the couch, still dented with the imprint of his head. On the coffee table, an open can of Sprite sat next to a bag of Fritos. He picked up the can and took a swig, finishing it. The stuff tasted real enough: flat, sweet, warm.

He flopped onto the couch, leaned back, and heard a muffled voice within Yeyestani's room.

"Not a chance," the voice said. "No way."

A second voice answered. "They've done it before."

"Not this season."

"The season's just starting."

"For the Mets, maybe. Not for the Buckos."

Sports talk. The voices came from a radio that Yeyestani played constantly in her bedroom. "It's my beacon," she often told him. "A homing signal, for when I get lost in dreams."

The radio had played all day, keeping Yeyestani company while she nursed a summer cold that seemed on its way to becoming something worse. He had checked on her once, but she made it clear she wanted privacy:

"Close the door, Akeo. If I need you, I'll call."

So he spent the day on the couch, watching TV and wondering if she would ever give him the money he needed to open a body shop in Windslow Bottoms. That was the real reason he kept vigil. It wasn't from a sense of duty. It was desperation, the kind that young men feel when teetering on the brink of adulthood.

The day faded as he waited. Light shifted through the curtains, yellowing as it crossed the room, and then, toward evening, her bedroom door opened.

"Hey, Akeo!"

He looked around to see her dressed and standing in the hall.

"Wake up, Akeo. We're taking a walk."

"You're feeling better?"

"Well enough to take you to the highlands."

"What for?"

She entered the living room. "Do you still want that body shop?"

"Yeah."

"Then follow me. We'll make a deal. You follow me now, you'll get your money tomorrow."

Had he imagined those things? What if he had just now awakened on the couch? What if his walk into the highlands had been a dream? Was that possible?

He looked down at his shoes, lifting one to inspect the fresh clay clinging to the sole. He picked at it, knocking a clump onto the carpet. It was real enough. At least it *seemed* real.

Down the hall, Yeyestani's radio played on. Was she in her room, sleeping, dying?

"Yeyestani?"

He waited for an answer.

None came.

He got up and entered the hall, walking until he reached the bedroom door. He pushed it open, peering in. A bedside window emitted the haze of a distant streetlamp. Near the door, a radio dial glowed across a water-stained nightstand. All else was darkness and shadow. He couldn't see her, but he felt her presence. She lay right in front of him. "Yeyestani." He caught a whiff of something sweet. Something musky. Okwe herbs? He sniffed again, recoiling as he caught the full force of the smell. Something was wrong in the room. He reached for the wall switch, snapped it, and squinted as the space filled with light from a lamp beside the bed.

Yeyestani lay beneath her covers, eyes open, staring at nothing, pupils coated with dust. But the eyes were far from the worst of it. The real horror saturated the bed, staining the blanket and sheets, clotting in the folds. It was blood. Old blood. Blood that in places had scabbed into patches of crusty shadow. There was so much blood that it would have seemed unreal were it not reinforced by the terrible stink in the room. And in the midst of that smell, Yeyestani lay dark and still, curled like the shriveled husk of a locust.

She was dead. She had to be dead. He knew this for certain as he stood within the open door, but even as the realization gripped him, Yeyestani shifted. A hand emerged from the blanket, fingers curled, beckoning. And then, softly, a voice: "Akeo." Her lips didn't move, but the voice rang clear. "Come here, Akeo." The blanket crackled. "We're almost finished." She reached for him, took his hand. "I've one more thing for you. The rest you'll have to learn on your own." She gripped him weakly, but he didn't resist.

She pulled him closer.

Something slipped from the bed, clattering against the floor.

He looked down to find a stone knife lying at his feet. It looked old, handmade.

"He came back," she said, gripping him tighter. "Kwetis came back, like he promised."

There was something terribly wrong with her arm. Its underside had been sliced like a gutted fish, laid open with a deep incision that ran from wrist to elbow.

"He told me it was time," she said.

"Who?" His voice cracked. "Who told you?"

"Kwetis."

He knew the name. Yeyestani spoke of him often: Kwetis, the nightflyer, the dream-realm spirit who sometimes lived within the physical form of a skyborn caretaker. Yeyestani claimed Kwetis could travel through time, infiltrate dreams, and alter the course of human events.

"Kwetis told you it was time to cut yourself?" he asked.

"No. He said nothing of cutting. He spoke only of blood . . . blood and rock. He told me it was time to give back to the earth."

Again, Axle looked at his feet. She had wanted to give her blood to the earth, but instead she had spilled it over the bed, onto the threadbare carpet.

"It's all earth," she said, reading his thoughts. "You'll understand . . . one day . . . soon . . . you'll see."

The blood was not fresh. In the blanket's creases, it resembled caked clay. And her hand felt cold, like stone.

"When did you do this?" he asked. "When did this happen?"

"This morning," she said. "Ten hours ago, while you slept on the couch."

That didn't make sense. How could she have done this to herself *before* leading him into the highlands? Unless he had dreamed the journey. Unless he had only just now awakened after an evening nap.

"That's not it," she said. "What you're thinking, that's not the way. You didn't dream it."

"You're saying I was really in the mine?"

"No. Not was . . . *are*. You're still there, Akeo."

"How can I be at the mine if I'm here?"

She stared, eyes dull with settled dust. "A person can be many places," she said. "In a room . . . in a memory . . . in a dream." Her eyes narrowed. "Where are we, Akeo? Where are we now?" Her face trembled, or maybe it was only his shadow moving across her as he pulled free of her hand. "You understand, don't you, Akeo?"

"Understand what?"

"When you walked to Windslow Mine, you walked with my memory."

Outside, far away, an engine roared.

"Memory is spirit, Akeo. Remember that. Don't ever forget it. Memory is spirit, and spirit is dream—past and future, one moment." She reached for him again. "You need to know that if you are going to serve *Awenyahsa*."

"*Awenyahsa*?" he said. "You mean the crater?"

"The mountain."

Outside, the engine roared louder, coming nearer.

"But the mountain's gone, Yeyestani."

"No, Akeo. Not for you." She touched his hand.

The engine roared toward the bedroom, crashing down from the dirt trail that ran between Coals Hollow and Windslow Road, thundering onto the gravel lane that wound through the heart of the trailer park.

He glanced toward the window.

She pulled him back. "That doesn't concern you," she said. "Not yet. Not here."

Headlights panned the curtains. And then—*WHAM!* An oblong shadow flew past the window. It looked like a mailbox: gate open, flag up, tumbling. . . .

"What's going on?" he asked.

She didn't answer right away, remaining silent while a second set of lights flashed by. He glanced toward them, wincing as the beams arced through the window. They were brighter than the first, bluish white, propelled by an incredible roar. He had never heard anything like it . . . and yet, it seemed familiar.

"You're at a crossing," she said. "A place of past and future . . . memory and dream . . . flesh and spirit. It's a test, Akeo. If you pass, you may yet become a skyborn, a great caretaker with a nighthawk's soul."

But of course, he did not want such things. He wanted a garage in Windslow Bottoms. He wanted his life to make sense. He wanted to go home.

"Yeyestani, I—"

The room darkened.

He blinked. The bluish light had done something to his eyes.

"We're almost finished," she said. "For now." She tightened her grip, pulling him closer.

Darkness thickened, blotting everything but the sound of her voice: "Remember the old stories," she said. "Remember *Awenyahsa*." Her voice took on a commanding edge, and with it the darkness vanished in a gust of sunlight, a glow that came on faster than any dawn he had ever known, as if the illumination had always been there, waiting for him to rise into it.

He looked down and saw the top of a pine-capped mountain, glacial shoulders nestled in a ruff of mist, central peak rising toward a low-hanging sun. He hovered in the light, wings extended, feathers splayed, body reclining on a bed of air. A redwing hawk hovered beside him, staring with an eye like polished stone.

"Look down," the hawk said, speaking without words, without sound. Its voice was sunlight on its feathers, tension in its wings. "This is the *Awenyahsa* of your greater grandfathers."

He circled, cleared a ridge and swooped down over the silver currents of the Monongahela River. Its name meant *broken cliff, fallen mountain.* Yeyestani had told him its waters were older than time. . . .

A clearing came into view. He banked toward it, picking up speed as he neared a palisade of woven branches. Rows of longhouses stood within the fortress. Smoke rose from vents in bark roves. . . .

So this was how it had been in the days before highways, trailer parks, and surface mines? He had heard the stories, but until now he had never appreciated the smallness of the village or the vastness of the mountain that a single generation of mining had reduced to a high-walled crater.

But how was he here? How could he fly like a hawk over terrain that had not existed for generations?

The doubt jolted him, nudging him out of the light, back into darkness.

"Not since '79."

"That was a come-from-behind team."

"They had heart."

"And it could happen again. Anything can happen."

"Right, and donkeys could fly. Next caller!"

Axle followed the radio voices until he once again found himself in Yeyestani's room. He had switched on the light when entering from the hall, but he could not see that light now. Nor could he see the radio dial glowing on the nightstand or the streetlight seeping through the bedroom window. Darkness encased him like a cocoon.

Yet he knew he had returned to the room. He smelled the stink of it, felt the tacky blood beneath his shoes, and heard Yeyestani speaking as she lay upon the bed. "You did it, Akeo."

"Did what?"

"Became a spirit, a piece of dream." She squeezed his hand. "You flew, Akeo."

He trembled. "And what am I doing now?"

"Now? Which now?"

"Here, with you. Is this real? Is this even happening?"

"It's all real. All happening. Layers on layers, like veins of coal in a mountain."

"I don't like it," he said. "It's confusing."

"Yes. It can be. You'll resist it. You'll make yourself forget. But you'll do it again . . . years from now . . . when you need it . . . when the Great Heart needs it . . . you will fly again."

He pulled away. "I don't believe any of this." He rubbed his eyes, his vision returning, blurry and dim. He saw the lamp now, its light spreading over the bed, illuminating the blood, spilling onto the door that led back toward the living room. He had left the door open when coming in from the hall, but it had fallen shut, sealing him off from the rest of the trailer . . . or whatever lay beyond. "I'm not really here," he said.

"Where then?"

He backed toward the door. "I'm asleep." He set his hand on the knob, its curved surface feeling more real than anything else in the room. "I'm dreaming."

"And where are you when you dream, Akeo? If your spirit is here, where is your body?"

"Out there," he said, meaning beyond the closed door. "On the couch." He turned the knob. "And that's where I'm going. I'm going back."

"To the couch?"

"Yes." He wanted to return to that quiet and familiar place, that place of reliable boredom where he could drink Sprite and eat chips and worry about getting a garage he couldn't pay for.

"But it isn't out there, Akeo." Her voice seemed at once close and distant.

"Walk away from me now, and you'll be on your own."

He opened the door.

Kirill watched Sam holster her rifle, securing the straps that cradled the gun across her back, barrel up between her shoulders.

"Describe Bird," she said. "How will I know him?"

"Braided hair, sleeveless vest, tattooed arms. He's hard to miss."

"Tell me about his pistol."

"Nine millimeter. Semiautomatic, but it can go full auto. There's a switch on the side."

She walked to the back of the Jeep. "Russian made?"

"That's right."

She opened the tailgate. "He get it from you?"

"Yes. Through my cousin. He's a collector."

"Who's a collector? Your cousin or Bird?"

"Bird. My cousin's more like a dealer."

She shook her head, looking disgusted. "Boys with toys." She reached inside the rear compartment and grabbed a heavy case, pulled it toward her. "He any good?"

"Any good?"

"With the gun?" She opened the case. "Is Bird a good shot, or was hitting the Mustang an accident?"

"No. No accident. He's a good shot. Practices all the time. Got a target range in his home."

She reached into the case, pulling out a night-vision monocular in a nylon harness. "We have to assume he's following the trail of spilled gasoline," she said, removing her boonie hat and slipping the monocular straps over her head. "And the driver won't get far, not the way he's losing fuel. If Bird keeps moving, he'll find the Mustang, but by then the people inside will have moved on. They'll be traveling on foot, harder to follow, and Bird—" She snapped on the night-vision monocular. A green glow pooled over her eye, down her cheek. "As I said, he's going to complicate things."

"You don't need to worry about Bird. He's on our side."

"Is he? Think about it. He sees me in the dark, how's he going to know I'm with you?" She took an ammo bag from the case. "He's wounded, pissed off, and carrying a semiautomatic handgun that can go full auto at the flick of a switch." She slipped the bag over her shoulder and closed the case. "He might be your partner, Kirill. But if I come across him in the dark I might have to put him down."

"Christ, Sam."

She slammed the tailgate. "You got a problem with that?"

Kirill hesitated.

"Good." She began loading the rifle. "Now what can you tell me about where we are? How well do you know this area?"

"Pretty well. I've been through it with a survey team."

She glanced toward the trail. "Does this path lead to the Mountain Downs site?"

"Yes."

"How far?"

"To the highwall? Quarter mile. Maybe more."

"All right." She started walking toward the posts that bordered the gasoline spill. "You take the Jeep. Drive back to your office. Wait for me."

"You're going to meet me at my office?"

"That's right."

"You're going to walk there?"

"I'll have to. You'll have the Jeep."

"It's seven miles, Sam."

"Only if I take the roads, which I won't." She paused, inspecting a patch of flattened weeds on the edge of the spill. "Looks like two of the Mustang boys got out to inspect the leak." She squatted, studying the ground. "One of them fell." She picked something dark and limp out of the mud. Kirill couldn't quite make it out.

"What is it?" he asked.

She dropped it again. It landed with a smack. "Ski mask." She stood, wiping her hands on her pants.

"Bird told me they were wearing ski masks."

She turned toward the trail. "So let me see if I've got this chronology right. Your attorney calls you a few minutes after 10:00. He say's he's in trouble and hangs up."

"I'm not sure he's the one that hung up. It might have been Bird. I think maybe Bird took the phone from him, broke the connection."

"All right. However it happens, the connection breaks. You call back, and this time you talk to Bird. He tells you that he and the attorney are chasing three guys in a Mustang. After that, you called me."

"Right."

"That was 10:13."

"I didn't notice the time."

"It was 10:13. We were on the phone for two and a half minutes. After that, you called the attorney back. That's your third and last conversation with him. The call ends with the shooting. You heard the whole thing."

"That's right."

"And what time was that?"

"I don't know."

"Did you call him right back after talking to me?"

"No. Not right back. I went to the bar, poured a scotch. Then I went outside to wait for you."

"Scotch? You have a liquor license now?"

"No. Special stash for special guests. I don't charge for it, don't display it."

She nodded, amused. That was one thing she and Kirill had in common, neither of them cared to be hassled over small stuff. They followed little laws, broke the big ones.

"Anyway," Kirill said, "after that drink, I called them again."

"So that was what? Five minutes after you called me? Ten minutes?"

"Maybe seven."

"So it was 10:22."

"Maybe."

"And I got to your place at 10:43."

"I don't know. I didn't notice the time."

"It was 10:43," she said. "When I saw you from the road, it looked like you were still on the phone."

"I was. I tried calling each of them one last time. First Peterson. Then Bird. Neither answered."

"So this gun battle went down sometime around 10:22. And now it's 10:56." She spoke without looking at her watch.

Kirill opened his cell phone and checked the glowing clock: 10:56. How the hell did she do that?

"So they've got maybe a half-hour head start, but I'm thinking—" She looked toward the mine. "I'm thinking they didn't have enough gas to get more than a few miles. They must have known that. That's why they didn't try getting to the interstate by way of Cliff Mine Run. The driver checked the gauge, saw the tank was nearly empty, and decided to drive through the forest and ditch the car in the mine."

"So by now they've ditched it?" Kirill said. "They've ditched it, and now they're walking through the mine, out toward Windslow Road Extension."

"Yes. That's what I'm thinking." She looked back at Kirill, fixing him with her mismatched eyes: one dark beneath the shadow of her brow, the other glowing milky green behind her night-vision monocular. "If your partner doesn't screw things up, I should be able to spot them from the highwall. There's just one thing . . . one more thing I need to know."

"What's that?"

"Do you want them clean?"

"Clean?"

"The hits. Do you want clean kills?"

Kirill turned, looking at the ruined Viper, seeing again how the remnants of Paul's head fanned across the custom platinum finish.

"No," Kirill said. "Not clean. Hurt them. Make it messy. Make them pay."

"You want their heads?"

"Heads?"

"Or maybe just their scalps? Maybe their livers?"

Was she serious? Or was she mocking him, knowing full well that he believed that dirty work was for soldiers, that it was important for generals to distance themselves from the blood of the field?

"No," he said. "No trophies. Just don't make it clean."

She nodded, turned, and took off down the trail.

He watched her go.

Even with the gun on her back, she ran with the grace of something indigenous to the forest, a long-legged deer bounding away in silence.

And then, in a blink, she was gone.

Walk away from me now, and you'll be on your own.

Axle opened Yeyestani's bedroom door and stepped into the hall that led to the living room. Blue-white phantoms flashed in the dimness, ghostly images of the odd light that had splashed through Yeyestani's window. He put his hand against the wall, feeling his way as he walked forward, realizing that the space had changed. He paused, his vision clearing, the phantom flashes coalescing into a pair of incandescent lights—bare bulbs hanging from black cords.

The living room was gone, replaced by a box-shaped room with pressboard walls.

And there were people here, two men and a woman standing around a large table while a third man sat slumped in a chair, his face turned toward a door that opened onto the wide chasm of Windslow Mine.

Axle knew these people, but from where? He stared, trying to understand and realizing that they were not familiar in the usual sense, not like people he *had* seen, but rather like people he *would* see . . . someday . . . years from now. . . .

One of them had removed his shirt, revealing a torso covered with scars. *Burn scars.* Axle knew this, although he could not remember ever seeing such scars before.

The other man wore his hair in a wild, tangled mane. He looked dangerous, tense, poised to do something crazy. He stood with one hand pressing the table, fingers twitching, clenching . . . unclenching. *He's going to hit the woman*, Axle thought, his mind crackling with a sense of absolute premonition.

"Listen, Reddy," the woman said. "Maybe—"

The man's hand clenched, flew up, and struck her hard on the side of the face. She fell backward, banging her head on an iron stove.

Axle reacted without thinking. "Hey!" He raced forward, not sure what he expected to accomplish, a kid throwing himself between fighting adults. And there was a gun here, too—long barreled, leaning against the table. He froze when he saw it, but no one reached for it. No one turned toward him. His challenge went unanswered.

The woman remained on the floor, dazed. The red-haired man moved toward her, both hands clenched, ready to hit her again. But the shirtless man moved, too, rounding the table to intervene. And through it all, the sitting man sat slumped in his chair, facing the door.

Axle tried making sense of it.

I'm like a ghost.

Emboldened, he hurried around the table, sidestepping the men and continuing on toward the exit. *I'm invisible,* he thought. *I'm seeing this, but I'm not here . . . not* really *here.*

He looked down at the woman. She leaned against the stove, trembling, disoriented, and her eyes—

He did a double take as he crossed in front of her. She met his gaze, her expression leaving no doubt that she sensed his presence. Her lips trembled, ready to call out.

"It's all right!" Axle backed toward the door. "I'm leaving." He turned to run, stumbling once again when he saw the face of the chair-sitting man: bloody, bruised, swollen . . . and undeniably familiar.

My father, Axle thought, seeing the likeness in the right side of the face, the side opposite the swelling. *He looks like my father.* Axle had never met the man, but Yeyestani had showed him pictures: father at the prom, at graduation, at the wheel of a giant coal truck. . . .

But there was no way this battered man could be his father. Axle's father had not died sitting in a chair, covered with blood. *No . . . not my father . . . my father didn't die this way . . . but someone else will.* The realization chilled him, filling him with a sense of things he was not ready to know.

There was only one thing to do.

He turned and ran into the night.

Outside, he found a Mustang parked midway between the shack and generator. It looked beat, with the mirror ripped away, door and fenders scraped to bare metal, black paint dangling like shredded skin. Beneath portions of that skin, a layer of candy-apple red peeked like oozing blood. And there was more blood, real blood, on the car's roof—long streaks of it that fanned like wings around the base of a jagged hole.

What did it all mean?

Yeyestani would not have brought him here to find these things if they were not important. He wished she were still with him, guiding him.

Walk away from me now, and you'll be on your own.

The moon hung low, shining across the mine, casting Axle's shadow against the highwall as he climbed the screw-thread road. Exposed coal veins lined the rock, blending with the darkness of his passing shadow. He touched them as he ran, feeling the chill of their slow time, eras folding back on themselves, the past bearing down upon the past, compressing, transforming. . . .

The path steepened as he neared the column of protruding rock. He stopped running, taking his time, trying not to look at the drop that loomed a few feet to his left.

His moon-tossed shadow moved with him, shifting away from the wall, falling against the path as he rounded the column. Then he stopped.

Once again, he had company.

A man stood before him, coughing as if struggling to clear his lungs. He had braided hair and tattooed arms, like the men in pictures Yeyestani had shared when talking about the old ways. But this man had nothing to do with old ways. And Axle, wanting nothing to do with him, stepped aside as the man pushed forward: onto the screw-thread road, down toward the ledge of machined rock.

Seconds later, a voice rose from the shack's open door: "Christ, Spinelli! There's someone coming down the wall!"

Again, Axle turned and ran.

He reached the summit.

Trees rose before him, jagged against the sky. He hurried toward them, stumbling onto the trail. His sides ached, but still he ran, hurtling onward until darkness forced him to cut his speed to a cautious jog.

The trail veered, following the inward curve of the wall, bringing him back to the place where an hour ago he had looked up at the overhanging roots and branches of a massive ledge-clinging tree. Now the tree straddled the path, branches tangled in undergrowth, roots broken against the alcove wall. He ducked beneath it, emerging to find someone racing toward him from farther up the trail. She wore clothes that merged with the darkness, but one of her eyes glowed milky green against the shadows of her face.

She ducked as she reached the fallen tree, and before he could step aside—

WHOOOOSH!

—she vanished in a gust of wind that had nothing to do with moving air. But the sound of her running lingered, as if she had passed through him and was now continuing on toward the crater.

How much more of this could he stand before he lost his mind?

Or had he already lost it?

He pushed onward, coming to a piece of sheet metal lying partially embedded in the rutted ground. It was the OSM sign, smeared with mud and trailing a piece of chain. Further on, he found more chain, a longer piece twisted like a metal snake in a pool of moonlight. The links looked wet. *Gasoline*, he thought, realizing he had been smelling the fumes for some time. The air reeked of it, and a short distance later, when he came to the posts at the edge of the clearing, he saw why.

A wide spill covered the ground. He avoided it, cutting through a line of brambles and into a glade that seemed different from the one he had passed through an hour earlier. Was it the same space? The trees looked taller, as if they had cycled through a decade of summers during the time he had spent at the mine. And beneath those trees sat a junked car with a smashed grill and rust-spattered trunk. But the rust wasn't rust, and the car wasn't empty. A piece of a man sat inside. . . .

Axle turned away, moving faster as he neared the portion of trail that led to Cliff Mine Run. Leaves hissed behind him, clattering in the still air as if something large were moving through the trees, but he didn't look back. He had seen enough. He wanted to be out of the forest, back home, safe in a place where things made sense.

But even as he moved forward, he heard the rumble of another surprise waiting beyond the clearing. It sounded like an engine. And there was light out there, too: muted and diffused, like a glow of headlights through trailside ferns.

He slowed his pace and slipped behind a patch of yarrow grass. Inching forward, peering between the leaves, he saw a heavyset man in a suit backlit by glowing foliage. The glow seemed to come from a car that had gone over the slope. And there was something else, a detail that Axle couldn't quite discern in the uneven light. It resembled a gigantic snake, long and black, stretching across the trail and coiling about the base of a leaning cedar. Maybe it was a downed power cable . . . a low-lying vine . . . an illusion. But whatever it was, the man ignored it as he studied the clearing.

"Hey!" the man said. "Somebody there?"

Axle held his ground, refusing to move, becoming one with the blades of yarrow grass until the man backed away, turned, and ran through the glowing ferns that lined the trail. And as the ferns swayed with the man's passing, Axle once again heard the rustle of something moving at his back, the sound of something entering the clearing, coming toward him.

Axle ran, his body becoming like the wind as he hurtled out of the clearing and down the trail, away from the thrashing hiss that stirred the forest.

Like the man on the trail, Axle ran without looking back.

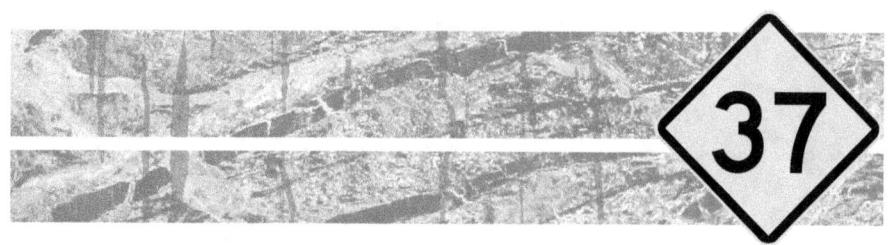

37

"Christ, Spinelli! There's someone coming down the wall!"

Axle blinked, awakening to find himself slumped in a chair, five feet from an open door.

"Damnit," Reddy said. "You hear me, Spinelli? There's someone outside!"

Spinelli hurried forward, looking different than he had the last time Axle opened his eyes. The man was shirtless now, covered with scars.

I've seen him like this before . . . nine years ago . . . I walked away from Yeyestani and saw him in this room.

The memory of it crackled inside him, as vivid as if it had just happened. . . . But it hadn't happened.

Yeyestani might have brought him to this shack, she might have opened the door and told him to come inside, but he had not entered. Instead, he had turned around, walked out of the mine, returned home alone. For nine years, that had been the memory.

But now his mind hummed with another version: one in which he had walked like a ghost past people he had not yet met: four people around a sawbuck table, a wounded man on a screw-thread road, a camouflaged woman on a forest trail, and a fat man beside a leaning cedar. False memories? They had to be. They could not have happened. And yet they now seemed palpably real.

"Talk to me, Spinelli! Look at the wall. You see him?"

Spinelli pressed his face to the inside glass of a boarded window.

"See the sombitch?"

Spinelli peered between the slats, cupping his hands to block the glare from the room's dangling lights.

"The ledge road," Reddy said. "He's coming down from the column of rock. See him?"

Spinelli tensed. "Christ!"

"It's him, isn't it?"

"Can't be sure. Too far away."

Tejay pulled herself from the floor and crossed the room to stand behind Reddy.

He hit her, Axle thought, recalling something he could not have seen, something that had happened as he sat unconscious in the chair. *Reddy slapped her face, knocked her down.*

The mark of Reddy's palm stained her jaw, but still she approached him, looking over his shoulder, eyes widening as she saw what lay beyond the door. "Shit!" She pulled back, slipping into a corner, placing herself so she couldn't be seen from the ledge road. "I thought you blasted him, Reddy."

"See," Reddy said, talking to Spinelli. "Tejay knows." He raised his shotgun. "It's Bird, all right."

Spinelli remained at the window, peering through the slats. "He's got that pistol with him!"

"We'll fix that," Reddy said. He pumped the shotgun. A spent shell flew from the chamber, but instead of the slap of a new round sliding into place, he got only the dull click of the pump. "Sombitch!"

Spinelli looked toward him. "What?"

"I'm out!"

"Out?"

"Empty. No ammo." Reddy slumped against the door. "What now?"

"Bluff!" Spinelli said. "Aim like you're going to blow him away. He won't know the difference. Act like it's loaded."

Reddy raised the gun.

"Tell him to stay where he is."

"Hey!" Reddy shouted. "Hey, Bird! That's close enough!"

Tejay leaned against an inside wall. She folded her arms, clenching them tight across her chest. "What's he doing?" she asked.

"Stopping," Reddy said.

"Hey!" Bird spoke from across the ledge, his voice weak, barely reaching the shack. "How about . . . a truce?" He sounded as if he were having trouble breathing. "All right? Truce?"

"Truce?" Reddy shouted back. "Why bring a pistol if you're looking for a truce?"

A pause, and then: "Insurance. Just . . . in case."

Reddy glanced at Spinelli. "What now?"

"Tell him to drop the gun."

Reddy leaned forward, halfway out the door. "Hey, Bird! Drop the insurance! On the ground! Right there. In front of you."

Silence.

No one moved.

"What's he doing?" Tejay asked.

"Putting it down." Spinelli shifted, trying to get a better look. "He's putting the gun on the ground."

"That's it!" Reddy said, shouting to Bird. "Now back away. Two steps. Hold it there!"

Tejay looked down at her folded arms. "What do we do with him?"

"Duct tape. We duct tape the sombitch."

"We tried that."

"Yeah," Spinelli said. "But this time we do it right." He backed away from the window and grabbed the tape from the floor. "Here." He tried handing it to her. "You'll need to use more this time. Make sure it holds."

"Me? You want *me* to do it?"

"No big deal, girl," Reddy said. "Just tape him up and bring him inside."

Her cheeks reddened. "Why *me*?"

"You did it before," Spinelli said.

"That was different. I had a mask. He didn't know it was *me*."

"Don't be proud," Reddy said. "He'll be getting a good look at all of us real soon."

"But he doesn't know *you*. He doesn't—"

"Hey!" This came from outside, Bird calling across the ledge. "I'm coming in."

"No!" Reddy steadied his aim. "Not till we say so."

"Damnit!" Spinelli said. "I'll bring him in!" He turned and grabbed his bloody undershirt from the floor. "But that means you take care of Axle." He pushed the undershirt into her empty hand.

"Take care of him?"

Spinelli picked up his jersey. His fingers streaked the hem with blood as he tugged it over his head and down across the scarred skin of his shoulders.

"What do you mean, *take care of him*?"

"Stop his bleeding." Spinelli turned, heading for the door.

"How am I supposed to do that?"

"Pressure." Spinelli kept walking. "Apply pressure. But don't hurt him."

"Shit!" She looked at the bloody undershirt, then at Axle. "He's *already* hurt."

Spinelli stepped outside.

"Yo, Bird!" Reddy said. "My man's going to tape your hands and bring you in. Be cool. Let him work. No one gets hurt."

"His eyes," Tejay said. "Tell him to tape Bird's eyes." She tossed the bloody undershirt back onto the floor beside Axle's chair. Then she returned to her hiding place in the corner. "C'mon, Reddy. Please. Tell him to tape his eyes."

Reddy ignored her. "The pistol!" he said, shouting to Spinelli. "Get the pistol!"

"Christ, Reddy." Tejay leaned against the wall, arms folded, head down as if she were trying to hide. "We're going to kill him, aren't we?"

"Yeah. Think so. Unless you got a better idea."

She glanced toward Axle. "Wasn't supposed to go like this," she said. "No one was supposed to get hurt. Remember that?"

"Sombitch! I remember you kicking Bird's ass in the SUV. That's what I remember."

"But I stopped. I didn't hurt him bad. I didn't *kill* him." Her voice dropped to a whisper. "Wasn't supposed to go like this. That's all I'm saying. Not like this."

Axle felt himself starting to drift again. His good eye grew heavy. He closed it. It was easier that way, easier to listen without looking.

"We gotta get out of here," Tejay said again, her voice fading. "I just want to go home."

38

*H*ome.

The word rumbled through Axle like slow thunder. But instead of conjuring memories of his childhood in Coals Hollow, it brought back the image of Yeyestani sitting atop the highwall, looking at a pair of spotlights rising from the southern horizon.

"Soon," Yeyestani said, "the son of one of those owners will return to his father's highland home."

Standing apart from the scene, watching with the omniscient stare of a dreamer, Axle watched his younger self turn to Yeyestani. He was surprised at how small he had been back then: short and scrawny, like a weed growing from the lip of the mine. "What son?" he asked.

But Yeyestani did not answer.

The scene was running on memory time, and as such it could be stopped, reversed, or accelerated at Axle's discretion. It could also be pondered, reconsidered, and revised. That was both the advantage and disadvantage of memory. Unlike videos or photographs, it could change, and when it did it was impossible to go back to the moment and see what had really happened.

Had the highwall conversation between him and Yeyestani really taken place? Had Yeyestani actually told him about Frieburg and Vorarov? And if she had, why had he not remembered it until after getting shot?

Because she didn't tell me. Because I'm dreaming, not remembering.

But the image in his mind's eye did not feel like a dream. It seemed too real, imbued with the weight and texture of reality.

He continued watching, and as he did Yeyestani reached out and touched the scrawny kid's arm. "Remember," she said. "Dream and remember. You'll understand. Someday. Trust me." She spoke to the boy, but her words seemed directed toward the man he would become, the ghostly voyeur from the future. "You'll dream the memory of now, and you'll understand."

39

Spinelli turned the roll of silver-backed tape over in his hands, hunting the end while he approached Bird. The man was badly wounded, almost as bad as Axle, but in the chest rather than the head.

"Is that your blood?" Bird asked.

"Is what my blood?"

Bird pointed. "On your hands . . . your shirt."

Spinelli looked down at himself, realizing for the first time how much of Axle's blood he had gotten on him. "No," he said. "It's not mine."

"But . . . it's someone's." Bird paused, catching his breath. "Guess . . . I got one of you." He grinned. There was blood on his teeth. "So we're even."

Reddy called from the shack: "The pistol! Get the pistol!"

Spinelli stooped, picked up the gun, and shoved it into his waistband.

Bird's grin broadened. "Feeling lucky?"

Spinelli didn't answer.

"I only ask because . . . that pistol . . . it's loaded . . . loaded and cocked. If I were you . . . I'd keep it . . . out of my pants."

Spinelli kept the gun where it was and tugged the end of the tape. *Zzzzzzzzck*!

Bird's vest, what remained of it, crackled with a sheen of clotting blood. His right arm dangled, longer than the left, as if disengaged from the socket. Nevertheless, he didn't seem to be in pain, just weak and out of breath.

Spinelli gave the tape another tug. *Zzzck*! "Turn around," he said.

"You . . . going to . . . tape me up? Like last time?"

"That wasn't me last time."

"No?" He looked at Spinelli's muddy sneakers. "Guess not. That guy had . . . heavy shoes. I didn't see them . . . but I felt them. Sure as hell . . . weren't sneakers." He looked at the shack, at Reddy. "I remember . . . that one . . . too." His eyes narrowed, sizing up Reddy. "He's . . . the shotgun man. That means—" He grinned as he looked back at Spinelli. "You're flashlight man. You're the one . . . made me stop." Bird lowered his voice. "Put it in park," he growled, apparently imitating the tone Axle had used during the heist. "Look at me!"

Spinelli wasn't amused. "I said turn around!"

Bird gave a lopsided shrug. Then he turned, his right arm swinging like so much rope, deadweight against his side.

"Hands behind you," Spinelli said.

Bird positioned his good hand against the small of his back. "That's the best I can do," he said. His chest gurgled, leaking air. "If you want the other hand . . . you'll have to . . . move it yourself."

Spinelli took hold of the dangling hand. It felt cold, dead. He wrapped tape around the wrist and pulled it back to bind it to the other.

"It doesn't hurt . . . as much . . . as you'd think," Bird said. "In case . . . you're wondering. There's not much pain . . . just a throb . . . more numb than pain."

Spinelli gripped both hands, lifting them away from Bird's back as he wound the tape around the wrists.

"I'm not . . . looking for trouble," Bird said. "I was . . . but not now." He gave a wet cough. Blood misted from his lips. "Now . . . everything's changed. Now . . . I'm on a mission. I'm looking . . . for someone."

"Who?"

"Not sure. He . . . didn't say."

"Who didn't say? What the hell are you talking about?" Spinelli finished taping Bird's hands. Then he grabbed him by the collar and turned him to face the shack.

"He said . . . he was a guardian . . . an earthborn." Bird coughed again, the sound coming simultaneously from his mouth and the open wound in his chest. "He came . . . after you . . . shot me."

"I didn't shoot you."

"Ah . . . guess not." Bird looked toward the shack, toward Reddy. "That . . . would've been . . . shotgun man."

Reddy shouted from the open door. "The hell you two doing?"

Spinelli gave Bird a shove. "Go," he said. "Inside."

Bird stumbled forward, wheezing as he advanced toward the open door.

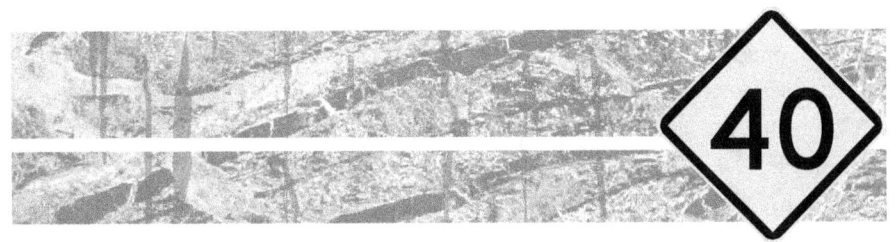

40

You'll dream the memory of now, and you'll understand.

The thump of stumbling feet drew Axle back from his dream. He raised his head and opened his good eye. Across the room, Spinelli led Bird in from the ledge.

"Here!" Reddy dragged the second chair from the wall. "Put him here."

Part of Bird's chest was gone. Blood spattered his neck, face, and arm. When he breathed, the wound sputtered like hot grease. He should have been dead, but here he was easing down into a seat, looking around with the poise of an Okwe warrior.

Spinelli knelt beside him, taping his legs to the chair.

"Man!" Bird sat back, looking around. "Stinks in here." He frowned at Reddy, noting the gasoline stains on his pants. "What'd you do? Go swimming . . . in high-test?"

"Shut up!"

Tejay moved deeper into the corner by the stove, positioning herself behind the chair, avoiding Bird's line of sight.

Reddy backed toward the table, giving Spinelli room to work. "Did you get his pistol?"

"Yeah." Spinelli put down the tape. "Right here." He pulled the gun from his waist, gripping the barrel as he handed it over.

"Careful," Bird said. "That's not your . . . momma's handgun."

Reddy leaned the empty Remington against the table and checked the pistol's chamber. "Semiautomatic?"

"Yes . . . at the moment. But . . . there's a switch . . . on the side. See? Flip that . . . it goes full auto."

Reddy found the switch.

"It's . . . modeled after . . . the Russian Stetchkin." Bird gave a blood-stained grin. "Not . . . that you . . . would understand."

Reddy flipped the switch. Then he raised the gun, aiming at Bird.

"The auto rate is . . . ridiculously high," Bird said. "Takes . . . getting used to."

"How many rounds left?"

"Not sure." His wound gurgled. "Not many. Less than a second's worth . . . on full auto."

Reddy frowned at the gun, then switched it back to its original setting. "What else you packing?"

"Well—" He sighed and looked toward the table. "I . . . was carrying . . . a briefcase."

"Yeah," Reddy said. "We need to talk about that."

"What's this?" Spinelli found Bird's cell phone, took it from its belt clip, held it up. "Ultra thin." He hefted it, feeling its weight. "Light as hell."

"Top of the line," Bird said. "You'd . . . probably like . . . something bigger."

Reddy snapped his fingers. "Give it here."

Spinelli tossed the phone to Reddy.

"Check his other pockets?" Reddy said.

Spinelli opened Bird's vest, reached in, pulled out a wallet: hand-stitched leather inlaid with soaring hawks. Spinelli opened the billfold. "There's cash in here." He pulled it out. "Ones and twenties."

"We split that," Reddy said.

Bird shook his head. "You guys . . . are too much."

"Fuck you."

Bird looked at the briefcase on the table. "Who . . . you guys . . . working for?"

"Working for?"

"Who . . . hired you?" He licked his lips. "Was it . . . one of the other developers? One . . . of the . . . casino families?"

"We work for ourselves."

"I doubt that." Bird shifted again, looking at Axle. "He . . . doesn't look . . . so good."

"Yeah?" Reddy said. "He looked fine until you shot him."

Spinelli flipped through the cash from the billfold. "Eighty-six bucks."

Bird kept staring at Axle.

"Eighty-six?" Reddy said. "What's that three ways?"

To Axle, Bird said: "Are you the one . . . taped me up . . . kicked me in the head?"

Axle tried responding, tried telling Bird that the heist had not been his idea. But he couldn't. He felt better than he had the first time he had regained consciousness—stronger, more alert, but still too weak to move.

Bird dropped his gaze, looking at Axle's rubber-soled boots. "He had . . .

big heels," Bird muttered. "The one . . . who kicked me . . . he had heavy heels
. . . like hammers." He looked around at Reddy's high-top sneakers, threadbare and soaked with gas and mud. "Interesting."

Reddy grabbed Bird's collar, pulling him upright in the chair. "The hell
you looking at?"

The chair shifted, wooden legs grating against the floor, bringing Bird
around until he saw the corner between door and stove. And in that corner,
standing with arms pressed tight across her chest, Tejay recoiled as if shot
dead by Bird's stare.

"You?" Bird said.

She made a futile attempt to turn away.

"You!"

Kirill returned to Sam's Jeep, closing himself in, shutting out the stink of blood and gasoline. The forest stood dark and still beyond the windows. No wind. No sound. It resembled a glass-enclosed diorama of plaster branches and acrylic leaves.

Sam was somewhere out there, beyond the trees, doing what she did best. She was a good soldier. He should have trusted her to work alone. There was nothing for him in this dark place, nothing to do but stare out the windows and muse about how fast his plans for the night had turned to shit.

He put the Jeep in gear, resigning himself to doing as Sam had instructed: drive to the club, await her return. But even as he turned the wheel his thoughts were on another time when, much like tonight, everything had turned to shit in the blink of an eye.

He remembered his old client, the rail-thin chef with the miserable betting record. Kirill's last encounter with that man had been one screwed up piece of business, an experience that still reminded Kirill that the world could not be trusted to play by the rules.

The chef, like many clients who had fallen out of favor with Kirill's Uncle Ilya, actually believed that the Vorarov family regarded him as a friend, or at least as an associate entitled to a little extra grace for old-times' sake.

"So how is Uncle Ilya?" the chef asked, still nursing his scotch.

Outside, shadows lengthened along 73rd and Lexington. The restaurant would start serving dinner in another hour. Both Kirill and the chef had places to be by then.

"How is my uncle?" Kirill shrugged. "Who can say? The doctors tell him he shouldn't drink, bad for the sugar. But what do they know?"

"You tell him I asked about him, OK?"

"I will do that."

"And tell him . . . about this other thing . . . the twenty-seven . . . tell him it's not a problem. I'm good for it."

"That's what you said when you owed him seventeen."

"Right, and it's still true."

"It might be, but there are other considerations."

"What other considerations?"

"How it looks."

"How it looks to whom?"

"To other people," Kirill said. "To other clients. You understand, my uncle needs to maintain appearances. It's much like the restaurant business."

"You know the restaurant business, Kirill?"

"Not so much, but you know what I mean." Kirill leaned forward. "Twenty-seven," he said. "I can wait here while you make some calls." He opened his jacket and pulled out a fist-sized Motorola, the sort of ultra-small convenience that was all the rage in the mid-90s. "Use my phone." He held his jacket open, letting the chef see the eight-shot Makarov hanging from a shoulder harness. "I have unlimited minutes." He placed the phone on the bar. "A man like you has many friends." He pushed the phone toward the chef. "Call them."

"You say I should get the money from my friends?"

Kirill buttoned his jacket. "Whatever it takes."

The chef drained his glass, crunched a sliver of ice, and shook his head. "No. The other way is better."

"What other way?"

"The other way I told you about. One more game. Roll it over."

"Twenty-seven?" Kirill frowned. "That's a lot of debt to roll over."

"Look, old friend." The chef took Kirill's hand. "I'm asking a favor. For old times."

Kirill did not like being touched, especially not by skinny men with bony fingers.

The chef squeezed Kirill's hand. "All right, Kirill? For me? We good here?"

Kirill said nothing.

The chef waited a moment, then he released Kirill's hand and pushed away from the bar. "I have to take a piss." He stood. "You think about it." He turned. "I'll be right back."

The chef headed toward the bathroom, walking past a line of tables, one of which was occupied by a young businessman reading the *Wall Street Journal*. At least, the figure sitting at the table *looked* like a businessman.

Kirill was not the only representative of the Vorarov family in the restaurant. Kirill had come to the Upper East Side with a Ukrainian named Oles Prutko, a bright new soldier who went by the nickname Snoop, after an American rapper who sang songs with titles like "Can I Get a Flicc Witchu?" and "Can U Control Yo Hoe?"

When he wasn't working with Kirill, Oles Prutko liked wearing baggy sweats and do-rags. He was a real character, a white boy with black ambitions. But those things didn't matter to Kirill. The important thing was that Prutko was hungry enough to be reliable. And he cleaned up well.

In a Versace suit, the Ukrainian Snoop looked like an Upper-East yuppie, one more upwardly mobile New Yorker out for a single-malt lunch. Prutko also had a great ear for language, and he could channel the vowels of white New Yorkers as readily as he could the consonants of West-Coast blacks. What he couldn't do, however, was read. English or Ukrainian, it was all tea leaves to the kid. Still, he looked convincing as hell sitting behind a Glenlivet and a *Wall-Street Journal*. To look at him, you'd never imagine he was eighteen-months out of a shipping container.

And he could follow orders.

Kirill remained seated as the chef left the bar. This was the signal. If Kirill and the chef got up together, all was well and Snoop Prutko could go on drinking and pretending to read.

But Kirill didn't get up.

The chef passed a young couple seated at a table by the hallway that led to the bathroom. They looked like out-of-towners, she in a summer dress, he in an open-collared shirt and cotton jacket. Kirill wished they weren't sitting so close to the men's room, but Prutko was a good soldier, clean and efficient. In any event, things were already in motion. There was no stopping them now.

Prutko looked up. He met Kirill's gaze in the mirror behind the bar. Then he folded his paper and started after the chef.

Prutko had been charged with two objectives: first, scare the chef; second, send a message. The message was for other clients, people who occasionally needed to be reminded that promises to Uncle Ilya had to be kept. The trick was to place the message as quietly as possible. To that end, Prutko had come prepared. Moving toward the restrooms, he removed something from his jacket pocket. It was oblong, about the size of a fist. He cupped it in his palm and pretended to dial. Then he held the thing to the side of his face. "Walter, it's me." He entered the men's room, still talking, a multi-tasking businessman making a cell-phone call on his way to the john. The charade would keep the chef from thinking someone was sneaking up on him, thus giving Prutko time to thrust the handheld stunner into the back of the chef's neck and zap him with a charge strong enough to knock him to the floor.

The chef wouldn't lose consciousness, but he'd remain dazed long enough for Prutko to kick or punch him in the face, choice to be determined by the elevation of the chef's head after he went down. The blow to the face had to be strong enough to leave a massive bruise. Then, Prutko would zap the chef again and leave the room.

In the unlikely event that anyone walked in, Prutko would go back to handling the stunner as if it were a cell phone. The charade would work, but not because the stunner looked like a cell phone. It didn't look like much of anything, just an oblong plastic shell. Anyone who looked close would see that it had no keypad, no ear or mouthpiece, but those were small details, easily hidden. In times of crisis, people saw what they were directed to see: a man on the floor, a bystander calling 911. And Prutko knew what to say to make the call sound real: "Send an ambulance. I'll stay on the line." Then Prutko would leave the room, instructing whoever had just entered to remain with the injured man. "Keep him calm. I'll watch for the ambulance."

The chef would remain disoriented long enough for Prutko to leave. After that, when the chef regained his senses, he'd insist he was fine. Just a fainting spell. He would know better than to file a complaint against Vorarov.

Later, with the bruise tattoo still blooming on his face, the chef would report to work at his fashionable midtown kitchen, and for a while the word on the street would be all about the importance of honoring obligations to Uncle Ilya.

Kirill put a twenty on the counter, picked up his Motorola, and rose to leave. He'd gone three steps when he heard something shatter in the men's room. It wasn't the thump of a man collapsing at a urinal. It was a roar of fragmenting glass, as if a fist or head had slammed a mirror, shattering it to pieces.

The couple at the rear table stopped talking. A stoned cook peered from the kitchen. The bartender looked toward the hall.

Kirill kept walking.

A man appeared in the restaurant's doorway, looking in from a line of sidewalk tables. He was young, handsome, neatly attired—the kind of upwardly mobile New Yorker that Prutko could only pretend to be. His expression left no doubt that he had heard the noise.

Kirill looked at the man and shrugged. *What can you do?* the shrug said. *Nice neighborhood. But it's still Manhattan.*

That's when the screams started: loud, shrill, full of pain.

Until then, Kirill had assumed that Prutko was beating the crap out of the chef. But the screamed words were not English.

"*Zupynk! Dopomoha!*"

They were Ukrainian.

And then—

BAM!

—the restroom door flew open.

The chef stumbled out. There was blood on his face, shirt, hands. In his right hand he held a blade of broken mirror that flashed with light from the street-side windows. His eyes flashed, too, catching the sun as he turned toward the tables. And then he ran, raising his glass dagger, charging at Kirill.

There was only one thing to do.

Kirill drew his Makarov and placed a 9mm shot in the chef's chest. The woman at the rear table screamed. The chef kept coming, propelled by the momentum of his charge, stumbling forward as Kirill fired again. The second shot struck the chef between his crazy eyes. There was no need for a third. The man fell, dropping the dagger, still reaching for Kirill.

Kirill stepped back, moving away as the chef's hand struck his lapel. There was no strength in the hand. No life. The chef was dead before he landed.

The glass blade shattered on the hardwood, playing counterpoint to the dead-meat thud of the chef's face.

Kirill turned.

The yuppie on the sidewalk remained as before, framed in the doorway, staring inside.

Kirill looked away, avoiding eye contact as he slipped the Makarov into his pocket.

He pushed past the yuppie and turned toward the intersection.

No one called out, but Kirill felt their eyes, watching as he veered right onto East 73rd.

He hailed a cab. The driver was a Serb. He could be trusted. "Just drive," Kirill said. "Stop when I say."

The Serb crossed Lexington as the signal ambered to red.

The restaurant vanished, eclipsed by high walls.

"Stop here!"

The cab pulled to the curb.

Kirill slapped a twenty into the slot and pushed out onto a crowded sidewalk.

Then he walked.

No eye contact here. People faced front, listening to Walkmans, talking on cell phones. He stayed with them for a few blocks, then slipped into another cab that had pulled to the curb near the Whitney.

A siren wailed in the distance, blocks away.

This time Kirill rode south, settling back to collect his thoughts, and realizing for the first time that there was blood on his jacket, streaks from where the chef had tried grabbing his lapel.

The driver was a Sikh: red turban, black beard, gentle smile. "Where to, sir?"

Kirill tried covering the blood. "West."

"West where, sir?"

"Keep driving. I'll tell you." He reached into his jacket, drew his cell phone, called for pickup.

Prutko had entered the country illegally. His body was as untraceable as a black-market gun. But Kirill was a citizen, easy to find. Uncle Ilya was not pleased.

"There was no need to shoot the chef, Kirill."

"He killed Prutko."

"Yes, but you should have walked away."

"The man was charging at me."

"I understand. But there was still no reason to shoot him."

"It was sloppy. I know. But what could I do?"

Uncle Ilya sat by an open window, watching gulls circle the beach.

"What could I do, *Dyadya*?"

"That question is not important, Kirill. It is not a matter of what you *could* have done. It is a question of what we must do now." Uncle Ilya paused, thinking a moment before saying, "We can fix this." He turned, looking at Kirill. His eyes were clouded with age, but they were nonetheless cunning. There were stories about how Uncle Ilya had become an underground chess champion during his years in a Gulag camp, playing with neither board nor pieces, tracking the moves in his memory.

"We can fix this." Uncle Ilya folded his hands, making a steeple of his fingers. "We have a soldier, a big man, like you, Kirill. He will say he was you, that he was the one who shot the chef. He is prepared to take any consequences, and I am hoping they will not be too severe. Our *mudaks* are already working on the case." *Mudak* was a nasty expression, extremely vulgar. It was Uncle Ilya's word for lawyers.

"And what about me?" Kirill said. "What do I do?"

"You'll need to go away. For a while. Just in case."

"To Russia?"

"No. Not that far, but maybe not so exciting, either."

"Where?"

Uncle Ilya peered with a cataract stare that seemed to focus on a point behind Kirill's eyes. "There is a piece of land in Pennsylvania. It was a coal mine. It is nothing now. But it might be something someday. I think you should go there. Keep an eye on things, open a business."

"What kind of business?"

"An entertainment business. Dancing. Movies. You know."

Kirill knew.

"We will get you the girls."

At the moment, it was a buyer's market for girls, with shipments being smuggled through east-coast docks. They came from the fragments of the old Soviet Union, from farms and cities where the old economies no longer worked and young people sought opportunities beyond the pale.

"How long?"

"You leave today."

"I mean how long do I stay out there?"

"Depends on how long it takes Pennsylvania to decide it wants casinos. We think it will be soon. In the meantime you can settle in, join the community. It makes sense. You know, good business."

And so it was that Kirill found himself in charge of a sex club in the middle of nowhere—in a place that was about as unknown as Las Vegas had been in the early years of the twentieth century. According to Uncle Ilya, the Jews and Italians had been in the right place at the right time when Nevada had turned its desert into an oasis of cash. Now Uncle Ilya believed that soon the same thing would happen in Pennsylvania, and when it did he wanted his people to be ready.

Sometimes, when he felt paranoid, Kirill wondered if maybe Uncle Ilya had been waiting for a reason to send him west to Pennsylvania. But most of the time Kirill believed it hadn't been planned at all. Uncle Ilya had just been doing his best with a bad situation.

That was how the game worked. Just when you got to feeling secure about something, the world knocked you in another direction. A person needed to know how to make the best of those changes. Being able to do that was a real survival skill.

Uncle Ilya had it.

Kirill liked to think that he had it, too, but there were times, like to-night—with Peterson dead and Frieburg walking wounded—when he wasn't so sure.

42

You?" Bird muttered.

Tejay sidestepped toward the stove.

Bird turned, following her. "You!" He seemed certain now. "I know you!"

"Yeah," Reddy said. "You know her. That's why she's hiding."

Tejay glared at Reddy.

"Might as well get out of the corner, girl," Reddy said. "He knows it's you."

Tejay took another sideways step, her face entering the shadow of the stove, her shoulders pressing the wall beneath a blackened chimney pipe.

Bird gave up trying to see her. He shifted again, facing front, looking at Reddy. "She your girl?"

"Yeah," Reddy said. "That'd be right. *My* girl. And now that we're all together, she's got some explaining to do."

"Explaining?" Bird looked suspicious.

"About your *money*," Reddy said. "Your *deliveries*."

Bird looked at the briefcase.

"Sombitch was supposed to be full of cash."

Bird sighed, his chest gurgling. "Damn!" He sat back. "Unbelievable."

Reddy continued. "She said you carried cash to the sex club. Every Sunday, she said. Briefcases full of bills."

"She said that?" Bird turned, trying to get another look at Tejay.

"Damn straight. That's what she told us. So the question is: What the fuck? Where's the cash?"

Bird grinned. "That's two questions."

"Fuck you! What's the answer?"

"*Every* Sunday?" Bird shook his head. "She said *every* Sunday?" Again he tried looking behind him.

"Tejay," Reddy said. "Damnit, girl. He's already seen you. Come out here."

But Tejay still wouldn't move. She remained as before, leaning back, arms crossed, trying to hold onto what remained of her secret.

"She didn't want you to know she was part of this," Reddy said.

"No doubt."

"But now you know. You know what this is all about. You know what we know and how we know it. So you might as well tell us."

"Tell you what?"

"Where's the money?"

"What money?"

"She said you'd have it. Every Sunday, she said. Like clockwork."

Spinelli had been holding back, but now he drew closer. "Look," he said. "Maybe there's a way out of this." He crouched beside Bird's chair. "Maybe there's a solution that can work for all of us." He spoke softly. The old Spinelli. Back in control, smooth as hell. "I've got a proposition."

Bird grinned. "So we're bargaining now? You ambush me . . . steal my briefcase . . . kill my attorney . . . leave me for dead—" He paused, catching his breath. "And now . . . *we're doing business?*"

"It's like this," Spinelli said. "You and Axle need help."

"Axle?" Bird said.

"That'd be him." Reddy pointed. "The dead guy."

"His name's . . . Axle?"

"That's right," Spinelli said. "You both need help, so what I'm offering—"

"Let me guess," Bird said. "I pay. You help. That it?"

"That's right."

"And I'll need . . . to keep my mouth shut . . . until you get away."

"Longer would be better," Spinelli said. "Maybe you could agree to keep it shut indefinitely."

"Indefinitely . . . as in forever? I keep it shut. You keep my money."

"Right, but in exchange for us getting you to a hospital."

Bird sat a moment, looking thoughtful.

"We have a deal?" Spinelli asked.

Bird shook his head. "I don't think so."

Reddy raised the pistol, pointing at Bird's temple. "I'm going to blow him away, man. I'm tired of this shit."

"Easy, Reddy," Spinelli said. "Take it easy."

"Yes," Bird said. "Take it easy . . . *Reddy.*"

"Sombitch! You told him my name."

"Chill!" Spinelli said. "It's all right. He can know it. We're working together, making a deal." He turned to Bird. "You've got to understand. It wasn't supposed to be like this. Hurting people was never in the plan."

"No?"

"Absolutely not."

"You never meant to hurt me? Just rob me . . . tape me up . . . kick me—"

"Kick you?"

"Oh, yes." Bird raised his voice, directing it toward the corner, toward Tejay. "Kick me!" His chest gurgled.

Spinelli glared at Tejay.

Tejay didn't respond.

Bird looked at Reddy. "Your girlfriend," he said. "I guess she thought . . . she had a score to settle."

"She can be a wildcat," Reddy said.

"Oh, yes." Bird grinned. "Don't I know! That's how they are . . . worker women. Down and dirty. They know how to dig."

"Shut up!" Tejay said.

"Ah!" Bird looked around. "The worker woman speaks."

"Shoot him, Reddy." She stormed forward, boots thumping the floorboards as she emerged from the corner.

Bird glanced at her heels. "There they are. Western heels. I bet . . . you wore those . . . for me."

"Do it, Reddy! Shoot him!"

"Hold on!" Spinelli said. "Christ, we're negotiating here."

"Looks like I've struck a nerve," Bird said. He looked at Reddy, reading his confusion. "She . . . didn't tell you?"

"The fuck you talking about?"

"Shoot him, Reddy!"

Bird shifted in his seat. "Listen, Reddy. I need to know . . . what she told you."

"*Shoot him, Reddy!*"

"Did she tell you . . . she was my *digger*?"

"Your *what*?"

Tejay said nothing. She seemed to realize it was over, that Reddy wasn't going to shoot Bird just yet and that Bird wasn't going to stop talking until he gave everything away.

"*Digger*," Bird said. "As in *gardener* . . . as in *landscaper*."

"The hell you talking about?" Reddy said.

Bird grinned. "I wonder." He leaned forward a little more. "What . . . did she tell you . . . about working for me?"

"She said—" Reddy glanced at Tejay, then back at Bird. "She said she was your helper."

"That's fairly broad."

"She said it was a temp position."

"That's true. The position . . . was definitely temp."

"She said she helped with books and shit."

"Books . . . and shit?" Bird looked at Tejay. "I suppose . . . that would be . . . *two* jobs."

Tejay was blazing now, her face red, eyes wide and angry. But she said nothing. She just let it go, watching it happen.

"Books . . . and shit," Bird said, pretending to think it over. "*Shit?* Maybe. But *books?*" He looked back at Reddy. "Are you saying . . . she said . . . she did my *books?*"

"Yeah."

"She said she was . . . my *accountant?*" Bird almost choked on the word, chest leaking as he stifled a laugh.

"No," Reddy said. "More like a temp secretary. She said that's how she knew about the money. About the deliveries."

"*Secretary?*" Bird looked at Tejay. "You've . . . got to be . . . *kidding.*" He paused, wheezing, catching his breath. "You told them . . . you were my *secretary?*"

43

Kirill accelerated along the wheel-rutted trail, leaving the clearing, heading toward Cliff Mine Run. The forest thinned to his right, giving way to the weedy slope that plunged toward a mountain creek. He glanced toward it, contemplating the proposed Mountain Downs Aqua Park that would feature one of the world's longest waterslides, one that would serpentine along the face of the contoured highwall and into a manmade lagoon complete with plastic cattails and palm trees. Thinking about those things brought back the sense of longing he had felt earlier. He wanted the resort to happen, and wanting it made him feel good. But the contentment lasted only a moment, shattering as something dark leaped from the trees and landed in his path. He swerved to miss it. It moved with him.

WHAM!

Metal crunched. The front end rose. He hurtled sideways, off the trail, through the weeds, onto the slope. The steering wheel spun through his hands as he tilted into freefall, toward something large and black beyond the side windows. He glimpsed it on the edge of his vision, a dark blur rising up to slam the side panel.

WHAM!

The seatbelt held him as the Jeep lurched to a stop. A pine cone thumped against the hood. And then, suddenly, stillness.

Nothing stirred but the gurgling creek, the hissing branches, the idling engine.

The blur beyond his side windows had resolved itself into the trunk of a giant pine. The Jeep leaned against it now, crunched against splintered bark, swaying gently as the pine recovered from the collision.

Farther down, ten feet below the base of the tree, a dark creek meandered over mossy stones.

I'd be there now if the tree hadn't stopped me.

He shivered and turned his gaze up along the slope, looking for the thing that had knocked him from the road.

Bear. He shivered. *Must have been a bear. Too big to be anything else.*

And yet there had been nothing bear-like in its movements. It had leaped from the forest, gathered itself into a crouch, and lunged at the left fender. What kind of animal behaved like that?

Gripping the wheel, steadying himself in the tilted seat, he tried believing that the beast had fled back into the forest.

Or maybe it's dead.

Somehow, he didn't think so.

Or wounded and dangerous.

That seemed more likely.

Panicking, he flipped open his phone, dialed Sam, and waited for the prompt asking him to state his name. But instead, he got the soft purr of a ringing connection.

One ring.

Then a second.

She wasn't answering.

He let it ring a third time before realizing his mistake. She had switched her phone to vibrate. No answer meant she was dealing with the Mustang.

"Christ!"

He closed the phone, breaking the connection.

Outside, the night remained still.

He was on his own.

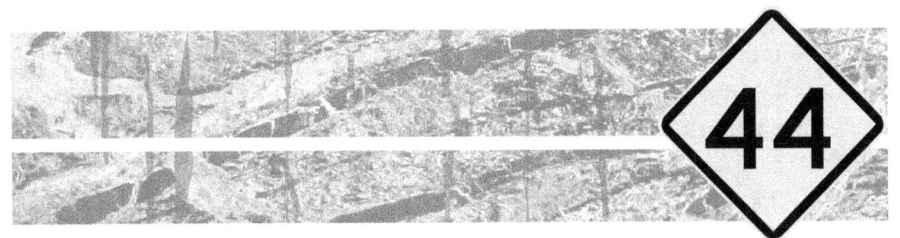

44

Axle stared at Tejay, studying the tension in her face, reading her memories. Since entering the shack, he had traveled deep into his own thoughts, but now, looking at Tejay, he found himself entering hers.

"*Secretary?*" Bird said. "You've got to be kidding. You told them you were my *secretary?*"

But Axle knew the truth. He read it in the lines of Tejay's face, the tilt of her mouth, the tension of her eyes. And as he studied these things, the walls of the shack fell away, and in their place appeared a sloping garden that shimmered in the light of a summer evening. . . .

He realized that he was not in the scene. He was invisible, a spirit looking down along a sloping landscape of hanging terraces and tiered beds. The arrangement recalled the contours of Windslow Mine, and to his right, completing the image, a wedge of fallen dirt and plants fanned out like the remnants of the rock fall that had killed his father.

Near a marble swimming pool, groundskeepers worked at securing a tarpaulin around the base of the slide, stretching a barrier to keep the collapsed mass from spreading onto the pool deck. Other workers moved along the garden's tiers, gathering tools and carting them to a pair of trucks parked in the shadow of the pool house. Everyone seemed eager to head home, everyone except a woman who stood beyond the pool in the shade of a dogwood. She wore her hair tucked beneath a dusty scarf, with a few strands of blond dangling around her forehead and ears. She was talking to a man in a sleeveless vest, and something about the way that man leaned toward her indicated that she was not talking about gardening.

"You?" she said, her voice remarkably clear in the quiet afternoon. "You!" She sounded at once amused and skeptical. "You're *him?*"

He nodded. "You sound surprised."

She looked him over, taking in his tattoos and braids. "You're *Maynard Frieburg?*"

"You can call me *Bird*."

"Bird?"

"As in Free Bird."

"Like the song?"

"No. Not really."

"You're, like, the guy who owns this place?"

"No. I'm not *like* him. I *am* him."

"Maynard Frieburg?"

"You seem unconvinced."

"No. It's not that. It's just—"

"What were you expecting?"

"Dunno." She gave a big-toothed smile. "I thought you'd be . . . I don't know . . . like older . . . maybe dressed like a banker."

"Who told you I was a banker?"

"No one. No one told me nothing. I'm not from around here. It's just that, with a big place like this, I figured you'd be . . . I don't know . . . you know . . . different."

"Aren't I different?"

"I mean *different* different. Jeez, I don't know. You know what I mean."

"Are you disappointed?"

She considered that. "No." She shrugged. "It's cool. I mean, you need to be yourself, right? That's the thing that—"

"Mr. Frieburg!" A worker called from the tarp-covered mound. "We're finished here."

Bird pivoted, stepping from the tree's shade, squinting at the stakes that held the tarpaulin in place over the stabilized landslide. "Is that tarp going to hold?"

"Yes. For now. Till we get back."

"Tomorrow morning?"

"That's the plan. We'll come with a full crew, tomorrow being Monday and all."

Axle put the details together: Monday, collapsed garden, landscapers. The scene before him was from earlier in the month, the Sunday after three nights of pounding rain had caused mudslides throughout the Windslow area. And in Windslow Bottoms, where most buildings occupied a flood-plain along Bottoms Creek, water had coursed through the streets. Axle had saved the Mustang by putting it on one of the service lifts, but every-thing else in his shop had been coated with layers of mud and raw sewage, forcing him to turn away business while he struggled with cleanup.

But Bird had money to burn. When a partial collapse of his tiered garden threatened to fill the clear water of his marble pool with topsoil, he offered a local landscaper overtime to work on a Sunday.

"Be early," Bird said. "I want this job finished by midweek. I'm having guests."

The man waved, nodded, then turned to climb into one of the trucks. A magnetic sign on the side panel read: Redwing Landscaping—Est. 1976.

Bird turned back to Tejay. "Do you need to go with them?"

Tejay shook her head. "I drove myself."

"Really?" Bird looked amused. "Wouldn't it have been easier to drive a car?"

"Huh?" It took her a moment. Then she smiled. "Oh, right . . . drove *myself*." She laughed. "You know what I mean."

"You drove?"

"That's right."

"So you can stay?"

She stopped smiling, feigning seriousness. "Why should I?"

The trucks pulled away, heading toward the cobbled drive that ran toward Windslow Road.

"Are you interested in gardening?" Bird asked.

"Not really."

"Plants?"

"No."

"Maybe I have some varieties you'll find interesting," he said. "My own crop. Quality stuff."

"Are we talking illegal substances?"

"Why, no, *officer*." He gave a disarming smile. "Of course not."

"What then?"

He leaned closer, his face turning gold in the angled light. "Blood ginseng," he said.

"Never heard of it."

"Not many people have." He lowered his voice, assuming a tone that was at once scholarly and seductive. "The People called it *katkwehsais*."

"What people?"

"The People. The ones who lived in the valley before settlers pushed them out."

"You mean, like, Indians?"

"No. Nothing like *Indians*. *Indians* are from *India*. I'm talking *Americans*."

"American Indians?"

"The tribe called itself *the Okwe*. The word means 'people.'"

"So they were, like, *the People*?"

"That's right."

"And why are we talking about them?"

"*Katkwehsais*," Bird said. "We're talking about blood ginseng. The Okwe cultivated it, smoked it."

"What's it do?"

"Different things."

"Like?"

He smiled. "Some say it's an aphrodisiac."

Axle found the verbal dance amusing. Detached as he was from human urges, observing more as a spirit than as a man, Axle saw at once that the dance would end badly. Bird's charm was all of the moment, all about the thing he wanted now. When he got that thing, everything would change. He would lose interest, shed his charm, resume a life that had nothing to do with the likes of Tejay.

"Aphrodisiac?" Tejay frowned. "What's that?"

"What's an aphrodisiac?" Bird studied her. "You're joking, right? You know what that means."

"Maybe." She shrugged, held his gaze. "But maybe you, like, want to show me."

Bird's smile broadened.

And then something strange happened. A voice came out of nowhere, distant, disembodied. Like Axle, it existed apart from the scene, inaudible to Tejay and Bird as they stood in the shadow of the dogwood. But Axle heard it. To him, it was as real as the tiered garden that sloped before him.

The voice was Reddy's.

He was hitting on you! Sombitch was playing you!

Axle tried turning toward the voice, looking to see if Reddy had somehow entered the scene, but the garden suddenly vanished, giving way to a room with linen-paneled walls and coffered ceiling. Time had passed. The room's tall windows looked out on moonlit trees. Bird had evidently taken Tejay to sample his crop of blood ginseng, and now the dance was crossing into serious foreplay.

Tejay stood beside an antique bureau, shedding clumps of dirt on the hardwood floor as she kicked off her work shoes. "I'm filthy." She looked toward the door of an adjacent bathroom. "I should wash up."

Bird came up behind her, his lips clamping the stem of a crackling pipe. "No," he said, taking the pipe from his mouth. "Don't bathe." He had removed his vest, exposing more tattoos along the backs of his shoulders. "I like the way you smell." He exhaled a puff of smoke and took her arm, raised her hand to his face, and ran his nose along her knuckles: smelling her. "Earthy."

She turned toward him.

He placed the smoking pipe on the corner of an antique bureau.

"I'm all sweaty," she said.

"Nothing wrong with that."

"I stink."

"So does humus."

She wore a T-shirt beneath her overalls. He pulled it up from her waist and slipped a tattooed hand beneath it.

"What's humus?" She slid her hands across his back, momentarily drawing them away as he removed her shirt. Her breasts were small, firm, pointed.

"You don't know about compost. Don't like plants. Aren't interested in gardening." He sounded amused. "What kind of landscaper are you?"

"No kind." Her overalls slid to her waist, then to her ankles. Nothing left now but a pair of bikini briefs: old, faded, drooping at the crotch. "Redwing was hard up for workers," she said. "He called me."

"How do you know Redwing?"

"I don't. I've only been in town a week. I stopped by his place looking for temp work. He said he'd call if he needed extra hands. Guess he needed them today."

Bird turned his back to Axle and took the smoking pipe from the bureau. The tattoos along his shoulders were bright red, like the markings of a chickenhawk. "So it must be fate," Bird said. His shoulders shifted as he held the pipe to his mouth and inhaled deeply.

"Say what?"

He didn't answer. Instead he kissed her, exhaling, filling her with smoke. Reddy's disembodied voice came again.

You're shitting me! You and him . . . you and this sombitch!

It occurred to Axle that he was still in the shack, listening to Tejay tell her story while Reddy interrupted. And yet, for the moment, that box-shaped room was little more than a dream. The real world lay within the linen-paneled bedroom, a world in which Bird and Tejay went from standing beside an antique bureau to writhing upon a massive four-poster bed.

Axle hovered close, watching their frenzied movements until Bird shivered, groaned, and pulled away.

Tejay lowered her knees, took her hands from his shoulders, touched his face. "You all right, baby?"

Bird looked at her. Then, abruptly, he turned to glance at a clock beside the bed.

"Something wrong?" she asked.

He wrinkled his nose and pivoted to the side of the bed, giving her the red of his shoulders as his feet slapped the hardwood floor.

She reached for him, grabbing empty air as he stood and hurried toward the bathroom.

Axle glimpsed the edge of a towel rack beyond the door, and then—*WHAM!* The door slammed, leaving Tejay alone with Axle's spirit.

A shower thundered in the bathroom.

Tejay pushed back her sweaty hair. "What am I doing?" She got up, grabbed her filthy T-shirt, and looked toward the shower's muffled roar. Axle read the uncertainty on her face. He sensed her dejection, her confusion. Did Bird expect her to leave? *Should* she leave? Did she *want* to leave?

She donned her T-shirt, stretching its hem past her hips to cover her thighs. Then she crossed to the bedroom door, opened it, and looked out toward a staircase and a dim dining room. There was something moving down there, a clatter of china and silverware that became more distinct as the shower stopped thundering in the bathroom. Servants were setting a table for a late Sunday supper.

Behind her, the bathroom door opened. Bird stepped out, skin clean, beaded from the shower. He looked at her. "You still here?" His hair was dry, his forehead embossed with the pink impression of a shower cap.

"What?" She turned, watching as he crossed the room. "What's that supposed to mean?"

He stepped into a deep closet. A wall switch clicked. Light spilled out, casting a wedge on the hardwood floor. Bird's shadow moved within the light. He was getting dressed.

"You want me to leave? Is that it?"

He emerged again, wearing a hand-tooled vest, stonewashed jeans, leather moccasins. He carried a briefcase. "Put your clothes on," he said.

"Where're we going?"

"Don't be presumptuous."

"What?

"Presumptuous," he said. "Is that another word you don't know?"

"Man! What's with you?"

He turned to look at her. "Sorry." He stepped closer, set his clean hands on her dirty shoulders, held her at arms length. "It's late. I lost track of time. I have to be somewhere."

"I don't get it."

"What?"

"I thought we had something going."

"We did. We had it going." He touched her chin, lifting it, looking into her eyes. "Now it's gone." He grinned, a weak parody of the smiles he had given her before. "Come on, now. A girl like you, you've had one-nighters before."

"Not like this."

"No?"

"Jesus Christ!" She pulled away, crossing her arms. "I'm not some throwaway whore!"

"No?" He considered the statement, eyes darkening. An idea seemed to occur to him, something too good to pass up. "Let's see," he said. "Let's see about that." He picked up his briefcase, set it on the bureau. "Let's try something." He thumbed the latches and raised the lid.

Tejay's eyes widened. "Jesus!" She stepped closer, staring into the briefcase. "What's that for?"

He reached in and pulled out a brick of shrink-wrapped bills. "Gambling," he said.

"You're going gambling with a briefcase full of cash?"

"This isn't about where *I'm* going." He ran a nail along the brick, breaking the plastic. "It's about you." He peeled back six bills, pulling them from the stack. "It's about where *you're* going." He held out the cash.

Her cheeks reddened. "You're unbelievable."

"You want it or not?"

She stared at the briefcase.

He seemed amused.

"How much?" she asked. "How much money is that?"

"In my hand?"

"In the briefcase."

"Why? You want more? You getting greedy?" He picked up the open stack again, pulling out three more bills, adding them to the six already offered. "Take it or leave it."

"You paying me? Paying me for sex?"

"Of course not." He smiled. "You *gave* me the sex. I'm paying you to *leave*." He closed the lid. "And it's my final offer."

She took the money.

"Now get dressed."

"You going to feed me at least?" She folded the bills. "Smells like someone's cooking dinner."

"For me, not you. Get dressed." He latched the briefcase and spun the dials, scrambling the combinations.

"I'm curious," she said. "Was it something I did? Did I piss you off or—"

"You're pissing me off now."

She grabbed her overalls, tugged them on, then grabbed her shoes and briefs and stormed from the room. Axle followed her, his omniscient vision watching as she descended the stairs, cut through a central hall, and entered a dining room where a large mahogany table had been set for one.

She stuffed her briefs into the back pocket of her overalls as she hurried past the table and into a large kitchen. A pair of elderly servants working at a cutting board ignored her as she headed for the back door. Evidently the help was used to strange women leaving quickly before dinner.

So you fucked him? Sombitch! You weren't his fucking secretary. You just fucked him!

Axle found himself positioned behind the mansion, looking out from the passenger seat of a battered Ford Escort. A hairline crack ran along the top of the windshield. Pocks of rust covered the hood. He knew the car. It was the same one he had seen in the frat-house garage, or *would* see, since the events he was observing had occurred weeks before he picked up Spinelli and his two-person crew in Morgantown.

The Ford Escort was Tejay's.

Twenty feet away, beyond the Escort's passenger-side window, a woman sat atop a short flight of concrete stairs. She smoked a cigarette, leaning back against a door.

Suddenly, the door opened.

"Hey!" The woman shifted, looking back as Tejay stepped out of the kitchen and onto the stairs.

"Sorry." Tejay pulled the door closed. "Didn't know anyone was out here." She descended the stairs and dropped her shoes.

"Did he throw you out?" the woman asked. She was young, but her voice was deep, aged with smoke.

Tejay pushed her feet into her dirt-caked shoes. "Yeah." She didn't look at the woman. "I take it this happens often."

The woman shrugged. "Couldn't say. I'm just visiting, living in the servant house." She nodded toward a wood-frame bungalow, the roof of which barely cleared a row of nearby hedges. "Those are my grandparents in the kitchen. They don't discuss his personal affairs, so I can't say how often he does anything. But it happens." She took a crumpled pack of Virginia Slims from the pocket of her windbreaker. "Smoke?"

Tejay frowned. "I'm trying to quit."

"Right." The woman extended her arm. "But one bad choice deserves another." She shook the pack until a filtered end popped free. "Go on. Can't be any worse for you than that hothouse ginseng he grows."

"You know about that?"

"I know."

Tejay climbed the stairs. "Thanks." She took a cigarette.

The woman flicked a butane lighter and leaned forward, lighting Tejay's cigarette. "Too bad for you it's Sunday," the woman said. "He seems to go out Sundays. Supper at nine, then he's gone till morning."

Tejay considered that. "Guess it takes a while to gamble a briefcase full of cash."

The woman laughed. "So that's what's in the briefcase?"

"Yeah. He showed me. Shrink wrapped bills. How much you suppose that is, a briefcase full of money?"

The woman shrugged. "A lot."

"You say he goes every week?"

The woman shrugged again. "Went last week. Before that, I wouldn't know. I was here last summer, but that was in the middle of the week, so I can't say what he was doing on Sundays back then."

"You know where he goes to gamble?"

"No idea."

Tejay leaned back against an iron rail, thinking as she smoked. *Sombitch! That's how you learned about the money!*

The scene changed again.

Tejay sat behind the Escort's wheel, her face aglow with dashboard light as she drove across the bridge at the edge of the Frieburg estate. She didn't turn onto Windslow Road. Instead, she drove straight as she left the bridge: across the center line and over the opposing shoulder. Roadside gravel crunched beneath her wheels as she brought the car around, facing the bridge. Then she pulled back into a cover of trees and killed her lights.

Her face vanished as the dashboard went dark. She shifted in her seat, turning as if to address someone between her and Axle.

"I wanted to see where he was going. So I sat in the car and waited for him to cross the bridge onto Windslow Road."

Axle realized he was no longer watching from the Escort's passenger seat. He was back inside the shack, sitting in the wooden chair, staring across the room as Tejay finished her story.

Reddy and Spinelli were back in the picture. And Reddy was fuming.

"Sombitch!" Reddy said, his face nearly as bright as his hair. "And I believed your bullshit! I believed you were his goddamn *secretary*!"

45

Axle felt exhilarated. He had not left the chair, and yet he had traveled, riding the wave of Tejay's words, living her story as she spoke it. The experience recalled Yeyestani's predictions: he was changing, learning, transcending. His spirit had flown, out of his body, into the past.

Now, across the room, Tejay assured Reddy that this time she *was* telling the truth. She spoke forcefully, compelling Reddy to direct his rage at a more vulnerable target: the duct-taped man with the broken shoulder.

"Unbelievable!" Reddy said. "This sombitch took advantage of you." He pushed the pistol against Bird's temple. "It's fucked up. And you!" He glared at Tejay. "You told me you were his temp!"

"But only because I knew you'd get angry if you heard how I'd been used. You always watched out for me—"

"Damn straight."

"I knew if I told you . . . if you knew what had happened—"

"I might have killed the sombitch."

"I know."

"I still might."

"Not yet," Bird said. "This is getting good. I want to hear the rest." He sounded stronger than before, no longer struggling to breathe.

He's like me, Axle thought. *He was dying, but he's coming back.*

"Finish the story," Bird said to Tejay. "You left my estate and parked by the bridge. Then what?"

"I followed you to the sex club. The place was closed, but you went in. You'd said the money was for gambling, so I figured there was a private game, high stakes, cash only. I've seen that stuff on TV. I figured I knew what was going on."

"So you decided to rob me."

"Yeah, but not right away. At first I only wanted to mess with you. I was pissed. I wanted to hit back. At first it was just daydreams, things I *wished*

I could do. But then I started believing I *could* do it . . . but not alone. The things I was thinking were too much for one person. That's when I went to see Reddy."

Bird looked at Reddy. "That would be you. They call you *Reddy* because of your hair, I suppose. *Reddy* for *red* hair."

"Yeah, and because I'm always *ready*, ready for anything."

"But of course that would be spelled differently, wouldn't it? I mean, it's either *Reddy* or *Ready*. It can't be both."

"The hell?" Reddy frowned. "The hell you talking?"

Tejay's eyes narrowed. "He's making fun of you, Reddy."

"No," Bird said. "Not at all. I'm just trying to understand. What happened when Tejay went to see you?"

"The fuck." Reddy shrugged. "I was drinking beer with Spinelli."

"Which would be you," Bird said, turning to face Spinelli. "And I suppose you're the idea man, the man with the plan."

"Something like that."

"And you did a stake out, followed me as I made the same run to the sex club last Sunday. Am I right?"

"Sombitch! You knew about that?"

"No. I didn't know then, but it stands to reason now. But here's the thing I still don't get." He stared at Spinelli. "If you're the *idea* man, and Reddy is the *gun* man, and Tejay is—" He paused. "Let's just call her the *femme fatale*."

"The *what*?" Tejay said. "What's that?"

"Doesn't matter," Bird said. "The question is . . . the thing I still don't get is *him*." He looked at Axle. "How's he fit in?"

"Driver," Spinelli said. "We needed a fast car."

"The Mustang?"

"That's right."

"I see," Bird said. "I guess the rest of you drive Escorts." He smiled. There was blood on his teeth, residue from the clots he had been coughing up and swallowing. But he wasn't coughing now. His breathing was regular, his voice strong. "I think I understand. Three of you robbed me while the idea man was somewhere else, north on Windslow, watching the road. But then after the robbery, the idea man needed to be picked up again. That's how Peterson and I were able to catch you."

"Not exactly," Reddy said. "We would have been long gone, but there was a problem."

"Which we don't need to go into right now," Spinelli said.

"Why not?" Bird asked.

"Because it's not important."

"Don't be so sure," Bird said. "Maybe it's all important. The more you guys tell me, the more I'm convinced that all of this had to happen just the way it did. It's like the guardian told me—"

"Who?" Spinelli asked.

"The earthborn guardian. It came out of the forest after you guys shot me. I was on the ground, dying—maybe dead—and the guardian came and said it wasn't my time. It said Kwetis hadn't arranged my birth just to have me die in the clearing."

Spinelli frowned. "Kwetis?"

"A spirit," Bird said. "A spirit from—"

"You saw a spirit come out of the forest?"

"No. *Kwetis* is a spirit. The *guardian* is physical, spawn of the earth, protector of the land. It was the guardian that came to me."

"Sounds like bullshit," Reddy said.

"Before tonight," Bird said, "I might have agreed. I've been studying Native myths and legends, getting in touch with my rumored roots, more for amusement than anything else. But that's changed now. Meeting the guardian put a whole new spin on things."

"You're saying you're a sombitchin Indian?"

"Okwe," Bird said. "Part Okwe. The guardian made that much clear. And something else, though the guardian didn't say so outright, it gave the sense that I'm part of an elaborate plan."

"What are you saying?" Spinelli asked.

"I'm saying that it would appear we've been brought here for a purpose."

"Sombitch! You're here because you were supposed to be carrying cash."

"Oh?" Bird raised his eyebrows. "Really?"

"Really!" Tejay said. "I saw it, remember? You showed it to me. Money in a briefcase. You said it was for gambling."

"Yes, *for* gambling, but not to gamble *with*."

"What's the difference?" Reddy said.

"Big difference." Bird looked around at them, and once again Axle was struck by how much stronger the man had become since entering the shack. Color had returned to his face. His chest no longer gurgled when he spoke. Though still taped to the chair, he was clearly in charge. "Do you guys read the papers?" he asked. "Any of you heard of Mountain Downs?"

Reddy and Tejay exchanged dim-witted glances.

"I saw some signs about it," Spinelli said. "Some readerboards in Windslow."

"Yeah," Tejay said. "I guess I've seen them, too."

"But you don't know what they're about? None of you are from around here?"

"Axle's the only Windslow boy."

"What's Mountain Downs?" Reddy asked.

"A casino. That is, it will be if we get it approved."

"*Indian* casino?"

"No. Tribal casinos have to be on tribal land. Windslow Mine never earned such distinction, not officially. And even if Vorarov and I could get the site approved, the profits from a tribal-affiliated Mountain Downs would have to be shared with the tribes. Our plan is better. See, the Commonwealth is getting into the gambling business. Licenses are being awarded. We plan to get one of them, but winning favors takes favors. The cash that Tejay saw in the briefcase was bread to be cast upon the water in hopes of a greater return."

Reddy glanced at Spinelli. "The hell's this sombitch talking about now?"

"Sounds like bribes."

"Ah-ha!" Bird said. "You really are the idea man."

"But where's that money?" Reddy said, turning toward the table, pointing with Bird's pistol. "What's all that shit in the briefcase?"

"That's material to be presented to the Gaming Commission," Bird said. "It's an overview of everything. Our casino isn't just going to be slots and cards. There'll be racing, too—and shops, condominiums, restaurants, amusements—"

"A full-blown mountain resort?"

"You got it. Everything but skiing. Seven Springs can have that. We'll take the rest."

"But it all hinges on gambling. Without that, you've got nothing."

"Right. And tonight Vorarov was going to review everything before our attorney took the package to Harrisburg. You've dealt with our attorney. Ambitious fellow. Drives a Viper, or should I say *drove*?"

"Enough!" Reddy said. "Enough talking." He looked at the others. "I'm getting a headache."

Bird nodded. "Probably gas fumes."

"Just shut up! I'm getting sick of you, man." Reddy turned to Spinelli. "You still got his wallet?"

"Yeah."

"All right. So it's not a complete loss."

"Not bad," Bird said. "Eighty-six bucks. Not bad for a night's work."

"I said shut the fuck up!"

"Beats putting your girlfriend to work as a digger."

Reddy pistol whipped Bird across the temple, the impact echoing dull and hard, like a hammer on stone.

Spinelli winced. "Jesus, Reddy."

Bird rocked to the side, chair legs rasping against the floor as he recoiled from the impact. But the thing that Axle noticed—a detail that was perhaps lost to the others in the room—was the way Bird's shoulder clenched with the force of the blow. His flesh had healed. The wounded arm was back in its socket.

Bird straightened up but said nothing. He stared at Axle, speaking with his eyes as a trickle of blood ran from his temple. *I'm all right*, his eyes said. *I'm stronger than they are. We're stronger. Both of us are stronger than the lot of them.*

Reddy turned to Spinelli. Eyes flashing, making it clear he'd had enough talking. "Go patch the tank," he said. "Do it now. And you—" He turned to Tejay. "Drain the generator. Get us some gas. When the tank is patched, fill it."

Tejay didn't need to be told twice. She turned and hurried through the door.

Spinelli remained inside, staring at Axle.

"Go on," Reddy said. "I'll finish up in here."

"Axle comes with us," Spinelli said.

"No. He'll just slow us down. And this one—" He looked at Bird. "This one's caused enough trouble already."

Spinelli hesitated, eyes narrow, mouth taut. He seemed on the verge of reasserting that they were all in this together, that Axle had not abandoned him back on Windslow Road and that there was no way they could abandon Axle now.

"You hear me?" Reddy said. "Patch that tank!"

The pecking order had changed. Spinelli, the idea man who earlier had proclaimed that the night would proceed with no one getting hurt, clearly did not have the stomach for what needed to be done inside the shack.

"This has turned into a goddamn mess," Spinelli said.

"Yeah!" Reddy pushed the pistol against Bird's temple. "And I'm the clean-up man."

Spinelli seemed about to say something else, but then he turned and walked away.

Three quick steps and he was out the door.

The forest changed as Sam followed the trail. Trees thickened to her left, becoming a mass of vines, trunks, and tangled leaves. To her right, a shale wall curved inward, leading to a fallen tree that cut diagonally across the path. Something stood beneath the branches. She slowed. The shape dissipated, resolving into a patch of rotting bark, hanging moss, shriveled leaves. Strange, though, for a second it had almost looked like a kid hiding in the shadows.

She passed beneath the trunk and emerged to see the trail straightening again, leading toward a wide, open space. *The highwall. I'm almost there.*

She continued on, jogging until she emerged from the forest and onto a rocky plateau that ended at a machine-gouged valley. The path continued here—across the bare rock and then down along the valley wall, descending at a 17-percent grade before curving out of sight around the base of a protruding column of rock. She'd probably be able to see the Mustang, either deserted or smashed to pieces, once she rounded that curve.

Moving cautiously, mindful of the sudden drop, she started down.

Something flashed in her night-vision monocle as she neared the protruding column. It looked like a puddle among the rocks: too bright to be water, too evenly shaped to be a natural formation. She crouched for a closer look and realized she was looking at a side-view mirror made of die-cast zinc and plaited chrome—a relic from a time when cars were made of metal, not fiberglass and plastic. Strangely, it seemed to be partially coated with black latex. She picked it up. The glass was cracked, the frame gouged and pitted as if it had broken off after scraping against the wall. Otherwise it was in fine condition, the kind of accessory one might find on a car that had been lovingly restored, well maintained. It was not, however, the sort of thing a car enthusiast would hide under a topcoat of black rubber—unless, of course, he were trying to temporarily alter the look of the car.

She dropped the mirror and walked on, slowing her pace again as she reached the bend in the trail. Here she found something shimmering on the column of vertical rock. It looked like blood. She sniffed it. It was fresh.

The partner's blood. He paused here, resting against the rock before continuing on.

And there was something else, a far-off throb like the chug of a gas generator. It came from beyond the bend in the path. She turned to investigate but stopped when something buzzed against her hip. The sensation lingered a moment, stopping as abruptly as it began.

What now?

She drew back into the shadows.

The tingle came again.

What is it now?

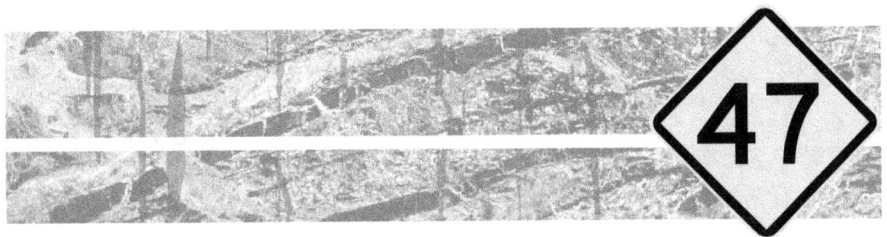

Lying on his back on the weedy table of rock and clay, applying duct tape to Axle's gas tank, Spinelli just wanted to be miles away from this screwed-up business. He didn't care about the money any more. He didn't care about Axle. And he sure as shit didn't care about Reddy and Tejay, both of whom he blamed for the way everything had gone south.

He tugged the tape, pulled off a six-inch strip, and ripped it with his teeth. Then he pushed his heels against the ground, sliding deeper beneath the car until he came to another bullet hole.

The holes in the bottom of the tank were larger than the ones in the trunk and bumper. These were the exit holes, and the bullets had evidently changed shape before leaving the tank. He tensed, unnerved by the possibility of what might have happened if a spark had ignited the leaking tank while the car's interior had been full of fumes. Spinelli knew all about gasoline, how unstable it could be. It was a lesson he'd learned the hard way, and he had no desire to learn it a second time.

The exit holes looked like miniatures of the fist-sized opening that Reddy's shotgun had blown in the Mustang's roof. The metal protruded in triangular jags, curved back like flower petals. They made it difficult to get a tight seal with the tape. Initially, he had tried flattening the jags with the pad of his thumb, but it was like handling barbed wire. Now he settled for an easier approach, applying layers of tape and hoping they would hold.

Don't have to get us far. Just out of the mine. Into Windslow.

It had been years since he had hotwired a car. He wasn't even sure he could still do it, but he'd give it a try once they reached town. There was no way he was going to stay in the leaking Mustang any longer than he had to.

He had burned once.

He was damned if he was going to burn again.

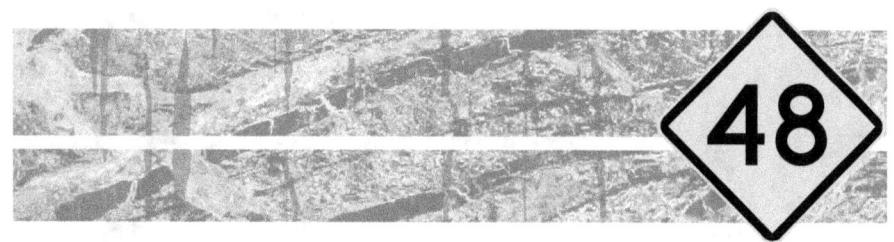

48

Bird held his poise as Reddy pressed the gun to his head. "Listen, Reddy. There's something I better tell you."

"Something *you* better tell *me*?"

"That's right."

"About what?"

"About how you and your friends are going to die on this ledge."

Reddy leaned closer. "Fuck you."

"Is that your answer to everything? Your all-purpose quip?"

"My all-purpose *what*?"

"Listen, Reddy. I'm giving it to you straight. You guys need to clear out of here right now. Forget the Mustang. Go on foot." He looked at the sealed door in the back of the room. "You might try going out that way. Pull off the boards, slip out the back."

"Not hardly!" Reddy said. "That door's sealed for a reason. This shack's on the brink, man. Nothing out that door but a big-ass drop. Front door's the only way to go."

Something thumped outside the shack, a jerry can clanking above the chug of the generator.

Bird looked toward the sound.

"That's just Tejay," Reddy said. "Getting gas."

"Right," Bird said. "And she's an easy target out there. The other guy, too . . . Spinelli . . . they're both easy targets."

"The hell you talking?"

Bird looked through the open door. "The three of you need to get off this ledge before the sniper starts picking you off."

"Sniper?"

"That's right."

"You're saying Vorarov's coming to take us out?"

"No. Not Vorarov. He doesn't do that kind of work himself. He's got someone else to do it. A soldier."

"Soldier?"

"That's his word for it. Soldier. Like a hired gun. He's got this one shooter on retainer, a mountain girl, militia trained. I've never met her, but I've heard. She lives alone . . . just her and her guns."

"A girl?"

"Woman, actually."

"A sniper woman?"

Bird nodded, looking grave. "One shot, one kill."

"A sniper woman's coming to get us?"

"Maybe. Maybe coming. Probably already here. My guess is that by now she's on the highwall, getting ready to take you down . . . one at a time."

Reddy turned toward the open door. "You expect me to believe that?"

"What's not to believe? When you shot us, Peterson was on the phone, giving Vorarov our location so he could send help. And I'm willing to bet that's exactly what he's done. He's like that, a real eye-for-an-eye man."

"You're bluffing."

"All right. You can believe that. Doesn't matter to me. Either way, if you run or stay, it's all the same. In a few minutes, I'll be alone with him." He nodded toward Axle. "That's what the earthborn guardian told me to do. Find him. Stay with him."

"Him?"

"That's right."

"He's dead."

"No. The Great Heart needs him. He's coming back, just like me."

Axle listened, hanging on the words, sensing their inevitable truth. *The Great Heart needs him.* He shivered, not on the outside where Reddy might notice, but inside. In the deep core of his soul, things were happening. He felt alive . . . more alive than he had ever felt before.

"Look at him, Reddy," Bird said. "Look at his color. He's coming back."

Reddy turned, frowning at Axle.

"The guardian touched us both, Reddy. And now we're both coming back. It's just taking him longer, is all. Trauma to the brain, that's got to take more time to heal than a blasted lung and broken shoulder."

Outside, Spinelli started shouting. "Hey, Tejay!" He sounded angry.

"Sounds like they're having trouble out there. Maybe you should go help them. That way the sniper can shoot the three of you together, get it over with."

Reddy looked toward the door.

"Tejay!" Spinelli's voice was louder now, angrier. "What are you doing?"

"Sounds like trouble," Bird said.

"Whatever." Reddy shrugged. "Spinelli can handle it." He turned back toward Bird. "Besides, you and me, we're not finished yet."

"Meaning?"

Reddy raised the pistol.

49

Sam felt the tingle a third time.

She drew back into the shadows behind the column of rock and un-clipped her buzzing phone. She checked the ID. It was Kirill. She took the call. "Damnit, Kirill. This better be important."

No response. The connection had failed.

She called him back.

He answered on the second ring.

"What is it, Kirill?"

"Sorry, I wasn't thinking. I shouldn't have called." He sounded shaken.

"Talk to me," she said. "What's going on?"

"We've got trouble."

"*We?*"

"Your Jeep . . . it's in a ditch."

"Christ, Kirill." She forced the whisper between her teeth, hoping he could hear the suppressed rage. "You drove my Jeep into a ditch?" She did not need this now. She lowered the phone and cupped it in her hands, composing herself before raising it again. "Listen . . . listen, Kirill. The Jeep's got four-wheel drive. You're in a ditch? You drive the hell out of it!"

"Can't. It's not that kind of ditch."

"What kind of ditch is it?"

"More like . . . a hillside . . . a forty-percent slope."

"A forty-*percent* slope is a near vertical wall, Kirill. You mean *degree*? A forty-*degree* slope?"

"Yeah. Maybe. All I know is it's steep. I would have flipped over if I hadn't hit a tree."

"Christ!"

"I don't think I did much damage. The airbags didn't deploy."

"My Jeep doesn't have airbags, Kirill. And it can drive a forty-degree hill. You might need the winch, but—" She paused. Did she really want him working the winch on his own?

"Winch?" he asked. "Where's the winch?"

She hesitated, becoming aware of a voice shouting from below. She tried making it out, but she couldn't, not with Kirill buzzing in her ear.

"Where's the winch, Sam? Can I operate it from inside?"

"Hold on," she said. "I'm putting the phone down. Hold on."

She set the phone on a cleft of rock and eased forward until her night-vision eye cleared the column. Now, for the first time, she saw what lay below: a ledge, a shack, a Mustang. . . .

A woman poured gasoline into the car, spilling fuel along the bumper.

"Tejay! What are you doing?" A man shouted from beneath the car, his voice audible above the chugging generator. "Goddamnit, girl!" He slid out from beneath the bumper. "You're spilling it!"

Sam heard him clearly in spite of the distance, as if the position of the ledge and the curve of the wall were conveying the sound directly to her ears.

"That gas," the man said. "*You're spilling it!*"

The woman kept pouring. "The spout's loose," she said.

Sam slid the rifle from its harness, raised her monocular, and sighted through the gun's night-vision scope.

"So tighten it," the man said.

"Tried," the woman said. "Don't get no tighter. It's like stripped or something." She went on pouring.

The man backed away from the car.

Sam read his expression in the crosshairs: tense, exhausted, and clearly troubled by the spilling gasoline. "Damnit, Tejay!" He winced as the tank overflowed. "That's enough!"

Tejay stopped pouring and set the can on the ground. It gave a hollow thump, coming to rest between her feet.

Even from a distance of five hundred feet, Sam could smell the fumes.

She slipped back along the wall and grabbed the phone. "I've found it, Kirill. The Mustang."

"Abandoned?"

"No. There's two people with it."

"Two?"

"Man and a woman?"

"No," Kirill said. "Bird said nothing about a woman. It's men. *Three* men."

"Bird told you they were wearing masks. He might have assumed—"

"*Three,*" Kirill said. "He said there were *three* of them."

Sam didn't have time for this. "I've got to go."

Kirill started to say something more.

She cut him off, folded the phone, and clipped it back onto her belt. Then she raised her rifle and moved back along the column of rock.

A roll of duct tape lay on the ground behind the car.

Resourceful, Sam thought. She had heard of using duct tape to repair fuel leaks. It generally didn't work for long. Gasoline dissolved the adhesive. If the patches weren't tight, or if the leaks were much larger than pinholes or hairline cracks, the tape wouldn't hold.

"Are those patches holding?" the woman asked.

The man wiped his hands on the weeds at his feet. "Think so."

"They going to keep holding?"

"Maybe." The man stood. "For a while, at least. Let's get out of here."

"Hey, Reddy!" She turned toward the open door. "Reddy! Let's go!"

All right, Sam thought. *The third one is in the shack.* That left only Kirill's wounded partner unaccounted for.

"C'mon, Reddy. We're leaving!"

Sam had found her targets. Now only one problem remained: how to honor Kirill's request.

Make it messy.

She looked at the open can near the woman's feet.

An idea formed.

Kirill folded his phone and looked up along the slope. Nothing moved. The way looked clear, but just to be sure he lowered the window and snapped on the spotlight. Shadows shifted as he panned the beam. No animal in sight. That was hopeful, but it didn't change where he was: rammed against a tree, stuck in a world of shit.

"*Yobany stos*," he muttered, swearing in Russian. Profanity always packed more punch in the language of his youth. "*Sooka!*"

But cursing wouldn't get him off the slope.

Sam had mentioned a winch. How hard could it be to work such a thing?

He snapped on the Jeep's interior lights and studied the dash. Winch controls were clearly marked: a button to arm the motor, a toggle for reeling the line. It looked easy enough, but first he needed to leave the cab and anchor the cable to something at the top of the rise.

He sat back, or tried to. His center of gravity now ran diagonally, from left shoulder to right hip. When he tried sitting straight relative to the seat, his weight pulled him toward the passenger side and the massive pine that grew beyond the side window. Could he get out at this angle? He popped the latch and pushed the door. Its light weight surprised him. He opened it easily, pushing it wide and holding it in place as he swung around to set his feet on the running board. The Jeep shifted. Side panels groaned against the tree. Needles fell, spilling over his lap. When the Jeep moved, so did the tree. He had to be careful. If the pine gave way, he'd never make it back to the trail.

As a young soldier, he had worn his upper-body strength like a badge of authority. Strong men had cringed at the sight of the young Kirill. But now he was older, a general. He hired people to do his muscle work, and years of giving orders had turned his strength to fat. Lifting the lightweight door might have been easy, but heaving his ass out of the tilting seat was going to take some doing.

Keeping one hand on the door, he gripped the edge of the seat and strained forward until his feet touched the tilting ground. Then he pulled himself upright, released the door, and leaned back against the side panel. The tree swayed as the door fell shut. More needles fell, dusting his head, slipping down his neck as he moved hand-over-hand toward the front of the Jeep. The ground crackled as he walked, crunching beneath his shoes until he paused beside the dented grill. Surprisingly, there was no blood on the car, no fur between the slats.

"*Ahueyet.*"

He continued on, crouching to inspect the winch. He felt along its housing, found the hook, pulled. Something popped, but the sound came from his shoulder, not the spool.

"*Sooka!*"

The hook hadn't budged. The winch was locked. Cramps flared near the base of his neck. He tried working them free, rolling his head, flexing his arms. No pain yet. That would come tomorrow when he awoke to find himself unable to get out of bed. But for now he was still functioning, feeling along the housing until his finger brushed a lever, a curved handle. A release? He pulled it.

Click!

"Got you, you bitch!"

The thing wasn't complicated. Like all machines, there was logic to it.

The reel spun freely now, humming as he tugged. Then, gripping the hook, he stumbled up the slope, the line paying out behind him. It was six feet to the trail. It felt like sixty. He tired quickly, dropping to one knee as he reached the ferns that lined the ruts. He got back up and pushed on, sweating, his shirt bunching in his armpits, clinging along his back and waist.

He looked around.

The diffracted glow of the Jeep's high beams streaked the trail with angled light. No sign of the animal. For now, the way was clear.

Struggling forward, straining against the weight of the hook in his hands and the heavy cramps in his back, he dragged the cable toward the trunk of a large white cedar. The roots looked strong and firm, the ground hard with packed clay. He circled the tree, making a noose by clipping the hook back over the line.

He stepped back, inspecting his work.

It seemed simple enough.

What could possibly go wrong?

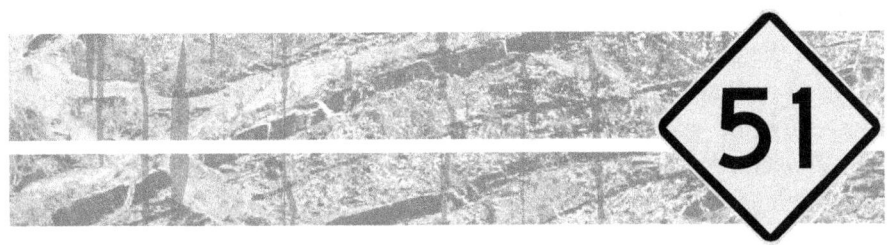

51

The stink of spilled fuel took Sam back. *Colorado*, she thought. *Incendiary Ray.*

She had met Ray at a gun show outside Beckley. That had been five years ago. She had been a different person then: restless, searching.

Ray handed her his book, *The Survivalist's Mission: Independence in a Dependant World*. She opened it. The type looked gray, as if it had been copied rather than printed.

She noted the publisher:

IRA
Incendiary Ray & Associates
Camp Survival, Colorado

The colophon, a heat ray incinerating the White House, looked as if it had been taken from a freeze frame of the film *Independence Day*.

"It'll change your life," Ray said.

She looked up.

A scar bisected his face, extending from temple to chin, passing beneath a leather eye patch. "Thirty bucks," he said.

A line of people stood behind her. She closed the book and opened her wallet. Cards fell from the billfold as she took out her money. She didn't carry family photos. No kids. No friends. Just a Visa, driver's license, and membership card for the National Rifle Association.

He noticed the latter. "You're the real deal, aren't you, sister?"

She handed him two twenties. "I try to be." She picked up the fallen cards.

"Had any training?"

"I'm in a club."

"I don't mean just guns, sister. It's about more than targets." He handed her a photocopied brochure with her change. "The website's on there. Log on. Look around. Sign up if you're interested. It'll change your life."

She took the bait.

Three months later she was 1,500 miles west, farther away than she had ever been before, but feeling strangely at home in the spartan accommodations of the place that Ray called Camp Survival.

The other visitors were a rag-tag group of lost boys between the ages of twenty and sixty. No other women, except for the ones who cleaned and cooked. As always, Sam was the outsider, and the position became even more obvious when Ray assembled the group for an ice-breaker at the camp's outdoor shooting range.

He had aligned three targets: a sealed gas tank and two jerry cans (one closed, one open). All were widely spaced and positioned in front of a vertical wall of rock. Overhead, an indigo sky shimmered with the first stars of evening.

To light the targets, Ray had rigged a pair of pole mounted flood-lamps, each trailing an orange cord that ran back to the camp's main building. Ray looked up at them, giving each a final inspection before turning to face the group. He wore desert fatigues, boonie hat, combat boots. In lieu of an eye patch, he wore a pair of aviator glasses: clear lens on one side, mirrored plastic on the other. A gun rack stood beside him. It held three rifles.

Everyone had been given earplugs, the kind that muffled gunshots, not voices.

"Let's talk about fire," Ray said. "Long-distance ignition." He scanned the group, sizing them up, making sure he had their attention. "We'll start with a quiz." He looked at a blond boy in the front row. He checked the nametag. "Anderson!"

Anderson straightened up, looking sharp.

Ray took one of the rifles, holding it chest high for Anderson's inspection. "Can you identify this weapon?"

Anderson hesitated. "It's a high-powered rifle, sir."

"Cut the *sir*. This isn't the US Army." He held the rifle closer. "What *kind* of high-powered rifle?"

"What *kind*?"

"I'm asking you."

Anderson hesitated again. "Sniper rifle."

"Model?" Ray scanned the crowd. "Anybody?" His gaze flashed on Sam. "Calder?"

She answered immediately. "M40A1."

He nodded.

She couldn't tell if he was impressed. His expression didn't change. His half-mirrored gaze returned only her own blank expression: steady eyes, level mouth, square jaw.

"Range?" he asked.

Sam responded again. "One thousand yards."

A murmur went through the crowd. Feet shifted. The boys were all looking at her now.

"Muzzle velocity?"

"Seven-seven-seven meters-per-second."

"Chamber pressure?"

"Fifty thousand psi."

Ray grinned. "You know your weapons, sister."

She nodded. "I try to."

Ray looked around, glaring at the men. He offered no comment. None was needed. "Listen up," he said. "Pay attention." He raised the rifle higher. "Fifty thousand pounds per square inch. Under that kind of pressure, a bullet is going to get hot, excess of 500-degrees. Gasoline ignites at 495. Now pay attention." He turned, pointing downrange, toward the fuel tank. "I ripped that tank from a Chevy Impala, topped it off, secured the cap. If I shoot it, what happens?" He glanced back, his gaze settling on a young man in the second row. "Walters. What happens if I put a bullet into sixteen gallons of eighty-seven octane?"

Walters barked back. "The gas is going to explode."

It seemed like the obvious answer.

Ray looked around. "Everyone agree?" He looked at Sam. "Calder?"

"I don't know."

Ray held her gaze a moment longer, then turned away. "Good answer." He looked at the others. "If you don't know, admit it. Never assume. Assumptions get you killed. At the very least, they make you look stupid." His mirrored lens flashed at Walters. "Now watch." He turned, shouldered the rifle, fired.

The muzzle cracked, a sharp report that was only partially dampened by Sam's earplugs. A second sound followed, deeper than the first, a roar of displaced air that served as a reminder that the bullet, at 777 meters per second, was traveling twice the speed of sound.

VhhhOOOM!

Then came a third sound, a muffled blend of muzzle crack and sonic boom, all of it rebounding from the wall behind the targets.

Thwack-OOOM!

But that was it. Nothing else. No explosion.

The tank remained as before, except that now it seemed to be pissing, loosing a stream of unignited fuel onto the rocky ground. Sam put it together. Of course, it was obvious. She had learned about this before, in another context: high school chemistry.

Ray turned. "You assumed wrong, Walters."

Walters shifted, said nothing.

Ray looked at Sam. "Calder. It looks like you know something. Share it."

"Gasoline," she said. "Gasoline doesn't burn."

Feet shuffled. Someone snorted.

She continued. "Vapors burn, not liquid. The tank's full. It's capped. No vapors inside. No vapors, no ignition."

Ray nodded. Leaking gasoline spattered behind him, changing pitch as it spread across the ground. "So maybe I should fire at the puddle. Put a bullet through the fumes. Would that work?"

"I don't think so," Sam said.

"Why?"

She hesitated, dredging her memory, coming up empty. "I'm not sure."

"Ratio," he said, looking at the others. "The vapor-to-air ratio has got to be between two and seven percent. Considering that," he looked at the others, "what's my best target for an explosion? The tank? The puddle? The closed can? The open can?"

Anderson answered. "Open can."

Ray turned toward him. "You sure? What if I tell you it's nearly empty, no more than an inch of fuel in the bottom? Want to change your answer?"

Anderson hesitated, no doubt sensing a trick.

"We're waiting, Anderson."

"It'll explode," Anderson said.

"Why?"

"Because . . . it's full of vapors. The fuel's mixing with air."

"It's mixing with air over the puddle, too. Why not go with that? If I ignite the fumes over the puddle, maybe the fire will follow the stream back up to the tank."

"Ignite the stream?" someone asked. "You said liquid gas doesn't burn."

"It doesn't, but the stream is evaporating as it flows, giving off fumes, mixing with air. That's how flamethrowers work, by shooting a stream of gasoline. Fact is, anytime you have gasoline outside a sealed container, you've got a chance of ignition." He turned back to the leaking tank. "So what do we say? If I shoot the puddle, will I get ignition?"

"No," Anderson said. "I don't think so. It's like you said, the ratio—"

"Let's test that theory." Ray took a butane lighter from his pocket. He spun the wheel, igniting the tip. "Go on." He offered the flaming lighter to Anderson. "Go down there, hold this to the puddle—"

"An open flame's different." This came from an older man standing beside Anderson.

Ray turned, checked the nametag, and said, "Different how, McGinley?"

"The bullet's traveling fast, going at—" McGinley glanced at Sam. "What'd she say, like twice the speed of sound. It might, I don't know, create a vacuum, alter the ratio."

Ray nodded. "All right, good. We're thinking now. Thinking things through." He took his thumb from the lighter, killing the flame as he turned toward Anderson. "So you're off the hook." He pocketed the lighter. "But tell me this. Why do you think it'll be the *open* can? What makes you so sure it'll ignite? What if the vapors are too rich, too concentrated? What makes you think any of those targets are going to catch fire?" He stepped back, looking everyone over. "Anybody?"

A hand went up in the back.

"Who's that?" Ray said.

A thin voice answered. "Reynolds." He was slim, clean cut, fair-skinned. Sam thought he looked like a minister. "The way I see it, one of those things has got to explode. You wouldn't bring us out here without a money shot. I say it's the open can."

Money shot? No, he probably wasn't a minister.

Ray nodded. "All right. So we're still thinking. And here's what we know. You have an open container, one where air and gasoline fumes are mixing. Then you add ignition—flame, spark, heat, whatever. You add that, you might just get some serious conflagration." He grinned. Then he turned, aimed, and fired.

VhhhOOOM!

The can shivered.

Thwack-OOOM!

No explosion.

Ray looked back at his stunned audience. "Lesson number one." He grinned, scanning the group. "Bullets alone won't ignite gasoline. Not hyper-velocity, not tracer rounds, not HE rounds. What you see in movies does not work in the real world. You got that? Bullets alone won't do it." His grin broadened.

Here it comes, Sam thought. *He's still got something to show us.* She had no idea what he was about to do, but his expression made it clear that they were about to see something big.

"You want to start a fire?" he said. "Then you have to find a spark." He turned, aimed high, and fired.

A floodlight shattered, raining glass while its chord broke loose and arced down toward what was now a wide spill on the rocky ground. Ray had set it up well, letting the puddle grow large enough to be an easy mark for the falling wire. It landed dead center, igniting the spill, vapors, containers—everything. . . .

VHOOOOOOOOMMMM!

A split second later all the targets were gone, engulfed by a black-and-orange fireball that billowed along the rock wall and thundered at the star-dusted sky.

Now, remembering that long-ago summer, Sam sized up the scene on the ledge below and saw a way to honor Kirill's request.

Make it messy.

She closed her eyes, took a breath, and opened them again. The gun was now a part of her body, the sight an extension of her eye.

The woman named Tejay was facing the shack, calling to someone named Reddy. Spilled gasoline slicked the ground at her feet. Beside her, the man named Spinelli climbed into the Mustang.

Sam relaxed, taking aim.

52

Kirill backed away from the tree-anchored cable, wincing as each step sent fresh pain through his back and shoulder. *Aspirin*, he thought. *Aspirin and vodka*. That's what he needed. It was an old cure, one that alarmed his American associates, all of whom believed that the alcohol warnings on aspirin bottles were based on scientific research and not a ruse by American drug companies who wanted to keep aspirin from becoming a cheap alternative to Tylenol. Americans didn't get it. They tended to ignore the reality of everyday conspiracies. Russians knew better. It was a cultural thing.

Kirill crossed the trail and looked down to where the Jeep sat idling on the slope, rumbling like a sleeping monster. So close, but he would need to be careful. One fall would do him in.

I can do it. Take my time. Take it slow.

He stepped through the trailside weeds, stopping when something popped in the distance. It sounded like a car backfiring. The Mustang? Had the bastards found gas? Yes, that was possible. The mine had a field office. He had never been in it, but he had seen it from a distance. It had a functioning generator. More than likely, it had gasoline.

The sound came again as he stepped back into the trail, and this time he wondered if he might actually be hearing gunfire. Maybe the bastards weren't getting away at all. Maybe Sam was picking them off.

He listened, waited for a third report, and realized as he did that he was no longer alone in the forest.

Something crouched a short distance away, partially hidden behind a clump of yarrow grass that grew on the edge of the clearing. It looked like a kid.

"Hey!" Kirill said. "Somebody there?" A witness was the last thing he needed.

But the kid didn't respond. He simply crouched, motionless, blending with the grassy spears until Kirill suspected there was really no one there after all.

Only shadows. And yet, a moment ago he had seen the kid with alarming clarity. How could he account for that? Had exertion addled his brain?

Enough of this!

Kirill was sick of this place. He needed to put it behind him and return to his boring office in his boring sex club—a place where shadows never appeared to be anything but what they were.

Turning again to face the slope and grabbing the cable that stretched beside him, he made his way back toward the welcoming glow of the Jeep's headlights.

And it was then that he heard another distant pop, higher pitched than the others. It echoed through the hills and then came again . . . and again . . . the unmistakable, semiautomatic pop of an artisan-made Stetchkin.

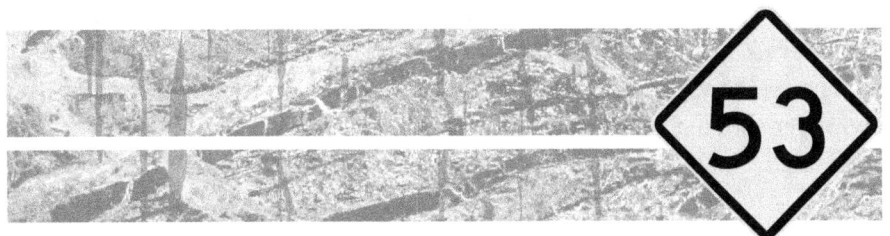

53

Reddy pressed the pistol to Bird's head.

POW!

The sound came from outside, the Mustang backfiring.

Tejay called through the open door. "Hey, Reddy! Come on!"

The Mustang stalled, cranked, and backfired again.

POW!

This time the engine caught, settling down into the smooth hum of a well-tuned idle. Headlights snapped on, spilling into the shack, stabbing Axle's eyes. He flinched and turned away. The movement was reflexive, done without thought. But then, with his back to the light, he realized what he had done. His body was his again. He could move.

He straightened up, flexing his shoulders, extending his arms. His shadow moved with him, rising over the boarded door behind the table.

"Hey, Reddy!" Tejay called again, louder. "We're leaving!"

Axle stared at the sealed door, noticing something odd about the wood beneath his shadow. Was he imagining it, or were the two-by-fours that bolted the door starting to bend inward? He blinked, clearing his vision. But the wood kept bending: creaking and straining as if bowing under a tremendous weight.

"Reddy!" Tejay shouted again, her voice turning shrill. "Finish it, Reddy! We're leaving!"

Axle turned from the door to see Reddy and Bird centered in the high-beam glare. Reddy held the gun to Bird's temple, but Bird didn't seem to notice. "The door," Bird muttered. "Jesus! Look at the door."

The headlights shifted, panning through the room as Spinelli tried turning the car around, maneuvering between shack and generator. Axle heard him calling to Tejay as the Mustang shifted into reverse. "Come on, Tejay! Get in!"

And all the while the sealed door in the back of the room kept bending, straining in its frame as the two-by-fours quaked with the slow snap of splintering pine.

Reddy looked toward the sound. "The hell—"

The door flew from its hinges, thrown inward by a winged shape that hovered beyond the frame. Axle stared at the figure, trying to comprehend. *I know this thing. I've seen it before.*

The creature grabbed the doorframe, folded its wings, and then—like a swimmer shoving off from the side of a pool—threw itself inward, clearing the table to land between Axle and Reddy.

Reddy took the gun from Bird's temple, swinging it around as the figure lunged.

CRACK!

The gunshot rang like a thunderclap, reverberating from the walls.

"Sombitch!" Reddy kept his finger on the trigger, squeezing off another shot, this one going wide as the creature grabbed the barrel. The shot hummed past Axle, splintering the far wall. More shots followed, punching holes in the ceiling until the gun emptied and started clicking.

"Do you want me to hurt you?" the creature said. "Is that what you want?"

Axle recognized the voice from earlier in the night, from the clearing above the highwall. This was the creature that had approached him as Spinelli and the others argued about the Mustang's leaking tank. Axle remembered its promise and command: *Answers come later. Just drive.*

And now Axle felt the answers quickening inside him, coalescing as he watched the earthborn guardian release the gun and grab Reddy's arm.

"Let me go!" Reddy dropped the gun. "Sombitch, let me—"

The guardian pulled Reddy closer, grabbed his throat, and lifted him from the floor.

"Let . . . me . . . go!" Reddy's voice came out in a strangled rasp as the guardian held him high, gas-soaked sneakers kicking against the overhanging bulbs. "You . . . som—"

The guardian slammed Reddy down onto the sawbuck table, pile driving him so hard that the top split in two . . . and suddenly everything went crashing: briefcase, papers, sawbucks, Reddy.

WHAM!

Outside, framed within the open door, Tejay stood with one foot toward the shack, the other toward the Mustang—caught between fight and flight with an open jerry can between her feet. She stared at the guardian, mouth open, eyes wide, apparently on the verge of shouting something to Spinelli when—*SNAP!*—the shack shivered with the sound of splintering wood, as if something had broken loose from the outside wall. The lights in the ceiling flickered and went out, darkening the room as the power line from the generator recoiled beyond the open door. Axle saw it all through the doorframe, watching Tejay frozen in the Mustang's turning lights. The power line swung toward her, twisting like a whip, its end sparking as it struck the spill at her feet. The ground ignited, the light of it striking her features, illuminating her face in a final rictus of startled confusion. She seemed to know she was going to die. The realization of it filled her eyes, but her legs remained as before, rooted in ambivalence as the jerry can exploded.

Axle watched, unable to look away, squinting at the raging flames that rose along Tejay's body to engulf her shoulders and head. Her hair poufed upward, billowing into a swirl of blackened smoke. She screamed, or maybe it was the squeal of the Mustang's tires as Spinelli tried leaving the scene. Either way, Tejay was gone, reduced first to a pillar of flame, then to a smoking char that reeked of seared flesh, melted polyester, and cracked petroleum. Axle caught the stink of it as a swirl of heated air wafted back through the door, and now, at last, he turned away, snorting to clear his nose and throat, covering his face as he looked back to find the light from the fire flooding the shack, fanning out around the guardian as it towered over Reddy.

"Get away, you sombitch!" Reddy scuttled backward across the collapsed table. "Get away!"

The guardian held its ground, standing between Reddy and the open door.

"Sombitch!" Reddy grabbed his empty Remington. "Get away!" He stood, holding the shotgun by its barrel, wielding it like a club. "Get away. I'm going out!" He swung the gun.

The guardian stepped aside, letting Reddy get his first good look at the burning ground outside the door. By now Tejay was gone, reduced to a lumpy stain, looking like a wedge of upthrust magma. Reddy couldn't have known it was her, and he must have thought she had given up on him, that she was in the Mustang, leaving with Spinelli.

"You sombitch!" Reddy swung the gun again, trying to drive the guardian farther away from the door.

The Mustang roared, swerving back into view as Spinelli cut the wheels, fishtailed, and struck the shack. A tail light shattered, spewing shards over the front step. The engine revved. The car jerked forward, picking up speed as it steered toward the rocky ground on the edge of the abyss.

"Hey, Reddy!" Bird said. "Looks like Spinelli's leaving without you."

Reddy leveled the gun, keeping it between him and the guardian as he stepped toward the door.

The guardian leaned back, looking down at him. "You want to leave?"

Its voice filled the room, reverberating like breaking stone. "Go ahead." It reached out, grabbed the gun by the stock, and tugged the barrel from Reddy's grip. "I won't keep you."

Reddy turned and bolted through the door, shouting as he ran. "Hey, Spinelli!"

The Mustang kept moving, skirting the fire.

The guardian dropped the shotgun, then turned to look at Bird.

"I did what you told me," Bird said. "I found your man. I stayed with him." He strained against the duct tape. "Now get me *out of this chair*!"

The guardian backed away and turned toward Axle. There was something in its eyes, a look suggesting familiarity that went back farther than their meeting in the clearing. Axle expected it to speak again, but instead it leaped over the broken table and out the shack's rear door.

Wings unfurled, caught a gust of spirit wind, then folded. An instant later it was gone, plunging straight down into the darkness of Windslow Mine.

After returning to the Jeep, Kirill once again knelt on the sloping ground and reached along the winch housing. Working by touch, he tugged the release handle until he felt the thump of engaging gears. Now the winch would turn, reel in the line, lift the Jeep back onto the trail. Well, *maybe* it would lift it. Beneath his burgeoning confidence was the knowledge that he really did not know what he was doing.

He stood, brushed dirt from his knees, and moved back along the fender to the driver-side door.

His neck and shoulders spasmed again as he climbed into the cab and settled back into the tilting seat. Sweat saturated his shirt. He would need a shower when he got to the club. A long shower. Then he would put on fresh clothes, pour a drink from the locked cabinet behind the bar, down some aspirin, and wait for Sam. It would all be behind him then. But first he had to operate the winch.

He looked at the controls. One button. One switch. What could go wrong?

He pressed the button.

A diode came on, glowing red. Above it, a single word: ARMED.

That's good, he thought. *Armed is good.*

He hit the switch.

The winch motor hummed.

Leaning on the wheel, he watched the cable tighten. And then, with a groan, the Jeep shifted. The steering wheel skidded through his hands. The front end lurched to the left.

"Yes!"

The Jeep eased forward.

"Come on, you little whore."

The side panel creaked as it left the tree. A shower of dead needles drifted down, dusting the windshield. He cleared them with the wipers as the

Jeep turned and began its short climb toward level ground. And then—

WhuMMMPH!

The Jeep shuddered and stopped.

What now?

He gripped the wheel.

The winch kept turning, straining, changing pitch as the tightening cable filled the cab with the double-bass drone of quivering steel. Could the cable break, fly back and shatter the windshield? It would probably take his head off if it did that.

"*Yebany v rot!*" He was back to swearing in Russian. "*Mne vsyo ostop-eezdelo!*" The latter was a colorful expression. No equivalent in English. A cry of exhaustion, the exclamation of someone who'd already been screwed a hundred times too many. He was sore, tired, and raw. He wanted it to end: "*Mne vsyo ostopeezdelo!*"

He shifted to low and toed the accelerator. The droning subsided. A little more gas. Something crunched beneath the wheels. The front end rose and jerked forward.

"C'mon, bitch! Go!"

He nudged the accelerator.

The Jeep kept moving: up the slope, through the weeds, onto level ground. He shifted to neutral, killed the winch, and came to a stop with the headlights blazing toward Cliff Mine Run. He might have relaxed then, but as he sat back he saw a dark shape crouching in the right sideview mirror, reflected above stenciled letters that warned of objects being closer than they appeared. It leaned out from the same stand of yarrow grass where Kirill had imagined seeing the teenage boy. But there was no chance he was imagining this beast: wolfish face, broad shoulders, powerful arms. The rest of it lay hidden in the tall grass, but there was no avoiding its eyes, glowing red in the brake lights. It was looking right at him.

"Christ!" He tried calming himself, telling himself he had the advantage. Whatever the animal was, it couldn't possibly keep pace with a speeding Jeep.

Kirill shifted to low, moved his foot to the accelerator, and then froze.

"*Sooka!*" What was he thinking? He wasn't going anywhere.

Not yet.

Not until he climbed out of the cab and released the winch cable that still anchored the Jeep to the trunk of the trailside cedar.

Reddy bolted from the shack, chasing the Mustang.

"Hey!" He fanned the air, waving. "Hey, Spinelli!"

Spinelli kept driving, away from the flames and toward the rocky ground that rimmed the ledge. The fire could not reach the Mustang there, or so it must have seemed to Spinelli as he crept along the bare rock that rimmed the edge of the abyss.

"Hey, Spinelli!"

Reddy ran faster, past the scorched stump of something that lay between shack and generator. He considered running around the flames, but there was no time for that. Spinelli would accelerate as soon as the Mustang cleared the fire. Then he would steer away from the brink and drive full throttle toward the screw-thread road that descended toward the base of the mine. From there, it would be a short drive to the lower bends of Windslow Road Extension.

"Spinelli, you sombitch! Wait for me!"

Reddy's only chance of catching the Mustang was to run straight through the fire. If he did that he'd head off the car before Spinelli accelerated away. And Reddy was sure he could pass through the blaze without getting burned. One leap and he'd be on the other side, as unscathed as a finger through a candle flame.

But there was one problem.

Reddy's shoes, socks, and pants were soaked with gasoline. Each leg was a fuse. He didn't consider these things until he was airborne, kicking his feet through the heated air, fanning the flames.

Before he hit the ground, his feet were on fire.

Spinelli hated fire.

When he was thirteen, his stepfather took the family on a cross-country trip that wound through the Appalachian foothills and toward the rolling piedmont of North Carolina. The stepfather called the trip a vacation, but from the start Spinelli suspected there were other motives. North Carolina was a right-to-work state, and the stepfather, who had not held a steady job in over a year, was desperate for a turnaround.

Spinelli spent most of the trip wedged in the back of the family's Impala, between a ten-year-old stepbrother and the plastic baby seat that held his two-year-old stepsister. It was August. Outside, the air was dry, unseasonably cool, but the backseat was stuffy and warm.

Marco, the stepbrother, claimed he suffered from carsickness, a condition that always earned him a window seat on family outings. He was an obnoxious kid, all farts and boogers, and Spinelli hated him.

On this trip, a nylon sleeping bag covered the cracked vinyl cushions of the backseat. Nylon, vinyl, and Marco—a terrible combination.

"I am Electro Man!" Marco said, finger raised.

"Knock it off," Spinelli said.

Marco had been doing the Electro Man thing on and off for the last hundred miles, ever since he had discovered the static potential of rubbing his ass against the nylon sleeping bag. He steadied his finger, pointing at Spinelli.

"I said knock it off, Marco."

Marco gulped back a belly full of air, letting it out in a long articulated burp: "I aaaaaammmm Electro-maaaaannnn!"

"I'll break it off, Marco."

"What?"

"Your finger."

"Not a finger. An electrode!" He jabbed.

Spinelli jerked from the shock, slamming the baby seat.

The baby shrieked.

Spinelli grabbed the finger, twisting.

"Ow!" Marco tried pulling away.

Spinelli held on, bending harder.

"Hey!" Spinelli's mother looked back from the front seat. "Goddamnit! Knock it off." She reached across the seat, smacking Spinelli on the head. "You know he's not in the mood for this!"

The *he* she referred to was not Marco. Marco was always in the mood for making trouble. But Marco's father, Spinelli's stepfather, was another story. He had been silent throughout most of the trip, seldom speaking unless it was to tell Marco and Spinelli to quit acting like babies. But at the moment, *he* was not in the car. He was outside, pumping gas at a self-service pump. At least, that was where he had been the last time Spinelli looked around. But now he was on the other side of the car, opening the door beside Marco, reaching in to grab Spinelli's wrist. "What the hell are you doing, Spinelli?"

The stepfather's last name was Corsoe.

Spinelli was the only *Spinelli* in the car.

"Marco started it!" Spinelli said.

"Don't care who started it!" He twisted Spinelli's wrist, making it pop, forcing Spinelli to let go. "I told you! I've had enough of this crap!"

Spinelli sat back, staring at his stepfather's vice-like grip, saying nothing.

"You hear me, Spinelli?"

Spinelli's wrist burned, but he didn't cry out. He clamped his lips and nodded.

His stepfather let go. "Now get out!"

"Out?"

"Out of the goddamn car!" He turned to Marco. "Let him out."

Marco did as he was told, clearing the way for Spinelli who slid across the nylon sleeping bag and into the dry evening air.

"Make yourself useful!" His stepfather pointed to the side of the car. "Pump the gas!"

Spinelli turned and walked toward the service island.

His stepfather remained by the open door. "And you, Marco! Cut that electro shit!"

"Yes, sir."

"Next time I'll let him break your goddamn finger! Hear me?"

Marco nodded.

"Get in the goddamn car."

Marco climbed back inside. He closed the door. Then his father did the same, climbing into the front and leaving Spinelli outside to finish the pumping.

The pump was still running when Spinelli reached the service island. He saw the wavy distortions of the rising fumes as they vented from the open tank. And he smelled them, too. God, he hated that smell. He would get Marco back for this, the little prick.

Amy, his stepsister, looked back as he approached the nozzle. She had stopped screaming, and now she grinned at him as if he had never bumped her baby seat and made her cry. That was the nice thing about babies. They didn't hold grudges.

He waved at her.

She smiled and waved back, slapping her hand against the glass.

Spinelli set his hand on the nozzle, intending to rest it there until the gas shut off. But something happened as his hand made contact with the metal. Something cracked beneath his fingers. He felt a jolt of static, and suddenly his wrist was wrapped in flame. "Shit!" He grabbed the nozzle, yanking it back. The flames followed his hand, surging in a fiery stream that arced across the doors. The nozzle was still on, its trigger locked into position, spewing fire.

Amy peered through the rear window, mouth wide, eyes full of wonder.

The front passenger door flew open. It was his mother trying to get out, but the fire was faster. It rushed in as the door swung wide, enveloping her as she leaned forward in her seat. She didn't scream. Didn't make any noise at all. She just sat there, poised in the open door, a human torch with one outstretched arm. And then she was gone, buried beneath the wall of black-veined fire.

"Get out!" his stepfather yelled. "Everybody out!"

But no one emerged.

It was then that Spinelli realized he was still holding the nozzle. He dropped it and ran. The hose twisted behind him as it fell, spraying his shoulders before striking the corner of the service island.

He charged toward the mini mart, a placard-and-glass building set against a backdrop of North Carolina pines. He saw his reflection in the storefront's glass: a terrified boy with wings of fire. "Help!"

People dashed outside, coming toward him. A big man took the lead. Crew cut. Broad shouldered. He swelled before Spinelli, flying forward to tackle him and throw him to the ground.

Next thing Spinelli knew, the man was on top of him, rolling with him, snuffing the flames. And that was the last thing Spinelli knew for the rest of the day.

The next morning, he awoke to pain.

Years later, Spinelli's life continued to pivot on that experience. Abandoned once by the biological father whose name he carried, Spinelli found himself abandoned again after the fire. A boy without a family, he left the hospital to travel through a succession of foster homes, finally lighting out on his own a few weeks after his eighteenth birthday.

He had come a long way since then. The school of hard knocks had taught him well, but although it had hardened him to the cruelties of the world, he nevertheless retained a deep fear of being burned. Hardly a day went by when he did not think about the look, feel, and smell of the gasoline that had scarred him for life and killed his mother and stepfamily. Through the years, that moment remained close, undiminished by the passage of time, a burning flame that never went out.

Spinelli understood exactly what he was dealing with when he steered the Mustang from the flaming ground. Under any other circumstances, he probably would have left the car and fled on foot.

But he had seen Tejay die.

He had seen the electric wire snap and fall into the puddle of spilled gasoline. A moment later he had heard the crack of the high-powered rifle and knew that it could only mean one thing. Vorarov had come to settle the score. The fat Russian had found the Viper and followed the Mustang's trail of spilled gasoline. And now he, or perhaps someone who worked for him, had taken position on the ledge road and was prepared to pick them off from a distance. Spinelli's only chance was to stay in the car, maneuver around the fire, and follow the haul road down into the pit of the mine.

But there was another problem. He saw it in his rearview as he drove away.

It was Reddy, coming at him, igniting as he leaped across the burning ground.

For a moment, Spinelli felt himself looking into the past, at a terrified boy reflected in a plate-glass window.

Flames climbed Reddy's feet and legs, spreading over his waist, rising along his shoulders, becoming a set of smoky wings as he reached the car and threw himself against the driver's side door.

"Sombitch!" Reddy grabbed the latch with one hand. With the other, he reached through the open window.

"*Sombitch!*" He grabbed the wheel. "You leaving without me?" Reddy seemed oblivious to the flames spreading along his arms. Getting inside the car was all that mattered. "You sombitch, Spinelli! Let me in!" He tugged the wheel.

The Mustang veered toward the brink.

"Let go!" Spinelli tried prying Reddy's hand from the wheel. *"Reddy, let go!"*

Reddy was hard enough to deal with under normal circumstances. A flaming Reddy was a clear impossibility. And the Mustang's front end was now veering dangerously close to the brink.

Spinelli glanced left, into Reddy's eyes, into pupils that blazed as if the back of his head had been burned away and his skull was filling with flame. One look, and Spinelli knew that Reddy had the wheel in a death grip. Only one option remained: leave the car.

He pushed away from the wheel and scuttled into the passenger seat as the forward tires slipped over the edge.

WHAM!

The front bottomed out, but the rear wheels kept turning, forcing the car forward along bare rock.

Spinelli grabbed the door handle. He tugged it, disengaged the lock, and pushed out as the car slid past its center of gravity.

The door flew open.

The trunk rose.

Spinelli jumped.

57

Though hardly an expert on Pennsylvania wildlife, Kirill felt certain the creature behind him was something new, an uncatalogued species of wolf, a genetic freak caused by the pollution in Windslow Mine. It looked dangerous, but at least for now it seemed content to sit and stare from a distance.

It's afraid to come closer. Afraid I'll ram it again.

Kirill needed to believe that, otherwise he'd never get out of the cab and disengage the cable.

I'll work fast, he thought. After all, how long could it take to disengage the line? Five seconds? Ten seconds max?

He took his foot from the brake and eased the Jeep forward, pulling alongside the cable-wrapped trunk, closing the distance between tree and cab. Then he engaged the handbrake and opened the door.

Chimes sounded, warning of a key left in the ignition.

The creature cocked its head, listening, watching.

Keeping the door open, Kirill got out, disengaged the hook, and tugged the cable to pull it free. No good. The cable wouldn't budge. Something held it to the base of the cedar. He glanced back at the creature. It hadn't moved, but the tension in its arms and back suggested that it might spring at any moment.

"*Sooka!*" he said, speaking to the animal. "*Oo ti bya, galava, kak, oon a bizyanie jopuh!*" He spoke words on impulse, telling the creature that its face looked like a monkey's ass. It was the sort of thing he used to say to the gang of bullies that used to hang around outside the rear entrance to his mother's Leningrad flat. The gang had called itself the *Chyorny Vhod Svinets*—the Backdoor Bullets. Sometimes they beat him up. Most of the time they let him pass, something he was convinced they never would have done if he'd acted scared. That experience had taught him the importance of sounding brave even when you were shitting your pants.

He stared at the thing. *"Pluvat na teba!"*

The thing just stared back, watching Kirill as he turned and advanced toward the tree. A moment later, he saw what held the cable. It was the tree itself: the weight of the Jeep had driven the braided steel into the bark. On the side of the trunk opposite the trail, the cable lay so deeply embedded that it looked as if the cedar had been growing around it for years.

"Sooka!" He was screwed. *"Yebany v rot!"*

He looked at the animal.

It kept watching, leering with glowing eyes as Kirill gripped the cable in both hands and tugged it hard. His shoulder protested, but he put his back into it, tugging again. Bark ripped, dusting his hands as a few inches of line broke from the cedar's grip. He pulled again. Another section came loose. This was taking too long, and his shoulder was cramping, seizing at the base of his neck.

The creature leaned back. Perhaps it was frightened, intimidated by the man who could extract metal cord from a tree trunk.

Kirill sneered as he drew up the slack and tried again, pulling harder in spite of the pain in his shoulder. Bark flew across his face and hands. Another pull, then another. His back spasmed, but he kept at it, working into a frenzy until the whole length of cable lay on the ground at his feet. That's when he heard a new sound, louder than the ripping of tree bark.

CRACK!

It sounded like the snap of a giant sail.

He looked around, turning stiffly, his neck cramping as the sound came again.

CRACK!

The creature stood upright now, pivoting on powerful legs and holding its head high between a pair of gigantic wings.

If that thing flies, I'm screwed!

He steadied himself, doing his best to seem unfazed as he stepped away from the tree and toward the ringing chimes of his open door.

The creature responded, arching its wings, leaning forward. What did that mean? Was it going to take off? Swoop toward him?

Kirill lifted himself behind the wheel and slammed the door. Then, with the monster once again framed in the sideview mirror, he engaged the engine and roared off in a shower of dust. Instantly, the beast vanished, hidden from view as the Jeep raced out of the trees and onto the shoulder of Cliff Mine Run. Gravel exploded under the floor, clattering like automatic gunfire. The tires climbed the slope, lost traction, careened into a sideways skid. Kirill spun the wheel. Too late. The rear fishtailed, skidding across the asphalt to collide with a guardrail post.

WhuMMMMPH!

The cab reverberated with the thump of crunching metal and breaking plastic.

Scratch one tail light!

Sam was going to be pissed as hell.

Screw it!

Tomorrow he and Sam could assess the damage. Whatever the Jeep needed, he'd take care of it. There was a body shop in Windslow, a little place in the Bottoms that he had heard did quality work for almost nothing. He'd have Sam take the Jeep there, send him the bill. Whatever the cost, it would be worth it.

Christ!

He shivered, gripping the wheel, glad to be driving on pavement, heading toward Windslow.

It's over! he thought. *It's over. I'm out of there. I've made it.*

But already something drew his attention back to the rearview: a sudden blast of light in the road behind him. For a moment he thought it was some bastard flashing his high beams. But it wasn't that. That would have made more sense than what he saw behind him now.

I've lost my mind!

Behind him, rising from the center of the downhill lane, sputtering and flashing behind the speeding Jeep, was the goddamnedest thing he had ever seen.

It couldn't be. It was ludicrous.

But it was nonetheless there, blazing up from the asphalt and coming right at him.

It was a pillar of flame.

58

S am watched the running man chase the Mustang, feet burning, fire climbing his legs. She had chosen her shot well. Tonight was one for the record books, a night when she had exceeded the sniper's goal of one shot, one kill.

And it was getting better.

The running man reached the driver side and threw himself against the door. "Sombitch!" Flames climbed along his back, spreading over the car.

What's happening? What am I seeing?

Flames spread along the Mustang's roof, door, and fender. The black paint was catching fire, igniting and curling away to reveal a bright red undercoat. *Black latex!* She remembered the mirror she had found on the trail. *The entire car is coated with black latex.*

And latex burned.

Flames spread along the man's shoulders and arms as he reached through the Mustang's open window. "Sombitch!" He grabbed the wheel. Smoke curled from his arms. "You leaving without me?"

And there was more.

In the crosshairs of her night-vision scope, she saw flames building under the car's rear bumper. The duct-tape patches had ignited, sending out creepers of fire that climbed the vapor trail left by the fuel Tejay had spilled over the back of the car. The Mustang had become a rolling bomb, and the fuse was lit.

And all the while the burning man kept struggling with the driver, pelting him with flaming arms, screaming at the top of his lungs: "You sombitch, Spinelli! Let me in!"

The car lurched, tilting toward the brink. A moment later, Sam heard the crunch of metal on rock, the rasp of breaking sandstone. The front end pushed out into empty air. And the rear wheels kept rolling.

She watched through the crosshairs, seeing it as if from a few feet away.

And as the cab filled with smoke and flames bloomed from the duct-tape patches, the passenger door flew open. The driver had climbed from behind the wheel, across the center island, and was now leaning out, bracing against the open door, looking toward the cliff. Then, eyes fixed on the table of rock, he leaped from the car.

By now the flaming man had scrambled halfway into the cab. Only his legs were visible, sputtering like wicks as the car angled nose-down into the crater. But it was the jumping man who held her attention. Her breath caught in her throat as he propelled himself toward the ledge. Was she really seeing this? He seemed to be soaring: arms out, legs splayed, face drawn taut by the wind of his flight.

Sam shivered.

He's going to make it!

He reached out. For an instant his fingers seemed to grab the ledge. . . .

But it was an illusion.

The view through the scope had flattened her perspective. In reality, the leaping man never had a chance. He missed the ledge by a wide margin. In a blink he was gone, vanishing with the flaming man and falling Mustang, leaving behind a patch of empty night and a curl of dissipating smoke.

Sam drew her eye back from the glowing crosshairs, lowered her gun, and looked down with unaided vision. Light flashed beyond the cliff, brightening as a thunderous roar shook the valley.

She shivered.

The Mustang had ignited.

One shot. Three kills.

She had never felt more alive.

Kirill neither heard the explosion nor saw the fireball that leaped above the trees. He had his own nightmares to deal with. First the stranded Jeep, then the monster in the clearing, and now the most insane complication of all: *a racing pillar of flame!*

The night had lost its mind. Nothing made sense.

The road veered. Kirill took the turn at sixty, skidded across the center line, and accelerated a few hundred feet in the wrong lane before the pavement straightened. He swerved back and checked the mirror.

The fire kept pace.

"The hell?" his voice trembled, speaking to the flaming pillar. "What the hell are you?"

He couldn't take much more of this. One more crazy thing and he'd lose it for sure, totally bug fucked: *Fsyoe zaeebahnuh!*

The road veered again. He took the turn at seventy, and still the pillar followed, always the same distance, neither gaining nor falling back. Would it eventually get tired? Slow down? Burn out? What if it didn't? What if it followed him through Windslow, back to the club?

"Christ!"

Up ahead, the road leveled, straightened, and dipped beneath a patch of runoff that spilled outward from a subsided shoulder. He remembered seeing the puddle before. Sam had driven across it, cutting her speed before splashing through. But Kirill wasn't about to slow down. Not with a flaming devil riding his ass.

He steered left, over the center line, preparing to cross the puddle's shallow end, but then he realized that shallow was not what he wanted. The more water the better. He turned the wheel, cutting toward the deep glassy water along the shoulder.

"*Sooka!*" He spoke to the fire. "Going to put you out, you bitch!"

The passenger-side tires left the road. Stones pelted the undercarriage, crackling like grease. And still the flame stayed with him, sparking along until—

WHOOOSH!

The Jeep hit the flood, cleaving the surface. For a moment the world vanished behind wings of jetting water. He glanced at the mirror. It was dark back there, too. No more fire. He'd put it out. But now he had another problem.

The Jeep was spinning, careening sideways over the wet asphalt. He hit the brakes and skidded to a stop across the center line. But it wasn't over. Outside something raced toward him. He saw it beyond his side window, a tentacle looping past the mirror, changing course as it crossed the hood.

He froze.

A curved claw swooped toward the windshield, coming right at him.

CRASH!

The windshield imploded, pelting the cab with shattered glass as the claw flew inside, slammed the seat beside him, and rebounded to strike the dashboard.

WHAM!

It left a dent the size of a grapefruit. But then, as if exhausted, it collapsed, landing with a thud atop the cup holder in the center island.

It didn't move after that. It just lay there, heavy, inert.

Kirill studied it, his pulse racing as he extended a finger toward its curved mass. He touched it. "*Sooka!*" His flesh sizzled. He recoiled, shaking his hand.

The damn thing was searing hot. And it had a reason to be, considering what it had been doing.

"*Yebany v rot!*"

It was the winch hook, almost molten from having sparked across a mile and a half of asphalt.

He understood it now. He had left the forest without retracting the line. The hook on the end of the cable had chased him the whole way, bouncing and sputtering against the asphalt as it rode the end of its tether. Then, when he spun out, the cable had whipped around the Jeep, winding tight until it slammed the windshield.

If the tether had been just a little shorter, it would have smashed through directly in front of him and taken off his head.

He shivered.

It could have killed him, but it sure as shit wasn't a monster, and seeing it for what it was made him wonder what other rational explanations he might have discovered if he had remained on the trail a little longer.

And then, as if to mock him, the Jeep began skidding sideways across the pavement like a vibrating cell phone.

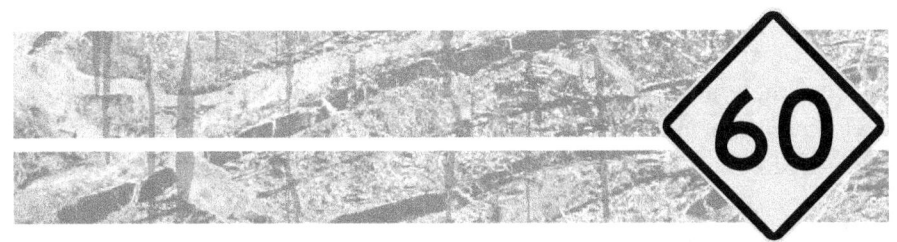

60

Sitting inside the shack, Axle watched what was left of his Mustang slide away from the flaming ground and into the empty air beyond the ledge. Reddy and Spinelli went with it: one struggling to climb behind the wheel, the other trying to escape from the passenger-side door. And then, with alarming swiftness, they fell, leaving a ghost of curling smoke.

"Hey," Bird said. "Hey, Axle! Get me out of this chair."

Axle ignored him, transfixed by the smoke beyond the ledge. He stumbled toward the door, catching himself on the frame. His legs tingled, weak in the knees, but getting stronger.

"Come on, Axle. Get me out of—"

An explosion cut him off, roaring from the mine as a fireball mushroomed beyond the precipice.

Bird flinched. "The hell's that?" He leaned forward, trying to get a look outside. "The hell's going on out there?"

"My car."

The fireball darkened as it rose, climbing into the night.

"My Mustang." Axle turned, looking at Bird. "Those bastards just drove my car into the crater."

"No shit?" Bird sounded amused. "So they're dead." He snorted. "Sorry for your loss. Now get me out of this fucking chair!"

Axle remained by the door, staring at Bird.

"What?" Bird said. "What are you looking at now?"

"You."

Bird's condition didn't add up. Blood still covered his chest. His vest remained frayed and spattered with pulp. A scabby trail crusted his chin, dried spittle from when he had been coughing up pieces of lung. But Bird was not coughing now. Nor was he bleeding. His wounds were gone, and the once-dangling arm was back in its joint, flexing as it strained against the tape.

"What's happened to us?" Axle asked.

"Can we discuss this later?"

Axle felt his own face, probing his blood-matted hair to find that his wound had healed as thoroughly as Bird's. No hole in his temple, no pain in his skull, just layers of crusty blood that might as well have belonged to someone else. "I was dying. So were you." He looked toward the shack's rear door, the splintered frame and the empty space beyond. There was nothing there now, but his memory still crackled with the image of what had been: a winged creature diving into the mine. "That thing," he said. "It healed us."

"Not a *thing*," Bird said. "It was an earthborn guardian, a man remade in the physical form of Kwetis."

Axle nodded, realizing that he knew these things, too. The knowledge welled within him, brightening as the fire on the ledge burned itself out and the room dimmed back into darkness.

"That's the second time I've seen him," Bird said. "First time was up above, after your friend shot me."

"My friend?"

"You know, the redhead. Called himself *Reddy*."

"He wasn't my friend," Axle said. "I'd never even met him before tonight."

"Whatever."

"No. Not *whatever*. Him and me, we were nothing. I hardly knew him, and what I knew I didn't like." Axle leaned forward, easing his shoulder against the frame of the open door. He felt something, a shifting in the wood, an odd flutter: the shack was vibrating. . . .

"I was lying on the ground," Bird said. "After the bastard shot me . . . I was just lying there. I couldn't breathe. I was dying. Then . . . I looked up . . . and there he was." Bird's voice was once again coming in short bursts, but this time the pauses seemed to be from gaps in his memory rather than holes in his lungs. "He said he was an earthborn guardian and that I needed to find you, stay with you until—"

"You hear that?"

"Hear what?" Bird cocked his head. "That ringing?"

"Yeah." Axle took his hand from the vibrating wall. *Ringing* was a good word for it, the low ringing of a giant gong.

"What is it?" Bird asked.

Axle looked toward the mine, watching as the sandstone along the precipice vanished beneath a layer of mist. No, not mist. It was the rocks themselves, trembling into a blur. "The mine," Axle said. "The mine's ringing. Vibrating. The whole mine—" He could see it now, a blurring of the ledge, the tremors spreading to the highwall.

"Goddamnit!" Bird raised his voice, shouting as the rumble became a roar. "Axle! Get me out of this chair!"

The sound seemed to originate from the top of the wall, from the point where Axle and Yeyestani had once sat and looked down at his father's grave. And there, standing on the brink, was the earthborn guardian: wings spread, arms akimbo, head back, bellowing. He was chanting, hurtling his voice into the mine until the rocks roared back. Sympathetic vibrations. The land was singing.

The weeds along the highwall's face moved in waves, shivering against quaking layers of shale, coal, and stone. They thrashed in the air, shedding leaves and branches that drifted down onto the screw-thread road. And it was there, where the road curved behind the vertical column of rock, that Axle sensed another presence: someone crouching in the quivering darkness, looking down, watching him.

The sniper was still up there. And now Axle saw her, vaguely, a tiny face with mismatched eyes: one dark, the other glowing with the pale green of a night-vision scope.

61

S am braced against the vertical column as the ringing in the rocks gave way to a subwoofer roar. The ledge quivered. She knew she should get off the highwall, but the job came first.

Far below, a piece of unfinished business leaned from the shack's open door: a man, mid-twenties, jacket stained with drying blood.

Was he Kirill's partner?

Can't miss him, Kirill had said. *Braided hair, sleeveless vest, tattooed arms.*

This man had none of those things. What was she to make of that? Could Kirill have been wrong about the number of people in the Mustang? Or could this be the mystery man who had knelt in the clearing, the man whose footprints had vanished among the weeds? That wasn't likely, either. Those footprints had been huge. This man was small, not much larger than a boy.

So who is he?

A roar rose behind her as the vibrations spread through the highwall. She couldn't stay here. It was time to take her final shot and clear out.

Steadying her aim, she centered the crosshairs on the man in the door-way. He turned then, looking right at her. She felt a jolt, struck by something in his eyes. She flinched and pulled the trigger, getting off a shot as the roar behind her grew louder.

The man recoiled, falling back into the shack. And she fell with him, los-ing balance as the ledge folded beneath her. Debris tumbled from above, a rush of rock and grit pouring down as she dropped the gun and scrambled back to grab the weeds that grew among the veins and strata of the quak-ing wall. She clawed at them, seizing a spiny stalk as the ledge collapsed into the crater. Her gun fell with it: hand built, state of the art, expensive as hell—now lost amid cascading rock.

Christ!

She clung to the weeds, dangling over the void with the rock face giving way around her. There was only one thing to do.

Climb!

She tugged at the weeds, pulling hand over hand while her feet dangled free. And then, with a snap that resounded through her bones, a stem broke off in her hand. She swung sideways, kicking against the wall.

Foothold! Got to find a foothold.

Dust billowed, thick as smoke, coating her nose and throat, stinging her eyes. She couldn't see, could barely breathe, but she kept kicking, hoping her heels would find a wedge amid the rock. If she could find one foothold, she might find another. Two footholds and she could climb. All wasn't lost. She could do this.

Please, God . . . help me.

At last she found something, a protrusion no wider than her heel. She gave it her weight. It held. Trusting it, she leaned left, reaching toward a cleft in the wall, a jagged fissure. She wiggled her hand inside and made a fist. The rock cut her wrist, but for the moment she remained anchored, hanging fast while a new din exploded to her left. She blinked, cleared her vision, and looked toward the noise.

That's when she knew it was hopeless.

"No, God . . . please!"

She wasn't praying.

"Please, God!"

She wasn't religious.

In spite of her upbringing, life had taught her the foolishness of believing in the existence of a beneficent God, a father in the sky who could be petitioned in times of need. But there had been days when she had believed otherwise. As a child, coming of age in the shadow of a whitewashed church, she had been instructed to turn to God when all else was lost. That had been after the black lung took her father, leaving her in the care of a stone-faced mother who practiced corporal penance and believed her children should do the same. Her mother had taught her to pray, but Sam was not praying now. Her words were reflexive, regression in the face of death . . . and Sam knew she was about to die.

Blinking grit from her eyes, she saw the column of rock venting dust and debris as it broke from the wall, collapsed, and fell toward her. . . .

She closed her eyes.

"God, please no!"

She wasn't praying.

"No, God. Please!"

She knew she wasn't praying. It was only instinct. Regression. She knew it. Believed it. And the belief filled her as she shouted the non-prayer, her voice soundless amid the roaring chaos.

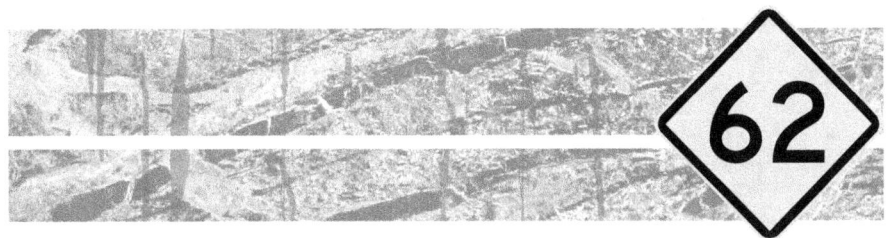

Axle fell back through the door as the crack of the sniper's rifle rose above the thunder of falling rocks. He landed, face burning, senses reeling. He touched his cheek, inspecting the damage, feeling a line of jagged splinters embedded in his jaw. That was the worst of it. The sniper had shot the doorframe. He'd been hit by splinters, not a bullet.

"What are you doing?" Bird said.

The floor heaved, tilting toward the abyss as the ledge gave way.

"Damnit!" Bird screamed. "Get me out of this chair!" He skidded as he screamed, slamming the wall beside the stove—a wall that now seemed more level than the floor. Everything else in the room moved, too. Stove, sawbucks, plywood, briefcase, papers, Axle—all tumbling together, piling up beside Bird on the horizontal wall. "Avalanche!" Bird cried, tugging at the tape. "We're going down!"

The roof flew away, leaping from its joists, revealing a churning mass of rocks and dust. Axle saw it, knew he was going to fall into it, and resigned himself as he and Bird skidded toward the brink. The stove fell first, clattering from the plywood and into the void. Bird followed, vanishing as a blast of wind rose out of the mine. Debris scattered, blue-backed documents breaking free of their bindings, swirling in a white-paper cyclone to the sound of flapping wings. An instant later, Axle felt himself changing course, hurtling parallel to the crater, looking back to see the shack breaking apart as it fell along the collapsing wall. A massive hand clutched his jacket collar, holding him aloft, whisking him away.

The guardian had returned, making good on its promise.

"Aw shit!" Bird screamed.

Axle turned to see a pair of tangled braids snapping in the wind. The guardian had grabbed the back of Bird's chair, and now Bird, who a moment ago had struggled to pull himself free of the duct tape, seemed to be praying that the tape would hold.

Axle read the panic in Bird's eyes, and then the guardian changed course, sweeping skyward so quickly that everything vanished. Axle's eyes rolled back. He blacked out.

A moment later, a lifetime later, he awoke . . .

. . . and he was flying.

63

Stalled on Cliff Mine Run, sitting behind a shattered windshield with a winch hook in the cup holder, Kirill gripped the wheel as a violent tremor pushed the Jeep sideways across the asphalt. Instinctively, he hit the brakes. But the Jeep kept moving, continuing on for nearly a dozen feet while a plume of dust rose above the trees. He couldn't see it clearly. The cracks in the glass distorted the scene, twisting the airborne dirt into strange patterns: a feathery arc, a wolfish head, and then—just before the cloud dissipated—a face with a pair of mismatched eyes, one opening onto a backdrop of night, the other filled with the orb of the moon.

But of course it was only dust. Nothing fantastic. No more supernatural than the winch hook that had followed him from the forest trail.

The Jeep had stopped shaking. *Tremors*, he thought, realizing that the rising dust had been kicked aloft by the same vibrations that had moved the Jeep. As for the source of the quake, that was Sam's problem. She was the one in the mine, at the apparent epicenter, not him.

His only real concern was that the Jeep remained stalled across the center line of Cliff Mine Run. He needed to move it: restart the engine, drive home, and get away from this madness once and for all.

He set his hand on the ignition, but hesitated as he saw something emerging above the trees. It hurtled upward, breaking through the dust, soaring into the light of the moon. What was it? He couldn't see it clearly. Cracks in the glass distorted his view, fracturing the sky into a mosaic of shadows. But there was a clear spot, a hole left by the winch hook, a jagged opening amid the cracks. He leaned toward it, pressed his hands to the dash, and squinted into the whistling air. He discerned it then, a cruciform shadow shooting straight up from the mine, and in its hands. . . .

What were they? What were the shapes in its hands? He stared, trying to make them out as they ascended into the sky.

People?

Yes, they looked like people, one in each hand: one dangling limp, the other bound to a chair. The image made no sense, but he kept staring until a horn blared to his right. He jerked back from the windshield and looked out the side window, toward the flashing headlights of an oncoming truck.

The horn blasted again as Kirill fumbled with the ignition, trying to restart the Jeep.

The truck downshifted, lurched forward, rumbled to a stop. It was a Chevy, hood riddled with rust. The side window rolled down. A head leaned out. "Move it!" The voice was young, indignant.

In no mood for a fight, Kirill wrenched the key, restarted the Jeep, and backed up across the center line, not stopping until he heard the scratch of branches against the rear panel.

The kid looked out his side window as he passed, revving the engine, acting tough as he stared at Kirill. He had a nasty face, dull features huddled in the shadow of a heavy brow.

Kirill stared back, feeling an urge to shift into low and plow the bastard over the shoulder and down the embankment. But the fight was out of him. He simply wanted to get back to the office, pour a drink, and wait for Sam.

The kid paused, glanced out toward the rumbling mine, then pulled away, throwing Kirill the finger once he was clear. Then he sped up, splashed through the runoff, and vanished around the uphill bend.

Kirill let him go. He had other things to worry about. For one, there was the question of the winch line. Could he drive with it wrapped around the Jeep, imbedded in the windshield?

Fuck it! He wasn't getting out of the cab in the middle of nowhere, not with the road vibrating beneath him and the mine venting plumes of gritty dust. And there was the monster, too, the flying thing that had already carried off two men. No, he was most definitely not getting out of the cab.

He shoved the Jeep into gear and steered into the downhill lane. It wasn't easy to see the road through the cracked glass, but he knew the way. Taking it slow, he pushed onward, heading home.

The road leveled as he passed the trailer park. A short time after that, stopped at the first of a series of out-of-sync traffic lights, he tried getting out of the cab to untangle the cable, but the door wouldn't open. The coiled steel held it closed, forcing him to fumble with the latches of the Jeep's modular roof, disconnecting the forward panel and pushing until it clattered out of its frame and down onto the road. Then climbed after it, sending new pain flaring into his back as he hefted himself onto the bar above the windshield. He swung his first leg over, stepped down onto the hood, and brought his second around. The hood clunked, bending inward beneath his feet as he walked across it. The dents didn't spring back. He hardly noticed. He was beyond caring.

Upon reaching the street, he turned and pulled the winch hook from the windshield. It broke free and landed on the hood. *BAM!* Another dent. He and the Jeep were both ready for the scrap yard.

"*Mne vsyo ostopeezdelo!*"

He stumbled around the cab, moving like a drunk as he worked the cable free. Then, he opened the door, started the winch, and retracted the line.

The yellow light still burned above the entrance of his club.

He parked a few feet from the door and stepped out to the distant hiss of highway traffic, the endless river of racing car lights that roared below his parking lot on the cutaway hill.

The deadbolt thumped as he turned the key. The steel door slid inward, welcoming him back to a world that made sense. The place smelled clean, but the scent of musk lingered. Sex hung in the air. But now, for the first time in ages, he found himself warming to it.

He crossed to the bar, took a bottle of Ikon from the locked cabinet, and headed upstairs.

His office was as he had left it. He took his first drink straight from the bottle. It tasted good. He went inside, not looking at the model of Mountain Downs that stood in the shadows. Instead, he walked straight toward his gun case, opened the heavy glass, and took down a fully restored, vintage Stetchkin. This was no high-end collector-edition copy like the one his cousin had sold to Bird. This was the real thing. He slapped in a twenty-round magazine and set the mode to semi-auto. The full-auto RPM was too high. He wanted to savor what he was about to do.

He crossed to his desk, opened a drawer, took out a bottle of aspirin. Generic stuff. Wal-Mart brand. Aspirin was aspirin. He popped the cap, shook out a half-dozen tablets, and popped them into his mouth. They crunched like beer nuts. The taste was harsh, chalky. He washed it down with another swig of Ikon. His back spasmed as he raised his head, drinking straight from the bottle.

"*Na strovie!*"

He toasted his health and drank again. Then he attached the wooden holster that doubled as the Stetchkin's shoulder stock. He was feeling the Ikon now, the alcohol settling into a glow that radiated back into his head. The pain was still there, but soon the aspirin would kick in. Everything would be as it should be.

He was home, back in a world with no surprises.

But even here the memories lingered.

In the room's dimness, superimposed over the model of Mountain Downs, he saw a winged creature—part hawk, part wolf, part man—rising out of the forest and shooting like an arrow toward the glowing eye of the moon. In one hand, it held a man dangling limp in the air. In the other, a man sitting in a chair. How could you explain a thing like that? What did it mean?

Fuck it!

He knew what he had to do.

He took another drink, raised the Stetchkin, cocked it, and pressed the wooden stock against his shoulder. The trigger was perfectly balanced. A little pressure was all it took.

He squeezed.

Across the room, Mountain Downs exploded in a shower of splinters and dust. He held the gun steady, firing across the mountain's western face, over cantilevered ledges, and onto the neo-deco façade of the twelve-story casino hotel. The tower shattered, its pieces falling down the steep face of the plaster mountain, crashing against the 1:240 scale race track that curved out from the model's base. Even set for semi-automatic, the gun emptied quickly. Then, with the air reeking of dust and cordite, he reloaded and took out the stables, mall, cineplex, and waterpark.

It felt good.

Kirill Vorarov was once again the master of his world.

Walk *away from me now, and you'll be on your own.*

Eighteen, frightened, desperate to return to Great-Grandmother's trailer in Coals Hollow, Axle crouched in a stand of yarrow grass and looked out at a man who stood between him and Cliff Mine Run. For a moment the man seemed to stare right at Axle. What was he doing?

Axle watched, afraid to move.

The man leaned forward, called out as if he saw Axle hiding in the grass, but then—instead of waiting for an answer—he turned and hurried away toward the diffuse light that burned beyond the weeds at the side of the trail.

Something had frightened the man, and Axle had no desire to stay around and find out what it was.

With the sound of something advancing behind him, Axle leaped from the tall grass and fled toward Cliff Mine Run.

The mysterious black cable still stretched across the trail, rising up from the slope to loop about the base of a tree. But its blackness changed as he approached it, losing its texture, thinning until it seemed to be little more than a tendril of fog. And then, suddenly, it vanished as if it had never been there at all.

He ran, out of the forest and onto the road that led toward home.

A mile later, his sides cramped and his breath thick with the hot-metal taste of exhaustion, he slowed his pace to a stumbling walk. How much farther? The road seemed to have lengthened since his trek into the highlands. The bends didn't look familiar. The trees seemed wrong, taller and older than the ones he knew. But he kept moving. He had no choice. He couldn't go back to the mine. . . .

There were times when the trees arched so thickly overhead that they seemed to belong to the days of the Okwe, when America's northeastern forest stretched unbroken all the way to the Mississippi. He feared he might wander in darkness forever, but then, at last, the yellow lights of Coals

Hollow appeared in the distance, simultaneously welcoming him home and warning him away.

He did not understand the how and why of the things he had seen at Windslow Mine, but he knew that they were true, that he had walked with a spirit, soared through ancestral skies, glimpsed the future, and held the hand of a woman who was even now lying dead in the back of her trailer-park home. He did not want to see that bloody bed again, but he kept walking, propelled by something that Great-Grandmother had called *oohaate*, the path that must be followed.

A can of Sprite stood on the coffee table. He crossed toward it, picked it up, shook it. Liquid sloshed in the bottom. One sip left. He drank it before turning toward the sound of talk-radio voices that wafted from Great-Grandmother's bedroom. Did he want to go in there? Did he have a choice?

He followed the sound.

She lay on her bed, curled on a mattress stained purple with her blood. Beside her, on a water-stained nightstand, lay a two-inch brick of shrink-wrapped bills, the old woman's life savings withdrawn from the Windslow branch of PNC Bank and left for him to start his body shop in the Bottoms.

Weeks later, when things quieted down, he made his first return trip to the Windslow highwall.

He walked to the shack and peered through the boarded window. He sat on the ledge and looked out at the trees that grew on his father's grave. He lay on his back and watched redwing hawks soar above the weedy hollow that had once been a mountain with rounded shoulders. And after a while he decided that his nighttime walk through the mine had been a dream, a lucid fantasy induced by the trauma of finding Great-Grandmother dead in her bedroom.

For nine years, the explanation satisfied him. He made peace with the memory, and then, gradually, he suppressed it—burying it beneath the conscious concerns that came with starting a business, going into debt, and facing foreclosure. But the memory remained, hardening beneath the weight of waking thoughts, awaiting excavation.

The highwall collapsed, and then . . .

. . . Axle awoke to find himself soaring above the collapsed face of Windslow Mine. He lay stretched upon the wind, gripping an updraft with splayed wings. His arms lay flat against his sides, hands pressing his hips to reduce drag. His legs, too, were extended along the line of his flight, serving as rudders. He banked on instinct, navigating the shifting currents of rising air as if he had been flying all his life, perhaps longer. It felt good, natural. He was in his element.

Below him, the remains of his ruined Mustang lay upended near the base of the collapsed highwall, smoldering beneath a column of smoke and dust. And to the south he saw the lights of Windslow, and beyond them the endless stream of interstate traffic, the cascade of lights that he had once hoped would carry him far from his dead-end life.

And now he was out of that life, flying above it, remade in the shape of something more than human. He was a spirit now, a fusion of his own intangible essence and the timeless being that was Kwetis, the nightflyer.

Banking left, putting his spirit body between the collapsed wall and the orange glow of the rising sun, he flew above the rippling veins of coal . . . the earth's sinew . . . the vault of spirits.

. . . *years from now . . . when you need it . . . when Awenyahsa needs it . . . you will change . . .*

At last it had happened.

He was Kwetis, the spirit for whom time was as fluid as air.

He became aware of changes in the wind, currents that blew from the four corners of the spirit world: the realms of experience, memory, prophecy, and dream. He felt them converge beneath his wings, carrying him high above a shifting landscape that pulsed like the face of a windblown sea. And as the world shifted beneath his wings, changes equally vast were taking place within him. His mind was opening, the purpose of everything becoming clear. He knew what he needed to do, where he needed to go.

A shack materialized beyond a vertical vein of rock, an igneous column that had welled from deep in the earth to form the core of *Awenyahsa*. He flew toward it, extending his arms to drag against the air. He lost altitude, coming down fast, landing in the wicker shadow of a chain-link fence that housed a generator with a 50-gallon tank.

The rising sun felt warm against his face as he walked to the brink and sat upon the sandstone precipice. He folded his wings and leaned forward, legs dangling, hands propped against his thighs. *Come to me*, he thought, sending his unspoken command back through the shack's closed door, across the ether that lay between him and the dreaming woman he had come to meet. *I'm waiting, Yeyestani. Come to me.*

The door creaked open.

He looked around, turning his head only, looking back between the folded arches of his wings. "I've come to thank you," he said, acknowledging a favor she had done for a previous incarnation of Kwetis. "You did well, Yeyestani." He saw questions in her furrowed brow. Was it because she knew that Kwetis would not return just to thank her? Or did she detect a piece of her future in his glowing eyes? Perhaps, though it would take her years to put it together, she sensed she was meeting the transformed spirit of an as-yet-unborn great-grandson.

And then, after a meeting that stretched deep into a dream-realm morning, he took back to the air, following the spirit winds forward in time and into the dreams of a five-year-old boy named Nathan Peterson. Here he fashioned horrors out of shadows, images beyond language. And amid the shadows, one recognizable shape: a wolfish man with gigantic wings.

The boy awoke instantly, screaming for his father.

This was perhaps the most delicate of all the manipulations. For it to work, the child needed to be so distraught that his mother would risk interrupting a business meeting across the state. Then, when reached by phone, the father had to be convinced to take the call in private, a decision that would lead to a crucial change in driving arrangements: Bird would take the briefcase in his SUV; Peterson would follow in his Viper after dealing with his son.

There were other places to go during that brief instant when the highwall collapsed and the immortal shadow united with the once-wounded spirit of the man who had called himself *Axle*. All of it, every visitation, every movement, was planned to serve the *oohaate*, to make sure things were where they needed to be. And then, when everything was in place, he flew back to a spring morning in Coals Hollow to make good on his promise to revisit the old woman he had named Yeyestani. Her dreams were strong, full of rich details, artifacts gathered from a life of experience. Such was the way with old people. When their lives grew sparse and empty, their dreams became museums of memory.

In her dream she was young, lying in a bed of grass. To her left, the rounded shoulders of *Awenyahsa* rested against a bank of clouds.

To her right, on the edge of a slow-moving creek, an adolescent boy slept on a threadbare sofa, legs propped on a coffee table. Between her and the boy, a closed door rose from a patch of yarrow grass. There were no walls. The boy lay in clear view, beyond the frame of the door. He recognized the boy. It was himself, from another life, another time.

"You have raised him well, Yeyestani."

She gave a half smile, an old woman's grin in a young woman's face: wisdom couched in innocence. In her eyes, a gleam of recognition, understanding. She knew why he was here. "Thank you," she said.

"Are you ready to finish your work?"

"Yes, if you are ready to begin." She turned, looking at the boy. "Hard to believe it's over. It happened so fast."

"You told me that, once. Big changes can occur in an instant, but they also take time."

"Like life," she said. "It takes time, but it passes in an instant." She reached out, taking his hand. "Remember me," she said. "And remember . . . you did not work alone."

He looked at her, trying to read her eyes. There was something there. For a moment, the dream was out of his control. She was in charge, reclaiming the role she had assumed throughout the final phase of her life.

"You did not work alone," she said again.

"What are you telling me?"

The half smile returned. "Think on it. The answer is in you." She released his hand. "For me, I have work to do, one last duty."

"Giving back to the earth," he said. "Blood for rock."

She nodded and turned away.

An instant later, he was flying once again.

You did not work alone.

There had, of course, been the earlier Kwetis, the deep-vein spirit that had put the *oohaate* in motion. But now he understood that there had been another helper as well. It was this other to which Yeyestani had alluded, a creature of flesh who had risen from a fall of rock in Windslow crater, an earthborn guardian who worked to serve an *oohaate* that would bring about the death and transformation of a son he would never know.

My father, Axle thought, the knowledge registering with a pang of emotion—something spirits were not supposed to feel. *The winged creature, the earthborn guardian—he was my father.*

The pang lingered a moment. Then vanished, leaving him with a sense that he would not feel such things again. And then . . .

. . . he awoke, leaving the dream realm to find that a spirit wind had carried his physical form high into the air, far above the collapsed mine and the twisted remains of his Mustang.

But his physical form had no wings.

He was a man again. And he was falling.

66

Spinelli felt nothing.

It was as if his body had fused into the surrounding rock, leaving only his disembodied awareness.

He was looking up from somewhere between two frozen rivers of scree that had miraculously parted as they plunged near him. He should have been buried alive, but instead he lay in a jagged valley, gazing at the sky. He vaguely remembered seeing the tons of falling rock surging toward him, but he could not remember having been afraid. It had been too unreal, like something from the memory of a dream.

And there were other memories, too. In one of them he had leaped from a Mustang and fallen into darkness. He could not remember landing, and perhaps that was because he had never really fallen in the first place. Maybe it had been a piece of a nightmare. Wasn't that the way nightmares worked? You dreamed the fall, not the impact. People did not die in their dreams. They simply awoke.

He considered that. A dream? Was it possible? He wanted to believe it. Believing would make everything safe.

Yes . . . a dream . . . only a dream.

Sometimes, back in the days when he had been living in the WVU frat house, when the nights were hot and the stuffiness of his cramped room made it hard to breathe, he would take a pillow and blanket outside and sleep in the vacant field behind the garage. Perhaps he was there now, awaking at dawn with his face to the sky? He pondered that, hoping it was true even as the details of his surroundings became clearer.

Above him, the sky was turning blue. Night's shadow drew back, chased by another dawn. To his left, the collapsed wall of Windslow Mine cut a gray swatch across the brightening blue. And he smelled smoke, harsh with the stink of scorched metal and rubber. Somewhere nearby, the Mustang smoldered. Now and then, he heard the ping of its cooling frame.

With a cramp of regret, he realized that the worst was true. He had fallen from the cliff.

And yet . . . he was alive.

He had heard stories of people who had survived falls from great heights: from buildings, trees, even airplanes. In one of those accounts the survivor had remained conscious at the moment of impact, feeling no pain as he struck the earth and bounced back into the air—over and over again like a rubber ball until at last he landed in a roadside ditch.

Spinelli could not remember bouncing, but he was definitely alive. His eyes were open, his vision clear, his thoughts coherent. So for a long time he simply stared, watching the sky, waiting for either a miraculous rescue or merciful death.

At last, with the rising sun, the latter came, but not before he saw something incredible.

On the edge of his vision, just visible beyond a ridge of rock, a man was falling from the sky.

Axle fell, tumbling. One moment he was looking up, gazing at the brightening sky. Then he faced south, toward the lights of Windslow, then down toward the mine, then east toward the rising morning. . . .

In the distance, a second figure fell with him. It looked like Bird, naked and pale in the silver light. He seemed to be going down over the lower bends of Windslow Road, tumbling in backward somersaults: a mirror image of Axle's descent. . . .

Axle extended his arms, stabilizing his fall, realizing as he did that he was as naked as Bird, skyborn, reformed so that he might advance an *oohaate* that was still far from finished.

The wind felt cold against his skin, freezing his face, chest, and loins as he angled parallel to the ground. Now, with the firmament no longer spinning, he was able to look at the twilight forests, valleys, and hills spread out like patterns in a blanket. Shadows shifted within the patterns, resolving into shapes as he plunged. A patch of gray became a rocky clearing. A shimmer of blue became a stream. A pulsing shadow became an owl flying low over the rim of the mine. The entire landscape was in motion, changing, reworking, pulsing in an endless process of becoming. And there were other things down there, too, things poised in shadows, awaiting emergence. And he would lead them.

Falling faster, wincing in the wind, Axle realized that all of it—trees, streams, animals, people—was no more substantial than swirling mist, momentary apparitions pressed between the slow time of rock and sky. And now they were his for the shaping. But first he had to return to earth.

Below, coming up fast, he saw the pointed top of a hazard sign. To its left, Saw Mill Creek ran through a bramble thicket. It was all racing toward him, blurring with the speed of his fall.

He closed his eyes, unafraid.

WHAM!

A force hurled him back, away from the ground, into the sky. He extended his arms, steadying himself as he soared through an arc that sent him plunging back toward the ground.

WHAM!

The blast hit him again, knocking him skyward, but with less force, into an arc that was far less severe than the first.

He fell again.

The ground raced toward him. His shadow was there, rising to meet him: a final embrace.

WHAM!

EPILOGUE

Cold.

Axle lay in a bed of mud and grass, leaning back against the bank of Saw Mill Creek. Water pooled around his legs, covered his feet.

The sun rose beyond a tunnel of weedy trees, its dome just visible through a break in the thicket, its light catching in the branches of a nearby oak. He knew the tree. It was the one Spinelli had sat in while waiting for Bird's Escalade to round the turn on Windslow Road.

He sat up, shattering the stillness as he pulled away from the water, looking down at himself as he stood in the cool dawn. This new body resembled the old one, but it was stronger, perhaps a little taller, definitely firmer about the waist and thighs. And his skin was pure, unbruised, unblemished.

Tall grass swayed around him as he stepped from the thicket. A sudden wind crossed the field, sending out grassy ripples that converged on the dead oak. And to his left, something snapped—a shrill report like the crack of a gun. The sound came again as he turned to see a black wing rising from a stand of thistles. It unfurled, billowing with the ripples of a spirit in flight.

But it wasn't flying.

And it wasn't a spirit.

CRACCCKKKKK!

It was a nylon windbreaker, its drawstring hood tangled in thorns.

It was Spinelli's.

He walked toward it, grabbed it, pulled.

The thorns opened, spreading like fingers, releasing the windbreaker.

He tied it around his waist, covering himself as best he could. It was hardly clothing befitting a champion, but it would do for now.

Climbing the shoulder near the hazard sign, he heard the approaching hum of a V8. He knew the sound.

A patch of glare cleared the bend. He squinted and saw the shattered glass of a side window. Music spilled through the hole: cedar flutes, digital drums, chanting voices. . . .

The driver's window whirred down as the SUV neared the sign. Bird looked out, shirtless. His tattoos were gone. "Nice pants."

Axle glanced at the SUV's muddy wheels. "You have trouble getting this thing back on the road?"

Bird shrugged. "All-wheel drive." He grinned. "It's an Escalade, man."

Axle stepped into the street and climbed in.

"So we're working together," Bird said.

"Drive," Axle said. "Your place. We'll get some clothes. Then contact Vorarov."

Bird drove out onto Windslow Road, toward the serpentine bends that wound toward the entrance to his estate. "He was there, wasn't he?" Bird said. "Vorarov. He was at the mine when the wall went down?"

"You know that?"

"No. The only thing I know is that you know everything. You lead. I follow. Am I right?"

"Yes," Axle said. "Two yeses. Yes, Vorarov was at the mine. Yes, you're my servant now. You have things we need in order to advance the *oohaate*."

"So what's the plan, Kwetis?"

"*Guardian*," Axle said. "I can become Kwetis in the dream realm. In flesh, I'm merely a skyborn guardian."

"So what are you guarding, Mr. Guardian? What's the plan?"

"We go to your place," Axle said. "We get clothes and money. Then we contact Vorarov and make sure last night convinced him to give up his plans for Mountain Downs."

"That could be a tall order." Bird toed the brake as he neared the first bend. "Kirill's really in no position to call it off. There are bigger interests involved."

"Which is where you come in."

"You think I'll be able to convince the Vorarov family—"

"No. That's not what I think. What I *know* is that you have money. You have connections. You and Kirill Vorarov will work together to make sure the commission rejects your applications. It shouldn't be hard. I'm sure your consultants will be glad to report that last night's rock burst resulted from serious instabilities at the site."

"Is that true?"

"As true as anything else you've been paying them to put in their reports."

"And then what?" Bird said. "We accomplish that, then what happens?"

They rounded a tight bend, driving across skid marks that were part of another life.

"Then our work is finished," Axle said. "Then we go back."

"Back to our lives as they were?"

"No. Back to what we were before the Great Heart brought us back."

"What? Back to being dead?"

"Yeah. Back to being dead."

Bird considered that. "Doesn't seem fair," he said. "We complete the *oohaate*—"

"No. Not us. We don't complete it. We're just part of the current wave. Others will follow."

"To do what?"

"Take it to the next level."

"By doing what? What's the goal?"

Axle looked out the window. "You don't need to know that," he said. "Enough talking. The less you know, the less you'll have to forget. Just drive." He turned toward the door and looked out through the raised window.

Beyond his reflection he saw the road's berm give way to a scraggly slope of sumac and stunted pine. Weeds grew in tangled clumps between the trees, staking their territory, riddling the ground with creepers that wound through seeding grass. And everywhere a flurry of insects hatching, preying, singing, mating, dying. He saw it now, a world of struggle, competition, conquest. Natural harmony was a myth. The world was a collision of forces, each seeking an edge, an advantage.

"What if they're like everything else?" Bird said.

"Who?"

"The spirits."

"Like everything else how?"

"What if they're just using us?"

Axle said nothing.

The SUV turned from the road, crossing over onto the Frieburg estate.

The landscape changed instantly.

Out on a sculpted lawn, a shadow darted between manicured trees. Just a cloud. But for a moment, through his reflection on the glass, Axle was certain he saw a dark figure crouching in the hollow of a garden wall. It leaned forward, burdened with the weight of folded wings, looking across the lawn, watching the SUV make its slow climb to the fortress on the hill. Axle raised his hand, pressing it to the glass in a sign of recognition. But the shape was already gone, leaping skyward, vanishing into the glare of a new dawn.

Read on for an exciting look at
Lawrence C. Connolly's

PROLOGUE

When his dead girlfriend's car broke down three miles from the West Virginia line, Dalton Davies got out, jumped the guardrail, and walked into the Pennsylvania forest.

He didn't have a plan, didn't know where he was going. He simply knew he needed to keep moving, putting distance between himself and the mess he'd left behind in Pittsburgh.

The sun was low over the hills as he entered the trees, shining yellow against the trunks and vines. It occurred to him that his clothes—T-shirt, cutoffs, and threadbare sneakers—were all wrong for a night in the woods, but he couldn't return to the highway. He needed to be elsewhere before the cops found the car. It would be simpler that way.

He came upon a coal-hauling road, humped in the middle, patched with weeds. He followed it to a ravine strewn with appliances, car parts, scrap wood, bottles, wire coat hangers, and something that looked like the rusted frame of a backyard swing set. It was Polly's kind of place. She'd been a junk artist before she went psycho, and he wondered if finding a dump on this particular evening was some kind of omen.

Dalton trusted omens.

Polly used to kid him about that, back in the days when she'd still had a sense of humor.

"You're a mystic, Dalton. A Sariputra in need of *bodhi*."

"Body?"

"*Bodhi*. It's like *satori*."

"The hell's that?"

"It's what you're looking for, my Sariputra."

"And what's a *sorry poochra*?"

She laughed. "That'd be you, Dalton." She punched his shoulder. "You're the *sorry poochra*. Definitely the *sorriest poochra* I've ever seen."

She had been like that when they'd first met, peppering her insults with

Eastern mysticism, always talking in circles and jagging him around—but in good ways. Those had been happy times. Even now, after all the crap that had gone down, he cherished those memories. And now here he was, on the day of her death, running away and stumbling upon a cache of junk that at one time would have had Polly jumping with anticipation.

"Damn," he said, speaking to her memory. "Wish you could see this place, Polly."

Sorry, Dalton. I can't see anything. Her words seemed to come from outside his head, emanating from the hiss and babble of a creek running through the ravine. *You killed me, remember?*

"I didn't kill you."

You didn't help me. It's the same thing.

"What could I have done?"

Anything but run away. Damnit, Dalton. When things get tough, you run like a pustule.

"So what should I have done?"

The creek babbled, flowing south. No words now. No answer. Just the sound of flowing water. Maybe that was because there was no answer. Or maybe because the only answer was one he didn't want to consider: that it was time to stop running, turn back, alert the authorities. He'd been ignoring that answer all morning, telling himself that his only option was getting away to a place where he could forget he had ever had a relationship with a manic-depressive junk artist whose final work had been painting the floor with her open wrists. "Angels!" she had said, looking up at him from the stained carpet, blood smeared like red wings. "I see angels! What do you see?" That was it. Her last words.

What do you see?

"I couldn't stop you, Polly."

Angels.

"I couldn't save you."

I see angels. What do you see?

Maybe his only option was to return to the car, tie something white to the door, and wait for the cops to check on him. When they did, he could tell them how he hadn't really stolen the car, just borrowed it. He could explain that he hadn't meant to bolt without calling 911, it was just that he'd been confused. It was like something had snapped when he saw all that blood.

Whose blood? The cop would say.

"My girlfriend's."

What happened?

"It's complicated."

Wind stirred the trees. Dalton shivered, sunlight shifted, and suddenly, near the base of the slope, he saw Polly lying in a drift of rotting leaves.

"Jesus!"

He stepped back, heart racing. This was crazy. She couldn't be here. And yet—

What do you see?

He stepped forward again, squinting, focusing, determining that it really was there. But it wasn't Polly. It wasn't even a real body.

"A mannequin!" His shivers deepened. "A sign!"

This one had to mean something.

He descended the slope.

The painted eyes seemed to follow him, staring from a face that looked more like Polly the closer he got. Wide eyes, straight nose, high cheeks, narrow jaw—it resembled the woman she had been *before* her junk-art mania had succumbed to depression, before her features had darkened and her gaze turned toward the angels in her head.

I see angels.

The slope was steeper than it looked, and more slippery. Halfway down he lost his footing, fell, and slid the rest of the way. Rocks and junk clawed at him, scraping his legs, pummeling his butt, covering his cutoffs with a muddy smear before he careened to a stop at the edge of the creek. The mannequin was beside him now. He looked toward it, and that's when he saw the other set of eyes.

What do you see?

The other eyes were real, alive, and looking right at him. They peered from the shadow of the mannequin's head: fixed, unblinking—snake eyes.

"Aw, shit!" He leaned away.

The snake didn't move. It just sat there: body coiled, neck cocked, eyes staring. Its head wasn't much larger than the tip of Dalton's thumb, but the shape of its eyes and the banded colors of its body marked it as a copperhead.

He scooted away.

The snake moved now, turning its head, tracking his motion, tasting the air with its hair-thin tongue.

Dalton rose to his feet. He took a step backward, intending to turn and climb out of the ravine when something struck the back of his leg, thumping a few inches above the heel. He looked around.

A second snake recoiled behind him. This one was larger than the first. Had it bitten him? The thump hadn't felt like much, just a tap. Maybe it was a warning tap. Did snakes do that?

He moved away, sidestepping now.

Both snakes watched, eyes fixed, tongues darting.

A rotting log angled over the creek, one end resting in the water. Dalton sat on it, looked at his leg, checked the ankle. The bite marks were there, two of them. They were like pimples, beads of welling blood. He touched one. It broke and flowed, dribbling down, staining his shoe.

The big snake kept staring.

"You son of a bitch! I wasn't even bothering you."

The snake flicked its tongue.

Dalton's leg was hurting now, pain spreading in waves. He tried getting up. The leg cramped. He stumbled and went down hard. And suddenly there were more snakes, a nest of babies emerging from the log. They struck at his hands. He recoiled. One of the snakes held on, clamping the soft flesh between thumb and finger. He tried shaking it away. The ropy body coiled, flexing against his palm.

"Goddamnit!"

He slammed the hand against the log, rubbing hard, reducing the body to a pulpy skid. But the head held on, jaws pulsing, eyes staring as Dalton pried it loose. The fangs retracted. They were nasty-looking: curved, smeared with blood, dripping venom. He tossed the head away, but the other snakes were on him now, biting his limbs, riddling them with punctures that oozed and smeared as he crawled backward through weeds. And then he was up, on his feet, and running along the creek. That was what he did best. When things got crazy, when the world turned shitty, he ran. Get away, that was his strategy. But why was he following the creek when he needed to get back to the road, flag down a car, scream for help?

He turned toward the slope, threw himself against it, and started to climb. His throat tightened. He couldn't catch his breath, feared he might pass out, but then he emerged: out of the hollow and into the presence of . . . not an omen . . . but a *miracle*.

A farmhouse stood before him: gabled eaves, covered porch, open door.

"Hey!" He stumbled forward. "Help!" He fell. A shadow streaked the ground in front of him, racing away on a gust of wind. He looked up. Nothing there. No clouds. Only the sun resting low atop the trees.

He stood, winced at the fire in his foot, and resumed his stumbling gait toward the house.

The door was open. Someone had to be home.

"Hey! Help me. I've been snake bit!"

He fell toward the porch steps, grabbed the banister, and nearly blacked out as his bitten hand spasmed from the pressure. He fell to his knees, everything hurting now, pain burning inside him as he crawled up the stairs and onto the porch. Then he knelt, blinking, clearing his vision. He'd been wrong about the door. It wasn't open. Not in the usual sense. He forced himself to stand, lurching forward, past a pair of dangling hinges, looking inside to see the door lying on a rotting carpet, dusted with years of grit. Weeds had taken root, spreading onto the floor, rising tall and spindly beneath the exposed beams of a fallen roof.

The house was in ruin, deserted. But still he pushed forward, entering the main room where wood, shingles, and flooring lay in a massive drift against the parlor wall. And beyond the drift, framed within a water-stained arch, he saw another room whose walls bore the outlines of a stove, sink, and refrigerator. The appliances were gone, and now other things stood in their place: strange constructions—incongruous. They didn't belong in a kitchen.

Are they really there?

He blinked.

Please be real.

He fell to his knees, rubbed his eyes, looked again.

What do you see?

The constructions remained fixed in his vision. One was a collection of books stacked in a case of cinderblocks and boards. The other was a bed of newspapers and cardboard sheeting. No dust on any of it. No weeds. The space looked clean.

Someone lives here.

"Hey! Can you hear me?"

The flying shadow returned, streaking through the open roof, blurring across the floor.

Dalton looked up, squinting at an exposed patch of sky. Something was up there . . . flying . . . circling. Dalton tried standing, but pain pushed him down again, onto his back, flat against the fibers of the rotting carpet.

I'm dying.

He clawed at his throat, staring straight up as the shadow came again . . . only this time it stopped, landed on a cornice, and looked down. Its head twitched between curving wings. Its eyes glowed.

Not real.

Dalton blinked.

I see angels. What do you see?

The thing leaned forward, grunting as it slipped from the cornice and glided down to a second-floor beam.

It resembled a man . . . a winged man with legs bent in too many places. Dalton couldn't see its face, only its eyes—sloe-shaped, glowing from within. "Are you real?" Dalton asked.

The creature stepped from the beam and dropped onto the fallen roof. It was close now. Too close. But Dalton couldn't move. Couldn't breathe. He could only lie and watch as the creature leaned forward a final time, arched its wings, and dove.

MORE FROM THE VEINS CYCLE

With *Veins: The Soundtrack*, author and musician Lawrence C. Connolly provides a series of instrumental soundscapes inspired by themes and scenes from his critically acclaimed supernatural thriller *Veins*.

Performing with his band, Connolly delivers a mix of trance, rock, and ambient compositions designed to complement the novel.

——§——

Axle and Bird are back from the dead. No longer merely human, they must now work to further the oohaate—the spirit path. Whether they will like what they find at the journey's end remains to be seen, but for now, there's no turning back.

An explosion at Windslow Mine has set things in motion. The forest is crawling with snakes, driven from their nests by underground fires.

And the snakes are not alone.

Other forces are emerging, rising from the earth's molten veins, preparing to reclaim a smoldering world. By daybreak, the residents of Windslow, Pennsylvania, will know that the world is burning beneath them.

By daybreak, the nightmare begins.

"Lawrence C. Connolly has the rare ability to completely transport the reader."
—ALICE HENDERSON
AUTHOR OF *VORACIOUS*

"... one of the genre's most masterful storytellers."
—MICHAEL ARNZEN, BRAM STOKER AWARD-WINNING AUTHOR

COMING FALL 2014

The final hours have come. Rocks burn, floodwaters rage, and serpents take wing as a storm of fire and rain threatens the world.

Amid this chaos, a young man named Axle lies near death in a shuttered bedroom. He has the power to save the earth, but to do so he must retrieve something from his dreams, an artifact of memory that he has spent a lifetime trying to forget. With a single ally standing guard, Axle's spirit searches the terrors of his past, following clues that may unlock a second chance for the human race.

All he needs is time.

Enter Samuelle, a woman whose touch can raise the dead and kill the living. Axle's rivals have given her a mission: find the dreamer, deliver the killing touch, unleash the storm that will destroy humanity.

"Delightfully dissonant. Unbridled imagination meets impeccable storytelling."
—JOHN DIXON, AUTHOR OF *PHOENIX ISLAND*

"This is a hell of a ride."
—Simon Kurt Unsworth, AUTHOR OF *THE DEVIL'S DETECTIVE*

FEATURING ART BY RHONDA LIBBEY

AWAKEN
YOUR
WONDER
— § —
FEBOOKS.NET

www.ingramcontent.com/pod-product-compliance
Lightning Source LLC
Chambersburg PA
CBHW071138260626
47162CB00003B/838